TIME FOR JUSTICE

NEIL SANDS

This book is dedicated to the memory of;

Archie Sawyer

1912-1995

A voracious reader - I hope he would be proud.

"It's every man's business to see justice done."

Sir Arthur Conan Doyle

CHAPTER 1

He waited silently in the bushes. Months of planning and years of mental turmoil had come down to this.

A fine mist of rain gently covered everything around him. The thickening clouds had covered the moon leaving the night dark and dismal. For him it was the perfect night, the perfect night to kill someone!

He was swearing to himself as he left the pub, "Fucking English bastards!" He hated them all and he knew they hated him. Sure, they laughed with him when they'd had a few drinks together and were boasting about their last blow job or when they got laid. He had no doubt that they'd laughed even more behind his back when he left, but he didn't care. Fuck them; fuck them all. He hadn't travelled almost four thousand miles to this poxy country to find friends; he had travelled here, first, to save his own skin and then, second, to make as much money the easiest possible way. Friends he didn't need, women he could get for free – and the money? That was easy to steal from the stupid English.

England really was the land of opportunity if you didn't care who you hurt and he certainly didn't.

The rain was falling heavily now, but he was feeling happy – the warm glow of the vodka in his veins made everything feel good. The dull-witted English bitch he lived with had been just what he needed, at least for now, and he looked forward to fucking her when he got home, if she wanted to or not.

Rounding the corner on Simms Lane he set off on his normal short cut across the railway bridge, whistling as he went. He then took a sharp left, taking the well-worn footpath through the trees.

He had picked his spot carefully, hearing the whistling before he could see his target approaching down the steps, head down in the rain, then looking up and shaking the raindrops from his head as he got to the cover of the trees. That would be his last conscious movement.

In two silent paces he stepped out from his hiding place, the sound of the rain on trees giving him cover he really didn't need. Holding the two wooden toggles in his hands he flipped the wires over the target's head in a well-practiced manoeuvre, pulling it tight in one swift move. The target was dead in seconds.

His breathing was still controlled, hands firm, mind alert – it had gone as planned.

The lessons had begun and things would never be the same again.

The call came in at just after 7 am. Detective Chief Inspector Dan Hooper was about to leave his house for the nick when his mobile rang. It was DS David 'Bronco' Laine.

"Morning, Guv, have *we* got an interesting start to the week; a body has been found in the trees next to the railway bridge in Turpins Road across from Simms Lane. From all accounts it's more than a bit gruesome. I wouldn't eat breakfast just yet and they need us there ASAP."

"On my way, Dave, should be there in ten. Have we set up a perimeter?"

"Yes, boss, all in hand. I'll meet you there," Laine replied.

Hooper thought, not for the first time, how lucky he was to have Dave Laine as his DS. The former Met Police

Special Crimes Unit detective was a twenty-year veteran, with no wish to move further in rank; his wealth of policing knowledge and his copper's nose for noticing things others didn't, made him the perfect partner.

Setting the alarm as he left the house and quickly pulling his Freelander out of the driveway, he felt the anticipation and excitement building. It had always been this way from his first days in the army, then throughout his ten-year career in No 1 Para and now in the police – he never needed telling when something special was about to happen, for that in-built sixth sense always told him.

As he turned into Turpins Road he was pleased to see roadblocks in place, the area sealed off with crime scene tape and Bronco Laine talking with Inspector Dave Armstrong who was, no doubt, duty officer.

Parking quickly, he retrieved a Tyvek coverall from his boot, which, these days had to be worn by anyone entering a crime scene. "So, what have we got, Bronco?"

"An IC-1 male approximately 40 years old and hanging from a tree. But that's only the half of it – you need to see it for yourself for he obviously hasn't got a head for heights."

As they reached the crime scene tape, Hooper stopped to sign into the log held by a young, female Police Community Support Officer and was led down the footpath, again marked with tape, to protect as much of the scene as possible, by the Scenes of Crime Officers, or SOCOs as they are called. At this stage, the less people trampling through the better.

It is a fact that many detectives have seen fewer dead bodies than your average uniformed officer, who are called to road traffic accidents and bodies found in houses, often weeks after they have died. Not so with Dan Hooper, he had seen more than his share of dead and mutilated bodies in his time in the Paras, but even he was taken aback.

Hanging upside down by his ankles was the torso of a

man. Naked, hands behind his back and headless! The head was placed in an upright position on the muddy floor just in front of the body and carved on the naked chest was the word 'GUILTY'. The Crime Scene Officers had erected a gazebo over and around the body to protect the area.

Hooper took in the scene slowly and carefully. "I get the very poor head for heights comment now, not one of your best, Bronco – who found it?"

"A runner just over ninety minutes ago, Richard Soper, aged 42, who is training for the London Marathon. He lives in Mount Rise; he had come through the woods from the far end, almost ran past it and called us on his mobile. He's sat in the back of Inspector Armstrong's car very shook up, but OK. We have taken a statement. If it's OK with you we can let him go and catch up later if we need to?"

Hooper nodded in agreement. While peering behind the body he saw the hands were fastened with a long, plastic cable tie. He crouched down very close to the decapitated head, looking at where it had come from.

"That has been cut through cleanly and quickly. I doubt he would have known a thing."

"Oh, doing *my* job, are you now, Chief Inspector? If I had realised that I could have stayed and ate the breakfast my wife was cooking me when I got the call."

Hooper stood up slowly and turned around to face the ruddy complexion of Gareth Hew Evans, a 6-feet 2-inch, 58-year-old former Llanelli front row and Home Office pathologist. "Gareth, it's always a joy to hear your dulcet tones, even if it is in these circumstances."

"Likewise, young Daniel. Now if you don't mind, let the hooker see the ball and we might just discover what caused this young man to lose his head in such unusual circumstances."

Stepping back to let the doctor closer, they were joined by Julie Burton who was the Crime Scene Manager – until the crime scene was released, she was in sole charge of it, no matter what the rank. She had been on the scene for the best part of half an hour and, with the team's photographer, had ensured that just about every angle had been photographed and videoed.

Hooper greeted her with a smile. They were good friends and often met for a drink after work. Contrary to what some people at the nick thought, there was no relationship other than 'just good friends'. Dan was one of the very few who knew that Julie's preference for a partner was female, not male. If anything, Dan often thought that him knowing made them even closer friends.

"Anything yet, Jules, or am I being premature?"

"You – premature, Chief Inspector? Surely not!" she replied with a smile. "Obviously it's very early, but on first impressions by the amount of blood, it's clear he was killed here, but the strange thing is, there aren't many footprints, in fact it looks more like the area has been swept with a branch to erase any. I will know much more when I can get a closer look."

"That shouldn't be too long, Ms Burton. From the body temperature and rigor mortis I would guess this poor soul has been dead for between seven and nine hours. I can't tell from lividity because the body has lost too much blood. I'll know much more when I get him back to the mortuary. As far as I know it was a quiet night, so I should be able to do the postmortem quickly. Anyone fancy joining me?"

"I will try," replied Hooper, "but if I can't then I'll send DS Laine."

At that moment, the Chief Inspector's phone rang its old-fashioned alarm clock tone. He, for one, couldn't abide ring tones of pop tunes and voices – perhaps he was getting old.

Hooper answered. "Morning Dan, it's Arthur." The voice of Chief Superintendent Arthur Jackson was calm as always.

"What have we got?"

"It's not good, sir. An IC-1 male, decapitated very cleanly, hanging naked upside down from a tree with the word 'guilty' carved in blood on his chest and, to top that, it looks like the area has been swept of footprints. I hate to say it, but it looks like a professional job to me. I just don't understand the naked upside down bit and the word 'guilty'. Is it some kind of statement?"

"Really, who knows these days with drugs? Anything is possible, but a professional hit on our patch is something new and, if that's what it is, we need to sort it ASAP. I want you to be Senior Investigating Officer on this, Dan, as you know the Super is away on leave in Italy for another thirteen days. If we can get it sorted by then it will be good for your record. I will let the Chief Constable know and get the press office to issue a statement, but you may need to do a press conference sooner rather than later as Sky News are already on it. I think we will keep the 'guilty' bit to ourselves for the time being. Pick your own team and report back to me at six this evening, I don't think any of us will be going far today."

"OK, sir, I've got DS Laine here now and I will get him to round up the team. I intend to call the first briefing at 10 o'clock."

After instructing his sergeant to call in as many uniformed officers and PCSOs to start door-to-door enquiries, he went in search of Julie Burton.

"Any sign of his clothes yet, Jules?"

"No, not yet; it looks like they have been taken, but we still have to do a full search. I doubt I will be back by ten, but I will call if we find anything."

"Great, thanks. The sooner we can find out who he is the sooner we can start looking for who did this, but it looks very professional to me – this isn't 'just' a murder, this is a statement."

CHAPTER 2

The next couple of hours flew by, the team of SOCOs having collected various blood samples, the body moved to the morgue and they were busy doing an inch by inch fingertip search, something they dare not rush. Every item was to be marked, photographed and logged before being sealed in evidence bags. All this was being watched by millions in their own homes live on Sky News with images being filmed from the circling helicopter. In their white coverall suits, hats, gloves, masks and shoe covers, the SOCOs looked very different from Joe Public's idea of a crime scene investigator popularised by programmes like *CSI*. The truth was much less glamorous and required not only great skill, but the patience of a bus-load of saints.

The DCI was just about to make his way back to his car to get everything set up for the first briefing when Dave Laine stopped him. "Boss, I think we might have a lead on whose body it is. Door-to-door say a woman in Duke Street says her boyfriend didn't come home from the pub last night; it isn't the first time he has stayed out, but he gave no inkling that he wouldn't be back last night."

"Who is he, Dave?"

"Well, she says his name is Helmut Schuster, she has only been living with him for about eight weeks, says he originally comes from Dresden in Germany. She has given a description and it could well be him. Unfortunately, she hasn't got any photographs, said he wouldn't let her take any.

NEIL SANDS

I have asked a uniform to stay with her and if needs be, bring her to the station later."

"OK, well done. What pub was he drinking in?"

"The George on Moor Lane. He could have used the bridge and footpath as a short cut."

"Cheers, Dave, I expect we will have to wait until after lunch to get any fingerprints off him – the Doc will want to do that himself."

"I saw Julie Burton cutting the cable tie that held his hands together before she bagged his hands. Matey may have left prints on it."

"I doubt it, he appears to be too professional for that, but we can always hope. I'm going back to the nick; you finish up here and get back by ten if you can, I would like everyone on parade for this one."

With one final look around, he made his way back to his car while removing his over-suit and took the short drive back to the police headquarters on Union Street.

He woke, after only four hours' sleep, as always. At 6 am, his head was a bit thick from the best part of a half-bottle of Teacher's whiskey he had drunk when he returned. Three extra strong Anadins and a glass of water, along with some fresh air would soon sort that out.

Slipping into tracksuit bottoms, tee shirt, trainers and beanie hat, he set out for his morning five-mile run. It was going to be a good day, the first of many good days. The bad days, he was positive, were all behind him now. There were more targets lined up on his list that needed taking care of and plans to be made. His overalls and the target's clothes had been burned on the way home. He felt alive for the first time in a long time. How could killing another man make him feel alive? 'Easily' was the answer to that. It had all gone exactly as planned and he couldn't wait for the next.

14

CHAPTER 3

Many police now used their computers, iPads, or Toughpads as the police now called them, but Dan preferred to do it in person as he felt it got better results.

"Right, good morning everyone." Hooper addressed the fifteen or so officers, both uniformed and CID, in incident room number two at the town's police headquarters. "The time is 10.03 on Monday twelfth March. This is the first briefing of Operation Nightjar. With the Super away in Italy, the Chief has made me SIO so I'll be brief as I want to get this over as quickly as possible."

Turning to the pictures displayed on the whiteboard, he said, "You can all see it's not a pretty sight. Death was approximately between eleven and twelve last night. The head was completely severed from the body, that isn't an easy thing to do, and makes me think we are dealing with someone who has killed before. The hanging naked upside down and the writing in blood implies he is making a statement."

"A bloody big one if you'll excuse the pun," chipped in DS Laine.

"I have made Brenda Shaw, the office manager aware that, everything you get, no matter how small, must go through her."

Hooper continued, "DI Roberts will be here as soon as she can get away from court; she will lead one investigation team. Stan, you're happy to work under June, aren't you?"

"Any time, boss. At my age, what a way to go!" joked the

48-year-old veteran. Having joined up in 1983 he had seen many changes in the job, not all to his liking or in his mind for the better, but he was a good, solid copper and, with just one year to go before retirement he was counting the days.

"Thank you, DC Jones, I don't think your humour would go down well with the DI if she was here."

"Sorry, boss; seriously, I enjoy working with her. What do you want us to start on?"

"I'd like you to start to sort through CCTV – let's cover an area of, say, a mile on all main roads around the area for anything from 10 pm until 1 am. Also, we can send out uniforms for any video footage from the public from anyone who was walking locally in the area. You can also check if there is any more from door-to-door."

"Bronco and I will go and see the girlfriend of the missing German and visit The George where he had been drinking."

"While we are dealing with him, Brenda, can you go on-line and check immigration for Mr Schuster? See what you can find. If it is he, there must be something behind such a killing and any background will help. Can you also check 'HOLMES' to see if there have been any similar murders of the past couple of years? In fact, go back as far as you can; matey may well have done something similar in the past. Julie Burton is still at the crime scene and, so far, none of the clothes have been found so we may need to widen the search for them as well." Pausing for breath he looked at the pictures again. "OK troops, let's do it. I can't help but think this is either a professional job or a total psychopath – in either case we have all got to be at our best. I want everyone back here for the next briefing at 4.30, unless anything comes up. Good luck, everyone, I think we're going to need it."

Brenda went back to her office. She loved her job and was looking forward to getting her teeth into a new case. She had worked for the police for nearly twenty years. Her late husband had been a PC but had sadly died seven years ago with cancer. She always felt that by continuing to work she was doing what he would have wanted. Brenda always enjoyed working on HOLMES, the Home Office Large Major Enquiry System, first introduced in 1985 and had now updated to HOLMES 2. It was developed after the case of the Yorkshire Ripper. The problem encountered with the Yorkshire Ripper enquiry was the vast quantity of information collected and stored (about forty tons of paper). It became impossible for any one person to have a complete view of the whole enquiry. HOLMES provides a computer system that not only automates the process of collecting and collating the information, but also helps to conduct the investigation in an organised and thorough manner. For Brenda, it was her perfect job.

CHAPTER 4

Number 62 Duke Street was a 3-bedroom semi, in not the nicest part of town. As Hooper and Laine pulled up in the DCI's Freelander, a group of hoodies standing on the far corner turned to see what was going on. A young uniformed officer positioned outside on the pavement greeted them with a smile.

"Morning, sirs, PC Martin." They all nodded. "It's a good job I'm here, those rascals would have the wheels off this faster than Lewis Hamilton's pit crew. Ms Durrant is still inside with her two children." There was still no sign of her boyfriend. "Any news, sir?"

"Not yet, Constable, we just need to find out a few more details from her. Keep a good watch on them, the car's mine since the cutbacks started. I have had enough of pool cars that stink of takeaways and BO and break down once a week, so take care of it, or else," Hooper said with a wink.

Walking up the front path, Hooper was struck by how neat and tidy the garden was compared to the rest of the street. There was just a small bit of lawn and a flower-bed where every other garden would have been filled with broken prams, car parts and rubbish.

The door opened before they could knock. "Ms Durrant?" She nodded. "I am DS Laine, this is Detective Chief Inspector Hooper and we would like to ask you a few questions about Mr Schuster. May we come in?"

She turned and led them through to the kitchen, which was

small but very clean and tidy. As they passed the front room a young boy and girl, both under five, were watching CBeebies.

"Can I get you a tea or a coffee?" she asked.

"No, thanks, this won't take long," said DS Laine, taking a notebook from his inside pocket. "Have you heard from your boyfriend since last night?"

"No, not a word," she replied. Angela Durrant was in her late twenties but had an aura of someone quite a few years older which made her appear tired and worn out. This wasn't helped by what looked like the remains of a black eye. Wearing a pair of old jeans that had seen better days, slippers and a round-necked blue jumper with a cardigan over the top, many would have called her look mumsy. She wore no make-up and her hair was held back in an elastic band. "Can I ask why you're looking for him?"

"I am afraid it's not very nice, Ms Durrant; you may want to sit down. Last night a man was murdered not far from here and the body may match your description of Mr Schuster. When was the last time you saw him?" Laine continued.

"Oh my God, that's awful." Her voice cracked and she put a shaking hand to her mouth. "Surely it can't be Helmut, you must be mistaken." She dithered for a second or two before regaining her composure. "Let me think for a second, you've shocked me." She took a deep breath and continued. "Well, after tea last night he went to the pub about 8-ish and I was reading the children a story. He goes there, to The George on Moor Lane, a few times a week, or at least that's what he tells me," she said, her voice sounding dismayed.

"Why do you say it like that?" Hooper asked.

"Well, to be honest, things haven't been very good lately. We met in a chat room on the Internet about four months ago. You see I lost my husband, the kids' dad, in a motorbike accident in November last year. He hit black ice on the bypass and went under a petrol tanker. He died instantly, they tell me."

Dan Hooper lowered his voice and said, "I do remember that, I'm so sorry."

"Thank you. It was awful at first; in truth, it still is. I was heartbroken, but you have to be strong for the kids," she replied with watery eyes. "I can't get out at night so to relax I go on-line. I got talking to Helmut, he said he was planning to come to England to work and was looking for lodgings. I didn't comment at first, but he kept mentioning it and then he offered to pay me fifty pounds a week rent for a room. I shouldn't have done it because it's a council house, so please don't tell them but I needed the money. Simon, that was my husband, had no life insurance, you see."

"I am sure there is no need to worry," said the DS.

"Well, at first everything was fine. He liked his room, paid a month's rent in advance, which really helped. I began cooking him meals and he was the perfect gentleman. I even got flowers on my birthday. He would be out a lot during the day, looking for a job. After about ten days he brought a bottle of wine for us to have with our meal, it was really nice. He was flirting with me, I knew what was going on, but I couldn't help myself and we finished up in bed." Blushing, she turned and filled a cup with water from the tap before clearing her throat and carrying on. "I felt very guilty the next morning and, again, he was fine, telling me how pleased he was that he had found me – that it was fate and how happy he would make me. But over the next few weeks, things changed. He became more demanding, short-tempered with the kids and me and started going to the pub more. I didn't mind the pub at all, but he would come home drunk and force himself on me, as you can see," she added, pointing to her left eye.

"A few nights he didn't come home at all, I don't know where he went and he hasn't paid any more rent. He obviously wasn't the man I thought he was." She stopped and looked both officers directly in the eye, first the DCI and then the sergeant. "I would be so pleased to see the back of him, but he is more than likely shacking up with someone else somewhere, than getting murdered – it isn't like he knows many people around here."

Hooper looked at her for a second or two and then asked, "How would you feel if we asked you to identify the body, Ms Durrant?" She visibly shuddered and finally sat on a chair. Her voice was trembling as she slowly replied, "I had to do that for Simon. Dear God, I don't want to go through that again; will it really be necessary?"

Again, Hooper took his time replying. "It may be the only way we have to identify him, but I am happy to wait until after the postmortem this afternoon and see if we get anywhere with his fingerprints. Do you have any family locally?"

This time she almost shivered. "No, I was an only child. My dad died when I was just twelve of a heart attack and, sadly, I lost mum five years ago after a long battle to cancer. I have an uncle and a few cousins in Australia, but apart from that, it's just me and my two lovely children, Darren who is almost four who misses his dad so much, and Daisy who was two last month. Thankfully she doesn't remember him although I do show her pictures of him."

Hooper continued, "What about your late husband's family?"

"Simon's mum and dad divorced some years ago. His dad re-married to someone from his work much younger than him and they moved to Devon where she was born – he didn't even come back for Simon's funeral. His mum moved back to Chelmsford, where she was born, after the divorce. That was bad enough, but Simon's death really knocked her for six. She lives with her sister, who is a widow, but both of them suffer bad health and, although I have been to see her once since it all happened, she hasn't been here since the funeral."

Hooper smiled a sad smile. "Thank you, Ms Durrant, I am sure none of this is easy for you especially after all you have been through. You told the constable who first called that you don't have any pictures."

"That's right. I went to take one a few weeks ago and he snapped, 'No pictures! I don't like pictures'. I thought it was strange but that was when things were starting to go downhill so I just left it."

"Can we take a quick look at his room and belongings?" the DCI asked.

"Of course, it's the boxroom at the top of the stairs."

To his colleague he said, "I'll leave that to you, Sergeant. Thank you very much, Ms Durrant, and we will be back in touch by late afternoon if we have no joy. In the meantime, if you *do* hear from Mr Schuster, please let us know. I don't think there is any need to leave the constable outside, do you?"

"No, I will be fine. I really hope you find out who it is by the fingerprints; I really don't want to go back to that place again."

"I quite understand," he smiled, turning to DS Laine coming back down the stairs. "Any joy?"

"Not really, Chief, a small suitcase, couple of pairs of jeans, a few shirts, etc, and a laptop, which I did take a quick peep at but it needs a password."

"OK, thanks again, Ms Durrant, we will be in touch. Here is my card; if you hear anything or need to be in touch, just call. Come on, Sergeant. We will just check out The George and then we need to get back to the station."

Saying their goodbyes as they left the house, they released Constable Martin from guarding the house and the Freelander.

"You can't help but feel sorry for her, can you? He feels about as dodgy as a nine bob note," expressed Laine.

"I know; life hasn't been kind to her. I'm not sure if I want the body to be his or not – let's see what The George brings."

CHAPTER 5

At that moment, his phone rang; it was Brenda Shaw. "Hi, Chief. Just to let you know I have had no joy with finding Helmut Schuster in Immigration or Interpol."

"Really? That's interesting. How about HOLMES?"

"No real luck, either," she replied. "One decapitation four years ago, but that was rival Yardie gangs in Tottenham – various writings in blood, but nothing like this."

"OK, Brenda, can you check the time of the postmortem again for me? We will be back soon." He hung up and told Laine the news.

"The fact is, Guv, with so many illegals over here we shouldn't be surprised; it's turned this country into a joke. It must make you wonder, though, if he is, in fact, German because if he was, he wouldn't need to be here illegally – Germans, like most of the rest of Europe, can just waltz in, set themselves up and claim for anything they need; it's no wonder the older generation gets so upset – if it isn't Eastern Europeans pickpocketing and scamming credit cards, it's Muslim extremists wanting to blow us up. It's no wonder so many of my dear old dad's friends, who fought for this country, feel it isn't theirs any more."

"Too true, Bronco. I think most of us think the immigration laws and border controls in this country are pathetic, but let's not let our superiors hear us say that. Herr Schuster is becoming even more of a mystery, I have a nasty feeling about all of this."

The George was a 1950s drinker's pub – no gastro pub grub here. You would be lucky to get a sandwich and, if you could, you'd be foolish to eat it. The blackboard outside advertised karaoke on Friday with Tom, and a tattered Carlsberg England flag fluttered from a first floor window. Four men in their sixties were stood outside smoking as the pair walked to the front door. The smell of stale beer greeted them. Only half the lights were on and there was one solitary man in his forties, dressed in tracksuit bottoms, old trainers and a Man United football shirt, playing the fruit machine. He turned to look at them. "Can I help you, gents? You don't look like my normal customers and I've a good nose for Old Bill. I'm Andy Mason, the landlord. I hope it ain't anything to do with that," he said, nodding to the television on the wall showing Sky's rolling news.

"Mr Mason, I am DS Laine and this is my boss, Detective Chief Inspector Hooper. We would like to ask you a few questions about one of your customers, a Mr Helmut Schuster."

"Oh, Herman the German. What's he been up to? Beating up his girlfriend again? The prick."

The DCI answered, "We can't say at this moment in time but when was the last time you saw him?"

"He was in last night, mouthy as usual. No one likes him – big head, big mouth and a nasty temper when he has had a few, which is most nights he is in here. I have had to warn him a couple of times when arguments have almost got out of hand, plus I have had my suspicions that he might have been selling a bit of weed, which I don't allow in here, just so you both know. If he is, he will be out on his German arse; have no doubt about that, gents."

"What time did he leave last night?" Laine asked.

"At closing time, just after eleven. I don't serve late, they only come out later if *you* do – that's a mug's game. This job's hard enough without overtime. Yes, eleven or just after. I was locked up at quarter past and he went well before that. Said he was on a promise, or to quote him: 'Tonight, I fuck the bitch hard."'

"Would you say he has made many enemies here, then?" asked Laine.

"So, is this about what's on the telly? Surely, you can tell me something."

The DCI answered, "As you can see on the news, a body has been found in the trees on the footpath near Turpins Road. The body hasn't been identified yet but Mr Schuster didn't return home last night, so that is one line of enquiry that we are following. It isn't made easier because we don't have any pictures of him to compare with the body and are waiting on fingerprints, but again, that will only help if we have him on file."

A smile spread across the landlord's face. "Well, in that case, gents, you have come to the right place – he is bound to be on my CCTV. The customers don't know I've got them, but there are three cameras – one in that smoke alarm above the fruit machine and ones in both those clocks – the one behind the bar covering the till and the one over the fireplace. Do you want to see?" Both policemen nodded. "Come on through to the office."

Walking between empty soft drink crates and boxes of crisps they squeezed into the tiny office. The landlord sat down at his desk and began logging into his computer. "I'll go back to about 10.30; he's bound to be on there." He brought up three images of the pub on one screen and in just a couple of seconds he paused the images. "That's him, Herman the German. Is he your man?"

There were two views of a group of men at the bar, one from the side across the room and one obviously from behind the bar. Both policemen turned to look at each other, gave a brief nod and DS Laine said, "Thanks, Mr Mason, you have been a great help. We will need a copy of this – if you can burn us a DVD, great; if not, I will get someone down here urgently to copy it. In the light of this, I have to ask you: do you think that any arguments could have carried on from here and that one of your customers may have taken things further?"

"If you mean kill him, no, of course not; if you mean gob in his beer when he goes for a piss, yes. I can't burn DVDs so you best send someone down. No one around here will be sorry for him, but I really can't see anyone killing him."

The DCI quickly got on the phone to his office manager, Brenda Shaw. "Hi Brenda, we have had some luck. CCTV at the pub shows that our body is indeed Mr Schuster's, or whoever he is. I need a techie down here to copy the CCTV and can we get DI Roberts and DC Jones down here? I want names of all the regular customers, especially anyone he had argued with, plus I want them all interviewed, with alibis checked out. I'm off to the postmortem with Bronco. I'll try to get the Doc to do the fingerprints first."

CHAPTER 6

He didn't bother showering after his run; he ate breakfast, dressed in old cargo trousers, a tee shirt and dirty jumper and then drove the few miles to where he knew he could score. Parking his car in a side street he walked to the Millfield Estate. He had made the same journey onto the estate frequently over the past two weeks. Climbing the two flights of urine-soaked stairs, he was greeted on the landing by a very large, barefooted Rastafarian, his dreads tucked into a rasta tam, wearing faded jeans and a long sleeved tie-dye tee shirt. "Ah, ya back again, man. Ya know da rulz; I gotta check ya fore you can go in. Got any sharps on ya?" Shaking his head, he held his arms out wide to be searched. "Ya good, ya know where to go."

The door on the council flat was reinforced with a heavy, metal sheet and large hinges on the inside. He pushed it open and just a couple of feet further in was a second door with a camera above it and a bell push. He rang the bell and waited a short time. The door opened, but before he could go in, a young boy no older than twelve strutted out wearing a white Adidas tracksuit and a New Era baseball cap sideways on his head, calling over his shoulder, "Nice one, bro. I see ya in a few days, yeah?"

The second door was now filled by the man he knew to be the dealer, standing just over six-feet tall to the top of his shiny, black shaven head and weighing in at a solid seventeen stones of steroid-induced muscle. A Gold's Gym vest was stretched across his chest, the bottom of it tucked into a pair of stars and stripes Baggies. He had a black and yellow U-Boat watch on one wrist and a huge, gold bracelet on the other.

"What'd you want?" he asked – no Jamaican patois slang from him, more Margate than Montego Bay.

"Scag and good stuff, not that shit you gave me last week."

As he breathed in, the gym vest was at breaking point and his bloodshot eyes pierced as he growled, "You get what you pay for here, cunt; if you don't like it, fuck off somewhere else, you piece of white shit!" and hit him full force in the solar plexus.

Falling back violently against the door, he banged his head on it with the whiplash.

"Wow, calm down, mate!" he gasped, holding his belly and trying to get air back into his lungs. "I've got a ton, but I should have a monkey soon. Look after me and I'll be back, that's all I'm saying – makes sense, don't it?"

"Give me the ton, then!" he growled. "I'll believe you've got five hundred sovs when I see it." He walked back into the room, opened a drawer under the table and took out a brown envelope. "Here's your scag and don't be so fucking lippy next time; you should be grateful I'm in a good mood today, else I'd have cut yer fucking ear off."

He took the envelope, shuffled his way out the door and the Rasta laughed as he made his way to the top of the stairs. "Ya don't wanna bad mouth the big man, he got a bad temper."

Nodding, he slowly made his way down the stairs, keeping a watchful eye all around him in case anyone tried to rob him of his stash. It wouldn't have been the first time someone had been mugged leaving a drug den.

In twenty minutes, he was in the van and soon back in his flat, grinning to himself about the punch he took and knowing that he was now one step nearer to the next part of his plan.

CHAPTER 7

Driving to the morgue, which was situated at the back of the General Hospital, Hooper's mind was working overtime. This was a very nasty and brutal murder. Both he and Bronco doubted anyone from the pub would be capable of such an act or have the sense to clear up afterwards. No, it all seemed much too pro for that. The landlord thought he might have been selling some dope, could it be that? Again, he doubted that, just for a bit of grass.

He pulled round to the rear car park and parked in a reserved space next to the morgue. He really didn't like these places, but today's postmortem shouldn't be too bad – if cutting up a dead body could ever be described as 'not too bad'.

As always, the first thing that hits you is the smell, not of death or blood and guts, but of disinfectant and bleach. It still got right to the back of your throat and often lasted a couple of days. He had only just entered the main door when he saw a smiling Doctor Evans, turning to him to speak.

"Afternoon, gentlemen, how is your day going so far?"

"Don't ask," replied Dan, "we have found out where he was living but the name, he is using a false one. I really need the fingerprints. I've got a mobile fingerprint reader in the car you can use."

"No need, my dear chap, I have beaten you to it. I thought you would be in a rush so I have just done them. Shall I send them over to the lovely Brenda?"

"That's great," replied Hooper. "The sooner we can find just who he is, the better. If you don't mind, I will leave Bronco here to witness your artistry while I return to the office and see what Brenda has found; is that OK?"

"Of course," replied the doctor. "Great," replied the DS.

By the time he got back, his office manager, Brenda Shaw, was waiting for him with a printout in her hand and a smile on her face.

"Good news, I hope?" he asked.

"You could say that," she smiled. "We have had a hit on AFIS – he is a German. Dieter Müller, aged 42, came to England two years ago and was living in Felixstowe. We got him because last November he was charged with CD60 – causing death by careless driving, with alcohol level above the limit, and CD90 – causing death while uninsured."

The DCI shook his head and asked, "What did he get?"

"That's the point; it was a very nasty case and he should have been held on remand before going to Crown Court and starting a long sentence, but some soft magistrate gave him bail. You can guess the rest, he did a runner and that's obviously why he changed his name."

"The times we hear that story – when will these magistrates learn? No wonder so many people feel let down by the justice system, it's a bad joke at times. What do we know about the victim?"

"Victims, Chief," she said, emphasizing the plural, "are twenty-three-year-old Mrs Suzy Palmer, her three-year-old daughter, Tamzin, and her unborn baby boy. She was five months pregnant, that's all I know at the moment. I'm getting the full file e-mailed over as we speak."

"That is nasty. Right, this changes things. Can you call round and get everyone back, including Bronco? I don't think there will be much found out there to help us now, but see if Julie Burton has time, we could do with her update. Tell them I want them all here in fifteen minutes sharp."

"OK, Chief. By the way, the press office has been on. They are arranging a press conference for 5 o'clock this afternoon. The Chief Super will sit in on it with you and wants to see you at 4.45 to go over what you should say."

"Great, that's all I need this afternoon. Thanks, Brenda," he replied as he quickly walked out.

Stopping to get a coffee from the machine in the hallway, he realised he hadn't had time for lunch, so he quickly ran up to the third floor canteen and picked up a tuna and mayo sandwich. Walking to the till he stopped and made a double take at the sandwich; with the smell of the morgue in his head still, as well as his nose, was this really what he fancied? Realising his mistake he quickly changed it for a plain cheese one.

"I hope there wasn't anything wrong with that, sir?" enquired a warm voice from behind the counter.

"Not at all, Sue, just not sure my stomach would handle that after the day I am having. And how many times I have told you? Please don't call me, sir, it's Dan if I'm on my own and Chief if not," he said gently, with a smile.

"Sorry, Dan, I wish a few more here were like you," replied Sue Thompson who, at thirty-two was already a divorcee with a ten-year-old son. In her black chef's jacket, checkered chef's trousers and black baseball cap covering her long, blonde hair, with just a few inches of ponytail poking out the back, Dan thought she looked really cute.

"I heard about the case, everyone's been talking about it and I hear you are Chief Investigating Officer. That's brilliant, I am sure you will do a great job. That's three fifty, please," she said, taking two x two pound coins from him. She held his hand in both of hers for a second or two longer than she needed as she gave him his change. They both smiled and

Sue felt a blush coming, so she quickly turned away.

Turning away himself, he just called out, "Thanks, Sue, take care." Walking slowly out he quickly brought his mind back to the case and the briefing that was beginning in ten minutes.

Sat in his office making notes for the briefing and finishing the coffee and sandwich, his mind wandered for a second, wondering if Sue made the sandwiches herself or if they were bought in. He liked the thought of her making them. He could hear his troops mustering in the incident room, so he picked up his notes and walked through. He was pleased to see that everyone he had hoped for had made it, apart from Stan Jones.

"OK, everyone, thank you for rushing back. The time is now 14.25 on Monday twelfth March and this is the second briefing for Operation Nightjar. There have been some good developments this morning and I feel the route to the killer has changed a couple of times, which is why you have been called back."

He went on to bring them up to date on his meeting with Ms Durrant and the landlord of The George, explaining about the new identity from the fingerprints and how Dieter Müller had skipped bail after the fatal car crash. As he was doing this, Brenda was writing the new details onto the whiteboard.

Carrying on, Dan turned toward DI Roberts. "Have you got anything for me, Jane? Oh, and how was court?"

DI Jane Roberts stood up in one of her five, identical Marks & Spencer black trouser suits that she wore every day for work. When it came to working weekends she would sometimes be slightly more casual, but as the daughter of a superintendent in Devon and Cornwall Police, Miss Roberts was on fast-track to the top and believed in dressing the part.

"Court was disappointing, Chief. Mark Jacobs – serial druggie, shoplifter, burglar and car thief. We had raided his house, found a wrap of heroin, a stash of cannabis, various mobile phones, DVD recorders, laptops and two flatscreen TVs, none of which he could account for and some with UV addresses on them, so he was bang to rights. We were all hoping he would go down for a couple at least, but the kind-hearted chairperson of the bench has given him, what she said is, his final warning, although it's about his third one of those already, together with a six-month community order and a fine of two hundred pounds. So, I have no doubt, as we speak, he will be casing a car or house somewhere so he can pay his fine. I hate to say it but it's getting worse; I sometimes wonder what the point is."

There was unanimous agreement from everyone in the room. The DCI was the only one not to comment. This was a regular and common complaint from front-line police officers these days that have lost faith in the courts and the justice system. Dan, however, didn't want his team to lose focus on the job in hand, so quickly prompted her to move on.

DI Roberts continued. "As you know, I am still working on the muggings and assaults on pensioners in the area. Two were just bag snatches from old ladies by teenagers on bikes and one, an 80-year-old male was knocked down and his wallet stolen, again by teenagers, so I need to stay active on that. But regarding this case, I'm afraid the main CCTV didn't give up anything, but I guess we need something more specific to look for – even on a Sunday night the main roads are still very busy. I have got uniform checking out local shop cameras, etc.

"Door-to-door did come up with something that might help. It sounded good so I went to check myself and have only just got back. A Mrs Cynthia Smith of Greystoke Drive, which is off Turpins Road, said she saw a man walking down the road at about 10.15 pm in overalls and what she called a bobble hat with no bobble – I think we call them beanies now. He was carrying a small rucksack in the direction of Turpins Road. Well, at a quarter to twelve she looked out again as she was going to bed and she saw the same man walking back but wearing jeans and a hoodie, no overalls."

"How reliable do you think she is?" the DCI asked.

"Well, I think she looks out the window more than she watches TV; she is in her seventies, a widow, but seemed 'with it'. She said he was quite tall, which, after I got her to define that, I think means about 6-feet. He was a white male in his late forties. I have just sent Stan back to the CCTV room to see if he can spot anyone of that description. I thought that would keep him happy for a few hours; I had heard about his comment this morning, the cheeky old git." Everyone in the room laughed at this. She continued, "As far as the pub goes, we got names and addresses and have uniform doing interviews as we speak, but I would be more than surprised if we get anything from that."

"OK, well done, Jane. I think it's worth going door-to-door again to see if anyone else has seen a guy with this description. He has to have recceed the area, he wouldn't have gone in cold." Dan turned to ask Brenda to put the description on the board, but she had gone to her desk to take a phone call. "OK, Julie, have your happy band of SOCOs got anything for me yet?"

"Well, the team are still on-site and will be there for at least the rest of the day. At the moment I can't be of much more help. We've had no joy with the rope, it's just a standard commercial nylon rope sold in shops and builder's merchants everywhere. We are still testing it, looking for any skin particles, etc. No joy either with the cable tie; it's heavy-duty commercial grade plastic, but again, any Wickes or B&Q stock them, and no prints on it. Obviously, there is lots of blood and so far, it is all from the dead person and most of it was under the hanging body, but we have found some blood splatters leading away towards the fence by the railway line. I said I thought the area had been swept of footprints, well, it had, and very well, but it had been more trampled here. He could have used that to get changed afterwards because he must have been well covered in blood."

"OK, thanks, Julie. I won't keep you if you want to get back to it. Anyone else got anything?"

DS Laine stood up. "Yes. I won't have the full report from the postmortem until the morning but Dr Evans assures us that the head was cut off by not one, but two blades of a garotte. The doctor thought you might know something about that from your time in the forces."

"That really doesn't surprise me, having seen the body and how the head was removed. They're not actual blades but very sharp, very strong wires. The French Foreign Legion has been known to use ones with twin wires, as well as our own SAS. They are silent and lethal if you know how to use one properly and this guy obviously does. I say 'guy' because I am sure we all agree it is far more likely to be a male, and it is all looking more and more like a professional job. Brenda, have we found out any more about the car crash?"

"Just off the phone with Essex Police. It appears that a Mrs Palmer was driving her Peugeot 205 along the A120 near Stansted. It was just after 6 pm on a wet evening. Some roadworks were about to start up and the workers were putting out the cones, using one of their motorway maintenance vehicles with the flashing arrows on the back. It would appear that everyone saw the flashing arrows and slowed down apart from Müller. He subsequently ploughed into the back of her car, ramming her into a flatbed HGV in front of her. The impact killed her and the daughter and the unborn baby never survived. But the shocking thing is, Mrs Palmer was decapitated."

A gasp echoed around the incident room. DCI Hooper

shook his head and said, "That has to be more than coincidence."

Brenda continued, "There's more, boss. Her husband is a sergeant in the Coldstream Guards and has been serving in Afghanistan. He was there at the time of the accident."

"Do we know if he is in this country now, and if so, where is he based?"

"He is in Aldershot in the UK now. He was flown back from Afghanistan for the funeral, where he was part of the United Nations Resolute Support Mission and was then on compassionate leave, but is now back at work," she replied.

"Right, I need to see him. Get on to the garrison commander and the military police provost; they will all know what he has been through. I don't want him treated like a suspect, at least not at this stage. Tell them we would like to interview him in the search for his family's killer. Also contact Aldershot CID and tell them what we are doing. I'll go down with Bronco in the morning. I'd like to be there for 9.30."

Turning to DI Roberts, he continued, "I think you need to carry on with what you're doing here until we see what tomorrow brings. I don't want to drop the CCTV search or anything else. Also, there are two sets of heavily bloodstained clothes somewhere and we need to find them. Right, everyone, just keep at it – this is a fast moving case, but let's not rush to conclusions in case we miss something. The next briefing will be at 6 o'clock tomorrow evening unless anything significant happens before."

As everyone started to leave, he turned to Brenda and said, "Could you do a background check on Sergeant Palmer and on his wife's family?" And to Bronco, "Bronco, we need to go back to Ms Durrant. I want to tell her personally what has happened and I think it's worth giving his room a proper search."

CHAPTER 8

He sat at the Formica kitchen table drinking a mug of strong, hot tea. Laid out in front of him were the drugs he had bought earlier, and a dirty syringe. He was contemplating his next move. He had never thought it would come down to this.

His childhood had been hard, never knowing who his parents were. He was brought up at Dr Barnado's in Barkingside on the outskirts of East London. Second-hand clothes and hand-me-downs were the norm; a very rare treat would have been an ice cream from Rossi Bros in the High Street and then looking at all the toys in the window of Marments next-door. His saving grace was joining the Army Cadets in Horns Road, Ilford – learning to read maps, taking guns apart, cleaning them and putting them back together again. Shooting a .22 in the small rifle range and being taken to the outdoor range at Rainham Marshes next to the Ford car plant at Dagenham filled his mind with both pride and adventure, he always knew what he wanted to be.

From the moment he signed up he only had one thought and one dream – to get to Hereford to be part of the world's toughest, most elite fighting squad. After two years as an infantryman in the Royal Anglian Regiment, he travelled to Sennybridge in the Brecon Beacons for Special Forces Selection. Mixed amongst men who were mainly from the Paras or Marines, he was the only infantryman who received tons of stick for it, but it was just water off a duck's back. Now, at just under 6-feet tall, he had enormous strength and stamina and was up for any challenge, physical or mental. Even the feared Fan Dance, a 40-mile march with full equipment, scaling and descending Pen y Fan, an almost three thousand feet peak in twenty hours, running four miles in thirty minutes and swimming two miles in ninety minutes, wasn't going to stop him.

From there he travelled to Belize for his jungle training – mixing with like-minded men, he found a camaraderie he had never known. Finally, he was accepted and became a member of the 22 SAS Regiment.

He loved his life in the Regiment surrounded by the lads, training, fighting, learning skills and travelling to so many different places. From Northern Ireland to Operation Desert Storm, from Bosnia and Kosovo, to one of his final missions in Sierra Leone. Every mission different, every mission dangerous, every moment carved in his mind forever.

After twenty years he took retirement and went straight into one of the many privately owned security companies filled with ex-special forces from around the world – to Afghanistan, Columbia, Nigeria and finally back to Iraq – wherever there were people willing to spend a fortune to be protected.

His bank balance may have grown, but it was a far cry from the Regiment; discipline was non-existent, drug abuse was rife and many of the men he was working alongside were people he had previously been fighting against a few years earlier, mercenaries from Iraq, the Balkans or the Congo. There were some from the USA, who were OK, but most were scum. He hated it and that was how his life changed forever.

CHAPTER 9

Angela Durrant looked petrified as she opened the door to the two detectives. "Please don't say I have to identify the body, I don't think I can face it," she said, with tears welling up in her eyes.

"No, you don't need to," replied Hooper. "We now have identification, but I wanted you to hear the details from us. You may wish to sit down."

The children were in the kitchen eating so she took them into the front room and sat on the couch, the two detectives remained standing. As the DCI told her about the false name, the time he had been in this country and the car crash, she began to cry. DS Laine got a glass of water from the kitchen for her and returned to talk to the children.

Drying her eyes with her hankie, she whispered, "That is awful to think I let a man like that into my house and my bed. I feel sick and dirty." Shaking her head she covered her face with her hands.

"You had no way of knowing, Ms Durrant. To have false ID shows what an unscrupulous man he was, you have to just put it behind you. If you don't mind, we would like to search his room again. Did he have a car?"

"Yes, it's a silver Vauxhall. It's parked across the road a couple of doors down and the keys are on the hall table. You know where his room is, I really don't want to go in there."

The boxroom had a single bed, an old wardrobe with a suitcase on top and a small bedside table with a laptop on it.

DS Laine placed the clothes in some evidence bags, sealed them and did the same with the laptop. DS Laine took down the suitcase, put it on the bed and opened it. It was empty, but he was just closing it when he stopped.

"Look at this, boss, there's something in the top, isn't there?" Running his hand over the inside of the lid he could feel something under the lining. Dan took out his Swiss Army knife and carefully cut along the edge of the lining. Inside was a plain, white, plastic shopping bag. He took it out, opened it and tipped the contents out onto the bed.

There were two passports, one Romanian in the name of Victor Dobrescu and one Bosnian, in the name of Goran Brdjanin. Both had different pictures of the same man, the person they knew as Dieter Müller. Next to the passports was another plastic bag; inside they found a large wad of money and a small notebook written in a language they didn't understand. There was also a credit card wallet with about a dozen credit cards in various names.

"Well, it gets even more intriguing, Bronco, so which is the real passport? I think we need to get someone from the Home Office to look at these. How much cash is there?"

Counting it into one hundred pound piles, Bronco replied, "One thousand, six hundred."

"OK, I have an idea that no one else will know how much is there and Ms Durrant is owed some rent, so how about we give her the months she is owed and a month's notice, so to speak?"

"Great idea, boss, she has been through enough shit."

"OK, I will give it to her. Let's have a quick look at the car, but we'll get it brought in for Forensics to give it a proper going-over."

They both left the room with Laine carrying the evidence bags; he picked up the car keys and went outside.

Hooper walked slowly into the front room. Angela was

still sat on the couch and he sat down beside her. "How are you feeling?"

"I'm OK, it's just another shock in a year of many. I'll get over it; I've got to for the kids. If I didn't have them I don't know what I would do."

"That's the only way to look at it and although you can't see it now, things will get better. I think you need to know we found two passports hidden in his room, so we still aren't really sure who he was. There was also some money there and, I have talked with my sergeant, and we both agree, with all you have been through, you should at least get the rent you were due and a little bit more. Here is four hundred pounds. I hope it helps, but I must ask you not to mention this to anyone, in the same way as you don't want the council to know about your lodger – I wouldn't want anyone to know about this."

He handed her the cash and stood up. For a second or two she just looked at it in her hand, disbelieving, then she slowly stood up and smiled. "Are you sure? I mean, won't you get into trouble?"

"Not if we keep it as our secret," he smiled. "I don't think I have met anyone more deserving. I hope it helps and you have my card – please let me know if there is ever anything else I can do to help."

She began to cry again, but then laughed and threw her arms around his neck in a big hug. "That is so kind, I don't know what to say – thank you so much." She kissed him on the cheek.

"Careful, you may get done for assaulting a police officer," he joked and then they both laughed. He held both her hands, looking her straight in the eyes and said, "You can't change anything that has happened in the past but you are obviously a lovely, caring person and a brilliant mother with two wonderful children, so look forward to the future – things will get better, I am sure."

With that he turned and walked to the door. "Oh, just so you know, someone will come to do a final search of the room and take the car away either today or tomorrow, I hope that's OK?"

"Yes, of course, and thank you again," she replied.

A quick look in the car revealed an ATM machine-scamming device and a lot of credit card receipts. Laine put these into another evidence bag and they both drove back to the nick.

CHAPTER 10

The press conference was being set up as Hooper returned. He quickly chatted with the press officer, Megan Barrett, who explained the format, liaised with the Chief Superintendent by bringing him up to speed and then telling him about his trip to Aldershot the following day.

It was agreed that the press conference should be kept short and sweet, providing just the bare facts at this stage.

The conference room at the police headquarters was about half full with reporters from both national and local newspapers, together with regional news and Sky News.

A table was lined with microphones and recorders and behind this were three chairs. On the rear wall hung a large police badge. Dan Hooper sat in the centre between the Chief Super and Megan, who opened the conference.

"Ladies and gentlemen, thank you for attending here this afternoon. Before we get underway I must point out that this is very early in a murder investigation so this will be very brief and there will be no Q&A afterwards. So, with that in mind I will hand you over to the Chief Investigating Officer, Detective Chief Inspector Dan Hooper."

Dan took a sip of water from a glass in front of him, cleared his throat and began.

"At just after 6.15 am this morning a body of a white male was discovered in trees just off Turpins Road. The body hasn't been formally identified so I am unable to give a name. It is, however, believed that he was not, I repeat – not – a

British national. You will all appreciate how early it is in the investigation, but we are asking for anyone who lives in or around the area of Turpins Road and Simms Lane and who were in that vicinity at any time from 11 pm last night until 6.15 this morning, to come forward. We are also looking for some clothes that will be heavily bloodstained. These would include a pair of blue denim jeans, a grey crew neck jumper and a black, zip-fronted bomber jacket. Anyone finding these or any other clothes, please don't touch them and contact us immediately. At this moment in time I am unable to give any more information, but we will give another press conference at the same time tomorrow when we hope to have much more for you then. Many thanks for your time."

As soon as he finished, a host of voices began to call out questions, but he just nodded, got up and walked out of the conference room, leaving Megan to finish off.

The Chief Superintendent followed behind and they both returned to his office without speaking. Only once they were inside the shut door did they speak.

"Sit down, Dan, that was just right, well done."

"Thank you, sir, I don't like doing them but it's a necessary evil. Let's hope we get something from it and it keeps them off our backs for another day."

"Quite right, you gave them just enough. Obviously, you will take it very easy on Sergeant Palmer, at least for the time being, but if needed, bring him back here for further questioning."

"Yes, sir, that's the plan."

"Fine; give me a call when you are on your way back, I'll want to know how you've got on."

They shook hands and Hooper left.

Hooper went back to his office and brought his policy book up to date. This is something done by all SIOs to record every detail of the case, what has been achieved and how lines of enquiry are being pursued.

CHAPTER 11

It was almost eight when he had finished. During that time, he had heard back from Stan Jones with no good news from any CCTV. Brenda also brought him up to date on the telephone calls from the press conference, none of which appeared to offer much help.

She continued, "I have the service record on Sergeant Ben Palmer, aged 27, born in Colchester, who joined up straight from school and is very well respected. Mother and father are both still alive and living in Colchester. The father works on the railways for Greater Anglia at Marks Tey station."

Bronco had been dealing with the passports and came dashing into the office. "Well, boss, this gets even more intriguing. I have been on to the UK Border Agency about the passports; they have no record of either name entering the UK. I also got on to the Bosnian embassy in London and, low and behold, Goran Brdjanin is a war criminal wanted for, amongst other things, expelling Muslims to various camps and killing and raping civilians near Omarska. He is, or rather was, one nasty bastard. I have sent the fingerprints to them to confirm, but I've looked at his picture on-line and it has to be him."

Hooper sat for a while taking this all in. "It just gets more and more complicated. It isn't just a sergeant in the guards that would want him dead but a few million Bosnians as well. I don't know where this will lead us but we have to follow just one lead at a time. Let's see what tomorrow brings in Aldershot. In the meantime, let's try to get a rush on the DNA. We need an early start so I think we should both call it a day for tonight. I will pick you up from home in the morning at seven."

Hooper stopped off at Tesco on the way home, placing a pre-cooked chicken, a packet of prepared vegetables and a bottle of Hardy's Crest Shiraz, in his basket. He was walking back to the self-service tills when he saw Sue Thompson at the checkout with a young boy. "Hello again, Sue. Twice in one day, that's a treat," he smiled.

"Dan, what a nice surprise. This is my son, Andrew. Say hi to Mr Hooper, Andy."

The young boy looked up and smiled. "I saw you on television today, didn't I, Mr Hooper?"

"Yes, I'm afraid you did, Andy. I wouldn't have thought the news was your kind of viewing though."

"It wasn't, but Mum wanted to watch in case you were on."

"Andy, do you mind?" She smiled and gave a look of mock anger.

"Well, we are workmates, Andy, so I can see why," Dan replied, laughing and looking from the boy straight into Sue's eyes.

"Kids – you can never expect them to say the right thing, can you? I thought you did really well anyway, so well done."

"Thanks, Sue. I doubt it will help the case much but you never know."

"Well, you appear to have your eating and drinking priorities right," she said, looking into his basket. She continued, "But pre-cooked chicken! You could do with a good woman to be cooking it for you."

"Now, that would be nice. Any volunteers?"

She smiled. "Well, you never know your luck, Detective Chief Inspector. Now, come on, Andy, time to get you home.

Enjoy your meal." She smiled again, picked up her shopping and turned to walk away.

They both grinned and nodded at the same time.

"Bye, Andy, take care of your mum." Hooper stayed to watch them go. It had been a long time since a female had made his heart pound like this, he thought, not since Catherine, and it hurt so much to think about her.

CHAPTER 12

The drive to Aldershot was surprisingly painless with both the M25 and M3 running freely for a rare change. The case was the only topic of conversation en route, both policemen trying to brainstorm different motives and suspects. They arrived at 160 Provost Company, the headquarters of the 4th Regiment Royal Military Police, in Maida Road, Aldershot, just after nine, turning in next to The Garrison Garage car sales. Their IDs were checked at the security gate and, after parking, they were led in to the main reception.

After waiting for a few minutes they were greeted by a captain followed by a sergeant.

"Good morning, gentlemen. I am Captain Peter Jones and this is Sergeant Carl Read." They all shook hands with Hooper who introduced himself before Laine. Jones continued, "Welcome to 160 Provost Company. Please come through to my office; I thought it would be more comfortable and informal than an interview room. Sergeant Palmer will be here at nine thirty. Can I get you a tea or coffee?"

Over coffee, Hooper explained the brief details of the case without mentioning the decapitation or the identity of the body.

They had just finished their coffees when Palmer was escorted in to see them and Captain Jones introduced everyone.

Hooper rose to his feet. "Sergeant Palmer, can I first say how sorry we both are for your loss; having read the case details, it really is a tragic case."

Ben Palmer was a little over six-feet tall with broad shoulders. He looked drawn as if he had lost a lot of weight and, although he still had a slight tan, he looked grey underneath, his eyes looking dead. His only reply was a single, "Sir."

Hooper continued. "Please take a seat and thank you for seeing us today. I realise that there isn't anything anyone can say to ease what you have been through, but I hope what I have to tell you may bring some closure for you. Yesterday morning at seven am, the body of the man you know of as Dieter Müller, was found. Our enquires lead us to believe that he was murdered between 11 pm and midnight on Sunday night." Hooper paused for any reaction from Palmer.

Looking Hooper directly in the eye, Palmer spoke very slowly in almost nothing more than a whisper. "I hope the bastard died a very slow and painful death, Detective Chief Inspector, but if you expect me to be happy or sad I can tell you I am neither. It won't bring my Suzy back, it won't let me hold and cuddle and tickle and tease my darling Tamzin and it won't let me see my son Benjie and watch him grow into a man. So, I won't be celebrating."

"I completely understand, Sergeant, but it's only right that you are given all the information and I hope it will at least give you some form of closure. The military understands both grief and trauma much more than ever before, so I hope you are getting all the help you need."

Palmer continued, "Nothing anyone can do will change anything in my life and, over the past few months, I have seriously wondered if I wanted my life to continue. As you rightly say, luckily for me, much more is known now about post-traumatic stress disorder these days and with the help of some very good people here I am dealing with the PTSD day by day."

Hooper sat listening and nodding his head in agreement. "I am very pleased to hear that, Sergeant. I was a captain in No 1 Para before joining the police force and I have seen and worked with many fine, brave men suffering PTSD. I know what it can do to a man and I know how hard it can be to treat it, so you have my utmost respect for how you are dealing with it. The last thing I want to do is to hinder your progress in any way, but I have to tell you a little more detail." Firstly, he went on to explain about the various names and aliases and that, in fact, Goran Brdjanin was a wanted war criminal. Secondly, he informed the sergeant about the way he was murdered, but without mentioning the blood written as 'GUILTY' on his torso.

Ben Palmer's eyes remained dead, but a half-smile spread slowly across his face. "Well, how about that? So, I guess you're now wondering if *I* did it. I wondered why two detectives would travel all this way just to give me this news. My CO could have done that; you really think I might have topped him, don't you?" The final words were said with a slow shake of the head.

"Sergeant Palmer, I wouldn't be doing my job properly if I hadn't come to see you. Obviously, we have to investigate every angle and lead and, in the circumstances, you can see why we had to speak to you. I don't see you as a suspect at the moment; if I did I would be required by law to caution you. As far as I am concerned, you are here of your own free will and can leave at any time, but if you were to leave then I may need to reconsider whether to caution you or not."

Palmer went to stand up, but Captain Jones stopped him. "Sergeant Palmer, you may be here of your own free will in DCI Hooper's eyes, but in mine you are here because I ordered it and you will stay here and answer any questions until I say differently. Do you understand, Sergeant?"

Standing immediately to attention, he quickly replied,

"Yes, sir." He then sat down, eyes focused to a point on the wall directly in front of him.

The Captain reiterated his point. "Ben, you know everyone here at The Garrison is behind you and supporting you, but the DCI has to do his job, so please understand that and answer his questions."

Hooper stood up and said, "Thank you, Captain Jones. Sergeant, I have to ask you where you were from 11 pm Sunday eleventh March until 7 am Monday twelfth March."

Still looking directly ahead he replied in a clipped voice, "I was in the mess on Sunday night for a quiz until just after eleven, sir. There were at least twenty-five other people there. I then returned to my room and didn't leave it until 8.30 the next morning, sir. I have no witnesses for that but the whole area is covered by CCTV, so that should prove I never left here, sir."

Hooper continued, "Did you have any knowledge of where Mr Müller was?"

"No, sir, I had heard he'd done a runner but didn't know where to. If I had have known I would have told the police, sir."

"Do you have any idea of anyone who may have carried this out?"

"No, sir, not to my knowledge."

"In that case, Sergeant, I think that's all I need from you today. I will need confirmation of your night in the mess and from the CCTV," and to the Captain, "Perhaps I can leave that to you to confirm for me, Captain," and back to Palmer, "but once that's done I hope I won't have to contact you again. On a personal note, I really do wish you well and hope that you can, in time, move on with your life." Hooper held out his hand to be shaken.

Palmer stood, paused for a second, and took his hand in a very firm handshake.

"Thank you, sir. I am sure you will understand me not wishing you luck in your search for your suspect, because whoever this Brdjanin, or whatever his name was, he certainly caused a lot of pain and horror in his time on earth and finally got his just desserts." With that he came to attention and saluted both Hooper and Captain Jones who returned the salute and said, "At ease, Sergeant, permission to leave," which he did, followed by Sergeant Read.

"So, what do you think?" Captain Jones asked Hooper.

"He didn't do it, I'm sure of that, but it might be someone who knows him. Could you get me a list of known acquaintances in the services, present or past?"

The Captain smiled. "To be honest, I think almost anyone in the services knowing about this case would have killed him if they had a chance, as I am sure you would have if you were still in."

"Of course, but I will be looking especially for someone with special forces training. I need to get back now, but if you could e-mail any info over to me that would be great. If I'm not there my office manager will pick it up. Thank you for your time, Captain, I will keep you informed."

Afterwards, Hooper and Laine shook hands with Captain Jones and he escorted them back to the car park. Standing by the Freelander, Hooper turned to the Captain and said, "Many thanks for your help. I hope that the case doesn't bring me back here, I really do."

With that he climbed in and drove away.

No sooner were they on the motorway than he called the Chief Superintendent as promised, bringing him up to date with the meeting. They discussed what should be released at the press conference that afternoon as the Chief wouldn't be in attendance and Hooper said he would move his briefing forward to 4 pm to bring him up to speed on the day's events.

The return journey was the complete opposite to the

morning one. A broken-down lorry on the M3 caused a five-mile tailback, followed by a crash between a lorry and a car between the M4 and M40, on the M25. It was now taking over an hour to do four miles. It was past 3 pm when they arrived back and Hooper was keen to see what had come in to his office manager, Brenda, during the day.

Grabbing a coffee from the machine he once again realised he had missed lunch but had no time to go to the canteen, as much as he would have liked to. He made straight for his office. Passing Brenda's office on the way he saw she was on the phone. She waved to signal she would be in directly. He sat down, turned on his computer and watched the inbox on his Outlook filling up.

Brenda sped into the office, knocking on the door as she entered. "Afternoon, sir. Just to let you know before the briefing that the Bosnian embassy have confirmed he was indeed Goran Brdjanin and they want to know if you would like them to hold back on releasing the news until you do."

"OK, great, yes – I think we should. I will release the other aliases as well – it might turn something up. This really has the makings of a strange case; I'm starting to wish the Super were here. Anything else?"

"Yes, I have heard from Captain Jones. Sergeant Palmer's alibi for Sunday night is a good one and he has had a team search the CCTV. He has no doubt Palmer was in his billet all night."

"Just as I thought. Is he also following up known associates?"

"Yes, sir, and will get back to you ASAP."

"Fine – thanks, Brenda. Anything else I need to know before the briefing?"

"No, I think that's it. It really hasn't been a very productive day."

"OK, well, let's see what the rest may have come up with."

CHAPTER 13

By just before four, the team was assembled in the incident room. Hooper walked in and stood in front of the bank of whiteboards.

"Right, good afternoon, everyone. The time is fifteen fifty-two on Tuesday thirteenth March. This is the third briefing of Operation Nightjar, dealing with the murder of the man we now know to have been Goran Brdjanin, a wanted Bosnian war criminal who has also used these other aliases that you can see here on the board behind me. I will be releasing full details of him to the press shortly, but wanted to get our briefing done first in case there is anything to add to what I already know. I will let DS Laine bring you up to speed on our morning in Aldershot."

With that, Hooper sat down on the top of the desk and listened to the detective sergeant explain about their day so far. DC Laine then stopped for a second and said, "One thing has just hit me, Guv, and I don't know why I didn't think before, but how did the murderer trace the victim? He was using fake ID, living secretly in another woman's house with no reason for anyone to know he was here, unless he was traced by the government of another country."

Hooper sat on that for a second and then stood up. "That is such a good point, Dave, and if that is the case, we could be dealing with a foreign hit man. I certainly hope it isn't because I hate to think where it may lead us, but we should certainly see if the Chief Superintendent can find anything about that from the Home Office or even MI5. Well done, Dave. Brenda, would you pass that on to the Chief Super? Now, I see we have a new face here, so let's go to you next, Billy."

William Clark was what most people these days would call a nerd – twenty-seven years old, dressed in green corduroy trousers, a striped brown tank top, horn-rimmed glasses, a shaved head, a tiny goatee beard and large, black ear spacers – it was an image he enjoyed and almost cultivated it. Working for the hi-tech crime unit, he specialised in computers and was often called in for cases of fraud and, more often, child pornography.

Clark stood up. "Thank you, sir, I have been checking on the computer found at Mrs Durrant's house. It was certainly owned by Goran Brdjanin and, apart from some of the most violent pornography I have ever seen, I found lots of e-mails, some encrypted between him and other wanted former Bosnian soldiers he is still in contact with. They will be passed on to the International Agency at the War Crimes tribunal. He had also been in touch with a very well-known Romanian criminal who specialises in ATM skimming devices and this fits in with the device you found in his boot. I have passed it on to the regional Serious Crime Squad who is having a clampdown on this at the moment. In a couple of old e-mails there are details of contacts for fake documents, but as far as threats or anything else linked to his murder, nothing at all I am afraid. There was just one more thing that might be of interest, though. I am not completely sure, but I think he had been hacked. I found something that looks like a very advanced phishing e-mail that had been opened. I tried to check where the e-mail had come from but it's buried deep in the dark web somewhere. It really looks very ultrahigh-tech and I will keep on looking, but it looks way above my pay grade."

"OK, Billy, many thanks. Let me know if you get any

further and I wonder if it's a security service looking into him." Hooper continued, "Julie, anything from the scenes of crime officer?"

Wearing a white lab coat, Julie responded with a sad smile. "I am really sorry, but I just don't have much to help you. All the blood samples are the victim's; the rain may have washed away any other DNA. We have carried out, with the help of uniformed, a search of the area for clothes and have found nothing. He must have taken them with him. I really don't have anything else to give you at this moment in time."

"That can't be helped, Julie – if it isn't there you can't find it; it just shows the person we are looking for knows what he is doing and has done it well. Stan, how have you been doing on the CCTV?" Hooper asked with a smile that made the rest of the room grin.

The veteran detective knew immediately that he was the butt of a joke and quickly picked up on it. "To be honest, boss, I have done a few things in my life where I have been warned I could go blind, but none as boring as watching hour after hour of cars and vans drive down our roads. I will be finished by tonight but, so far, have thirty-two vehicles that came in and left our patch in the time zone we are looking at. Once I have finished I will run them all and see if anything comes up."

"OK, Stan, keep at it. I would be amazed if he hadn't have driven in and out of the area. Jane, how about you?"

Looking as smart as ever, DI Jane Roberts was already standing with notes in her hand. "Nothing at all from the pub customers as we mentioned at the last briefing. We have had some joy with private CCTV though and I am just back from the wine merchant at the far end of the High Street." This was greeted by a drunken "Ttthank you, osifer" from Stan Johnson and a few laughs from the others. She continued. "Their camera picked up a man in a beanie hat in the High Street and, again, a man in a hoodie walked back, but we can't see his face in any of the shots as they are quiet blurred. I think he may have slipped down the alleyway next to the old Woolies store. As soon as we have finished here, I think we should get some uniforms doing door-to-door there and give the area at the back of the shops the once-over. We are still checking other shops in the area for their CCTV, as well."

"Good one, Jane; that may well become a lead. I want to use that picture in the press conference – could you arrange that please, Brenda? June and Stan, keep at it. Bronco, I would like you to take some time to just sit and run through everything we have so far, just to see if anything makes that old copper's nose of yours twitch. Thank you, everyone. I have to say, the more we find out, or indeed, don't find out, the more I think this is a professional job and, for that reason, if we get close to anyone, we really need to be on our guard, but – as always – we can only follow the evidence. Let's be positive about the man on the CCTV and hope that we get some luck with the vehicles as well. The next briefing will be at 8.30 tomorrow morning."

As they were leaving, Hooper handed the policy book to Dave Laine and he made his way back to his office to prepare for the next press conference.

CHAPTER 14

The conference room was full this time, at least twice as many television cameras than before. The table in front of Hooper and the press officer, Megan Barrett, was covered with microphones and small digital recorders. Two uniformed constables stood to one side of the table holding press releases to be given out shortly and a screen had been lowered from the ceiling on the left-hand side, with a projector hanging from the ceiling further back in the room.

Megan Barrett brought the conference to order and handed over to Hooper.

Clearing his throat, he began. "First of all I would like to confirm what was said at yesterday's press conference. At just after 6.15 am yesterday morning, Monday twelfth March, a body of a white male was discovered in trees just off Turpins Road. That body has now been formally identified as a Goran Brdjanin. It has been confirmed that he was on the International War Crimes Commission's wanted list for crimes committed in Bosnia, including expelling Muslims to various camps and killing and raping civilians near Omarska. You will all be given a full statement at the end of this press conference, but this is a picture of Brdjanin." The picture appeared on the screen. "The Bosnian embassy has been informed. We are continuing our investigations into his murder and are anxious to contact this man." The screen changed to show a blurred image taken from the CCTV. "I appreciate it isn't a very good picture but if anyone recognises him, can they please come forward as we would then need to eliminate him from our enquiries." He then went on to give the other aliases used by Brdjanin and explained that he had links to ATM scamming. Asking for anyone to come forward, who knew him or had any information about him, he closed the press conference, again, without asking for any questions.

Megan Barrett thanked everyone for being present, gave out both the hotline number for public contact and her own direct line, for any of the press to contact her.

As Hooper arrived back at his office, Brenda was waiting for him with DS Laine.

"Just a thought, boss, but shouldn't we check with Interpol if any other wanted war criminals have been murdered? I can't believe that he picked that place by chance to kill him and didn't do a thorough recce of the area and the victim's movements beforehand. Surely we need to go back over the past few weeks with CCTV and also check at the pub if he has had any outsiders in recently. Also, he must have checked out Duke Street."

"Good point, Bronco. We don't want to leave any stone unturned but I keep coming back to the decapitation in the car crash as being the link here, but yes, please check that, Brenda. Let's hope we get some leads from the press conference this time, we need something to get a breakthrough."

"Yes, you're right, Dave, we don't want to leave any stone unturned. Let's get DI Roberts to go back to The George and Stan Jones to check CCTV. Brenda, could you let them know for me?" Then he turned to his computer to bring his policy book up to date.

CHAPTER 15

His day had been productive. Waking with no hangover this time he doubled the length of his normal run, showered, had breakfast and was out by 8.30, parking the van just along from the first school on his list. Sitting in the back, looking out of the darkened windows of the back door, he watched the children slowly walking to school, some in groups laughing or chatting, some on their own like Nobby-No-Mates. All in various styles of uniform, boys with shirts out, ties undone, girls, some with skirts so short they hardly covered their underwear and a few couples had arms around each other. He sat patiently waiting until after nine when they had all gone in – no luck here – on to the next one for lunchtime. Before then he had some shopping to do so he drove well out of town, stopping in various shops, buying a bit here and a bit there.

At 11.45 he was parked outside another school. Again, climbing in the back he watched as some kids came out to go to the chippy over the road, a few walking to the far side of the shopping precinct to Greggs and some sat on a bench having a crafty fag. It was then that he saw him coming from an alleyway next to Greggs on a small kids' BMX bike. A group of three girls went across to see him, obviously impressed by his tracksuit and new trainers as they were hanging on his every word. Looking around all the time while he was talking to them, one girl took something from her school bag and gave it to him. It was quickly obvious that she had given him cash as he quickly checked it before reaching into a duffle bag hanging around his shoulder and handed her a package. With that he kissed her on the cheek, patted her bum, laughed and cycled off.

This had all been captured on his camera. He quickly got into the driver's seat and set off to try and follow him. It was easier than he thought; as he turned the corner at the end of the precinct the boy came past on the pavement. He waited for a while and then followed at a distance. After a few minutes the boy pulled up outside a fairly nice house. Dropping the bike on the path he took out a key hanging on a chain around his neck and then unlocked the door and let himself in.

He parked a little way up the road and watched for about an hour, but there was no movement. He drove to an Internet café on the far side of town. He had work to do.

CHAPTER 16

The next day dragged for Hooper. DI Roberts had been back to The George but had no luck. The manager said he only got locals; anyone else would stand out like a sore thumb. Stan Jones was progressing, slowly checking and then eliminating vehicles seen on CCTV. The press conference sparked lots of phone calls, all of which were sorted in order and would be followed up, but there was nothing that looked or sounded anything like a lead. The search and door-to-door in the streets around the side alley of the old Woolies didn't yield a thing either.

Both Hooper and Laine were getting more frustrated so decided to take a break and go to the canteen for lunch. Sue's face lit up when she saw them walking in. Looking over the shoulder of a young PC she was serving, she gave Dan a huge smile. "Good afternoon, Chief, I hope you are well. What can I get you today?" The grin never left her face.

"Well, what would you recommend, Sue?" Dan replied, with a grin of his own.

"Well, I am reliably informed my toad-in-the-hole beats a Tesco chicken any day of the week."

"Sounds good to me. What about for a sweet?" he replied, still grinning.

"Well, you could always nibble on my cupcakes, sir."

"Now, now, you two, find a room or at least a restaurant," Bronco butted in, leaving them all laughing, "and I'd like the lasagna, please, Sue," he added.

She quickly served them both as the laughing continued and they went to a table on the far side of the canteen.

DS Laine looked at his boss, lifting one eyebrow as he asked, "Oh, so things are going well there then, Guv?"

"I think Sue is lovely, don't you? But we both know what this job can do to any relationship and, to be honest, I don't think I have got over Catherine yet."

Lowering his voice and speaking as a good friend, not a workmate, Bronco replied, "I doubt you ever will, Dan. To lose someone you love and want to spend your life with so close to the wedding day would destroy most men; you deserve so much respect for how you have dealt with it, but there comes a time in everyone's life when you have to move on and perhaps Sue could help with that."

Dan sighed. Dropping his shoulders he nodded silently and began to eat his meal, his mind drifting back almost two years.

Catherine Raye was a teacher of English and drama in the local high school for girls, loved by everyone she met, including Dan Hooper, who got to know her at quiz nights in The Brewery Tap, a friendly, family run pub on Gipping Lane. Their friendship had blossomed and both said it was as close to love at first sight as anything could be from the moment she walked towards him at the bar with a sparkle in her eye and a cheeky smile on her face.

"I know you don't know me, but I think you should know that you caused a stir with many of my girls and the staff when you were called to the high school for the robbery last month, and well done for finding the culprit."

Dan looked amazed and, for a second, was left speechless. "Ahm, arh, oh thanks, I was just doing my job. I'm pleased it was sorted quickly; I wish a few more were that easy. But thank you anyway. I'm Dan."

"Catherine," she replied, holding her hand out, "and how do you think you will do in the quiz?" Still holding her hand, he smiled. "I guess about as good as usual, which means anything just above last. How about you?"

"Well, we are a team of teachers, we should know all the answers, shouldn't we? But let's see… how about if your team scores more than mine I buy you a drink afterwards and vice versa?" Still holding hands they both laughed and said "Deal" at exactly the same time, making them laugh all the more. And laughing was what they did most of, both finding a true soul mate in each other and a love that they never, ever dreamt they could find. Life for them both couldn't have been more perfect, but that changed in the blink of an eye.

Brenda coming in to find him broke his train of thought. "Sorry to interrupt your lunch, Guv, but the Chief needs to see you immediately."

He made his way to the Chief's office on the top floor. The door was open so he tapped and walked in. The Chief looked up. "Ah, Dan, sorry to drag you up here but some bad news. I've just had a phone call from Italy, from Terry Ward's wife, Diana. He has had a mild heart attack. The times you hear this happening when someone is on holiday. He is in hospital, but is OK. They will be travelling back in a few days, but he will need to rest for a few weeks. I have no problem with you continuing as CIO, but thought I should warn you that HQ may want to send in another super to replace him."

"OK, Chief, well, the most important thing is that the Super rests. All I can do is keep doing what we are doing, but there is almost nothing to go on. If you get back in touch with Diana or the Super, please wish them well." With that, Dan left the office and informed the rest of the team.

CHAPTER 17

He had waited until it was well after dark, dressing slowly and making sure everything was in place. His stash of heroin and a syringe, along with a few more important bits, all placed in a small backpack.

It was after eleven by the time he had parked the van by some lockup garages on the edge of the Millfield Estate. Sitting quietly in the dark for a few minutes until he was sure no one was around, he slipped out of the van and, with his head down, made his way through the alleyways and side streets of the estate until he was close to the tenement block. He stepped back into the shadows for a while, his eyes sweeping the windows and walkways above him – not that many who lived around here ever dared look out of their windows at night, let alone venture out. He knew when the time was right.

He could smell the sweet aroma of weed being smoked from the bottom of the stairs; it was almost as strong as the smell of the stale urine. Head down still, he slowed his pace as he made his way up to the second floor. Leaving the backpack on the stairs, as usual, he was met by the tall Rasta. "Ah, man, how ya been? Ya back again to score? Ya no da rulz, gotta pat ya down." He nodded as usual, holding his arms out wide to be searched. The Rasta knelt down to feel his legs; it was the last thing he would ever do. A vicious blow to the side of the neck, hitting the carotid artery, rendered him unconscious immediately. In one swift move the head was held, twisted and snapped like a twig – in less than two seconds he was dead.

Quickly dragging the body against the wall, he propped it up as if it was asleep. He retrieved his backpack, removing his first weapon, and went to the front door. Pushing the first reinforced door open, he looked up at the CCTV camera above the second door, rang the doorbell and took a couple of steps back, waiting for the door to open. The dealer opened the door, this time wearing Nike tracksuit bottoms with a white vest. "You again, you whingeing fucker, what do you want? Don't tell me you've got that monkey you were talking about." Reaching behind him he nodded, saying, "I told you I would get it, didn't I." Bringing his hand around from his back, the dealer's jaw dropped when he noticed it wasn't five hundred pounds; he was holding a high-powered Taser gun. This wasn't the kind used by the police, but a much more powerful version especially made by Axon Enterprise in Scottsdale, Arizona for use only by special forces.

Before the dealer even had time to register what it was, the two metal barbs hit him in the chest and over fifty thousand volts shook his muscle-filled frame. It would have been enough to down a dray horse, but not a seventeen stone steroid pumped, wild animal. Although the first burst stunned him, he didn't fall to the ground but roared like a wounded beast and tried to walk forward on shaking legs, one hand on the wall to help him keep upright and the other grabbing at the barbs in his chest. The Taser fired again, this time stopping him in his tracks for a second and causing yet another roar. It took two more bursts to bring him to his knees, pissing himself as he fell and with a final one to lay him out, totally spent, shaking like a grounded fish.

Working quickly, he took surgeons' gloves from his bag, dragged the dealer inside the flat using cable ties for his hands and feet and sat him in a chair. He took the heroin and syringe from his bag and set about loading it with the entire stash. He didn't bother searching for a vein in an arm but rather, pulling the head to one side he plunged the needle directly into the bulging vein in the dealer's neck.

Looking around the flat he saw there was an open wall safe. Inside was at least thirty Baggies of cocaine, heroin, a bag of pills, which he assumed would be MDMA, better known as ecstasy, along with a large stash of cash. This was a bonus as he had even more drugs than the ones he had brought to use on the dealer. He got the pills first, then the Baggies, opening them one at a time and emptied them into the dealer's mouth, washing it all down with some water from an open Evian bottle. He went to the safe, picking up four of the rolls of cash, which he guessed must have been five hundred pounds in each. I know just what I will use these for, he thought, stuffing them down the dealer's throat. He finished by winding some grey gaffer tape around the dealer's head, covering his mouth with five layers. He knew that if the drugs overdose didn't kill him, he would certainly choke on his own vomit or suffocate and die a revolting death.

Finally, he took a knife out of his backpack, cut the tee shirt from the bulging muscled chest and slowly carved 'GUILTY' from one nipple to the other.

After dragging the giant Rasta into the flat, he searched everywhere, ensuring that the camera above the door wasn't recording. It was just linked directly to a small television screen. From his backpack he took out the half a dozen pictures of the young boy he had printed off at the Internet café and left, leaving them with two of the three mobile phones he had found on the desk, before closing both doors securely. He would soon arrange for the bodies to be found. He had done what he had set out to do and it was time to think about the next one.

He felt elated as he carefully made his way back to the van – it had all gone so well.

It wasn't yet midnight and the roads were still busy so he

took his time keeping to the back roads and well within the speed limit. Locking the van in the garage, he entered his flat, downed a large glass of Teacher's, then showered and changed. He felt good, he felt positive; he felt like his old self and so he thought he should after two good kills tonight. He rested for well over an hour, wanting to be sure the drugs or the vomit had done its job, before going out again. Taking the phone with him that he had removed from the dealer's clothes and a very useful piece of equipment that changes your voice digitally, as always, taking care to avoid any cameras, he made his way to a towpath by the canal. Sheltered by overhanging trees and making sure no one was near, he called 999. "Emergency, which service, please?" Placing the voice changer over the phone he just replied, "Get the police to the Millfield Estate. Tell them Leroy Linton needs to see them urgently and he has a gun." He cut off before the operator could reply, removing the SIM card from the phone, breaking it into two pieces and throwing it and the phone into the canal. He then made his way back to his flat, hoping for a good night's sleep and for a change from none of his recurring nightmares. Tomorrow was a new day and he had more plans to work on for the next mission.

CHAPTER 18

The rest of the day had really dragged with no forward movement on the case. Dan was very aware that unless he could get another lead from somewhere, he might well be taken off it.

Everything about the case was going over and over in his mind, sifting through the evidence, certain he had missed something but worried that it was a professional hit and they would never find the killer. The press was getting restless and he really didn't know what to do next. No wonder he couldn't sleep and was almost relieved when his phone went off just after two am.

It was Bronco. "No time to sleep, Guv, we have another body, or should I say bod*ies*; we need to get to the Millfield, ASAP. Not the best place to go at night – it's been a virtual no-go area for the past year ever since those in power said they thought the police were picking on too many young blacks there and they didn't want to appear to be racist. We've sent two paddy wagons just in case there's a problem. It looks like the same MO and it looks like one of the vics is Leroy Linton. We received an anonymous phone call at 1.20 saying he had a gun, so firearms are already on the scene."

"The 'Leroy Linton' muscle-head steroid freak and the area's number one drug dealer – surely it's a drug war bust-up and nothing to do with this case!" replied Dan. "I'll be there in fifteen."

He was up, dressed and out in no time, driving as fast as

he could. He was there in ten.

Flashing blue lights were bouncing off the walls of the tenement blocks. There were two armed response vehicles with AFOs packing away their weapons, two public order vans with uniformed offices, an ambulance and a SOCO van. Groups of nosey neighbours stood on landings and groups of young teens viewed from a distance, trying to see what was going on – many filming on their mobile phones.

As Dan got out of his car, he was met by The ARV on the ground Commander, Inspector Simon Nunney, a former Army staff sergeant and Desert Storm veteran. "Dan, good to see you. We are all clear here – we had to put the front door in but apart from that, no problems for us, but it looks like you have an interesting case to deal with. I'll send our report in as soon as I get back."

"Thanks, Simon. Yes, it's a tricky one, alright." With that they shook hands and Dan made his way to the entrance.

DS Laine was already getting the PCs to persuade the public to stop filming and move everyone as far away as possible. "Everything OK, Chief? Julie is waiting for you inside," he called and got thumbs up in return.

His DS arranged for a door-to-door of the neighbours and, even though it was the early hours of the morning, most seemed to be up and out watching anyway. He signed in with another PCSO and was guided up to the flat by a young PC.

The first person he saw was Julie Burton. Seeing Dan she smiled, saying, "It looks like the same MO and it's another nasty one for you." She led him into the flat, pointing out the camera as they passed it and the security door, which had been smashed open by the police when they first arrived. One crime scene officer was taking pictures of the two bodies in the room.

"So, what have we got, Julie?" Dan asked.

"It's a bit early to say but, as you can see, we have two bodies. It would appear they were dragged in, judging by the marks on the floor. We will need to hear what the Doc thinks but, at a guess, that one's had his neck broken and the other one either choked or overdosed. I don't want to touch either of them until he has seen them. There's quite a bit of powder around this one's face, which looks like both cocaine and heroin and, going by the needle mark on his neck and the old syringe lying on the table, I would think he has been overdosed by someone else."

Dan looked around, studying the scene. "What about the camera above the door, any joy with that?"

Julie shook her head. "No, it's just linked to the TV set but not recording. I doubt his clients would want to be recorded but there are these pictures either left by the killer or they were Linton's."

At that moment everyone turned around as they heard the deep voice of Home Office pathologist, Gareth Evans. "Daniel, we must stop meeting like this, you frequent the nicest places. Let's have a look and see what you have for me this time."

The other crime scene officers moved out to give him more room. He first went to the giant Rasta lying on the floor, lifting his arm and lowering it and then putting both hands on the side of the corpse's head and slowly moving it. Taking a digital thermometer from his case he placed it against the ear of the body. With a nod of his head and a "Hmmm," he stood up and moved to the seated body. He took its temperature and turned to Dan. "Well, I would say the big fella on the floor had his neck broken either in a specialised way or the murderer was incredibly lucky, which I doubt. I would give the rough time of death at about midnight or a bit before. I will know much more about this other chappie when I get him back to the mortuary, but in the meantime I would like to have the tape removed from his face, if you don't mind, Ms Burton."

Knowing there may well be fingerprints on the gaffer tape, Julie carefully used a pair of fine-nosed scissors to get behind the tape and cut down next to the mouth. When she had cut right through, she peeled the tape back over the mouth and gasped when she saw what was in the mouth. Gareth Evans stepped forward to get a better look. "That's the strangest piggy bank I've ever seen," he commented, removing the first roll of notes but noticing more rammed in the throat. "I'll get the rest out when we get the body back, but someone else can count it," he laughed. It was not uncommon to use gallows humour in situations like this. "If I can have the bodies back as soon as possible, I will work on them later today." He concluded, "I wish you all adieu. Good hunting, my friends," and with that he left, passing DC Laine on the way out.

Bronco looked around the room and said, "Look at this place! They would never have been able to set something like this up if we had been able to police the area properly."

"I'm sure you're right," said Dan, "but it is what it is. How is the door-to-door going?"

He smiled and replied, "As you might guess, although most of the neighbours are doing impressions of the three wise monkeys – hear nothing, see nothing, say nothing – our lads are getting loads of verbal from the young morons. However, one of the PCs just pointed out that a couple of years back, Linton was the chief suspect in supplying the drugs that killed that Jess Baker girl when she died after taking ecstasy at The Vertex nightclub off the High Street."

Dan nodded. "Yes, you're right and they're right. We can ask Brenda to retrieve the file on that case when she gets in and see if anything jumps out and anything that we have on Linton that might help us. In the meantime there's nothing else for us to gain here, it has to be the same person. We've never released anything about the 'GUILTY' markings; we should let Julie and her team do what they do best. Let's just bag those two mobiles and take them back to Clarky in tech and see what he can find, but I can't help thinking it won't lead us to the killer. I suggest we both shoot home, have a shower and some breakfast and get back in for six. Can you call Smithy, the night sergeant, and get him to ring around the team to get them all in for seven, please."

CHAPTER 19

Dan was back at the nick by six thirty and DS Laine soon after. Unsurprisingly, Brenda Shaw was already there busy working on her computer. One by one, the team had arrived and by 6.45 they were all ready for the next briefing. Dan was busy on the phone to his Chief Super, Arthur Jackson, and then for an update from Julie Burton, a quick mouthful of coffee and then it was time for the next briefing.

The room quickly became quiet as Dan walked in and up to the front. "Morning, everyone, thanks for getting in so early. There has been a huge update on Operation Nightjar and this is briefing number four. As most of you will have heard, there have been two more murders on the Millfield Estate; one who is yet to be formally identified but we know to be Leroy Linton as he had 'GUILTY' carved onto his chest. We are waiting for details on the other, but I would guess he was the guard for Linton's drugs business. We are waiting for the pathologist's report, which we hope to get shortly, but Linton appears to have been given a huge drugs injection. He had drugs inserted into his mouth and rolls of money stuffed down his throat and then gaffer-taped over."

There was a loud murmur from the room and DC Jones said, "Well, that's a choker – talk about putting your money where your mouth is!" It caused a loud groan before Dan replied, "Thanks, Stan. Even *you* can't get away with one that bad. Moving on, the other has a broken neck, done in a very professional way. I'd like Brenda to bring us up to speed on what she has found out about the victims so far. Brenda, over to you."

She stood with a file of papers. "Thank you, sir. As you mentioned, no formal identity has yet been made, but from photographs crime scenes had taken, I think we can confirm that one is Fitzroy Livingstone, AKA Big Fitz, aged 38, no fixed abode, born in Deptford, London, has known Yardie connections and has served four prison terms for various drugs and violence offences. I had a quick chat with Julie and we think he was staying in the flat. The other is indeed Leroy Clifton Linton, aged 44, born in Trench Town, Jamaica, coming to this country aged 12 with his parents, Devon and Cedella Linton. The mother died five years ago from cancer and the father has a long record for drugs and violence and is currently serving a life sentence in Belmarsh for murder.

"We believe Linton lived in Glendale near The Maypole pub. His first conviction was almost twenty years ago for ABH and he was given a suspended sentence. Since then, it's a typical build-up from cases of possession with intent to supply, twice when he was obviously a street dealer – both times the magistrates gave him his last chance and he was stopped in a car, which was hired with false ID – it had five kilos of cocaine hidden in the boot lining. He claimed he was just driving the car for a friend and had no idea what was in it; the CPS wouldn't take it further. He has been questioned many more times for various offences, mainly drugs, but has always been able to avoid being charged. His most recent, as many of you will know, was a couple of years ago when we knew he was responsible for supplying the ecstasy that killed Jessica Baker, but again, he managed to avoid being charged due to the CPS saying there was insufficient evidence."

Stan was the first to comment, "Bloody typical! We do all the work, get the villain and time and time again we are let down by the courts or the poxy CPS." This started various comments from the team about how often the CPS does this and how hard work and good policing is let down over and over again.

Bringing the briefing back to order, Dan said, "OK, everyone, we all know the problems we work under, but now isn't the time to discuss it. Anything else, Brenda?"

"Well, just one thing, sir, that I thought I should mention… The late Miss Baker's father is also in public service; he is the local fire chief. I just thought that, with the last victim having had a part in killing a soldier's wife, there might be a link there."

"Good work, Brenda. Yes, that certainly is a thought."

He turned to ask computer science guru, William Clark, for an update as Brenda checked her phone and signalled that she had to get something from her computer. He nodded and turned to listen.

"Well, Chief, I have a bit to go on. I've examined the two mobiles both burners surprisingly, both have just been used for incoming calls whereby most drug dealers have ones for incoming but a separate one for outgoing. I have double-checked with Ms Burton who confirmed that they went over the flat with a fine toothcomb and there isn't another one there. We do, however, have the number of the anonymous tip-off call. It was withheld but we can still see it. It has only been activated for a very short time, the past twenty-four hours, and there were a couple of calls yesterday, but it was turned on at 1.19 this morning. The 999 call was made at 1.20 and it's not been active since, so I assume the SIM card has been removed and the phone dumped. I have checked which area it last pinged from and it would appear it was last used in a quarter-mile area bordering Marsh Lane, Colvin Road and Newton Road–"

DC Laine interrupted, "If you ask me, I would say the phone has been dumped and, as that area is very residential, the best place to dump it would be in the Lea Canal; it must be worth a look."

Dan agreed but went back to Billy Clark. "Anything else?"

"Only that I've also tried to analyse the recording; they've used a voice modulator and a very sophisticated one. I've had no joy so far but will keep working on it and hope to get something. Dan smiled, saying, "Thanks, Billy, that's great. I think it's best to let the drugs squad have the phones you have and the details of the other one, they may be of use to them."

Brenda caught the eye of the DCI and said, "Just to let you know, Dr Evans has said he will be doing the postmortem at 10.30, so you're welcome to stop off there any time after that."

Dan continued, "OK, thanks, Brenda. Could you arrange for a search team to check the Lea Canal? Billy will provide them with the rough area."

Turning to DI Roberts who was, as always, as smart as a new pin, he said, "Could you look into any connection between the last victim, Brdjanin, and this one? It might be that they had both upset a supplier; we all know the problems with county lines drug trafficking. You know DCI Dave Anthony in Drugs? Have a chat with him, see if it leads anywhere and then could you go and see Mr Baker, the dead girl's father. We need to let him know and see what his reaction is." And then to another colleague, "DC Jones, could you continue co-ordinating the local area, get uniforms looking for private CCTV and sounding out any locals that might talk. You then need to get back on CCTV traffic cams, looking for any vehicle within a two-mile radius that matched any you saw from the last killing. Bronco and I will take a team to Linton's house and do a thorough search but, somehow, I don't think it will help us find the killer – this is getting stranger by the day. Let's get to it, keep in touch and meet back here at 4 pm for the next briefing."

Jane Roberts approached DCI Hooper as he walked

away. "Guv, just to say I have had another mugging of an oldie, a 78-year-old lady on a mobility scooter. She tried to fight back when two yobs went for her handbag. The scooter turned over with her in it and she has a fractured hip, which is never good for anyone of that age. So, once I have done what you have asked, I need to interview her."

"That's nasty; these kids have no respect, do they. You need to deal with that – if you need any help, let me know."

"Thanks, Guv, we both know half the reason for no respect – apart from parents who don't give a monkey's, if they get caught the magistrates treat them like naughty school kids and not the villains that they are."

Dan agreed and asked to be kept up to date with how she got on.

He spent the next fifteen minutes on the phone to the Chief Super, to bring him up to date and to ask him to get press officer, Megan, to fend off any press enquiries for the time being. He didn't want to be doing a press conference yet; the last thing he needed at the moment was a load of questions he had no answers for. The Chief was in full agreement and also agreed to sanction more feet on the ground if needed and more desk staff to work on CCTV, HOLMES and the PNC.

CHAPTER 20

Glendale was a typical, late 1960s Wimpey development of semi- and detached properties with streets and closes named after trees. It was mainly open-plan with lawns, but no walls or fences around the front gardens. It was just after 8.30 am when Hooper and Laine passed The Maypole pub, turned right into Elm Rise and then first left, pulling up outside number 16 Willow Croft, a detached house that was obviously out of character with its neighbouring houses. A police van with a search team of six waited just around the corner.

Walking up the drive, past a black BMW 7 Series with darkened windows, an assortment of broken toys and a very dirty double pushchair lay on the front lawn, which needed cutting. DS Laine knocked on the door. They could hear loud music playing inside, 'Cause I'm lovin' the way you shake your ass, bouncing got me tipping my glass; I wanna fuck you, you already know.' Bronco shook his head. "Charming. Nice for the kids to listen to. Whatever happened to *The Wheels on the Bus*?"

Dan replied, "It's Akon, Dave, with Snoop Dogg from his *Konvicted* with a 'K' album – it sold millions."

"That's as maybe," Laine replied, "but I'd still prefer kids to hear *The Wheels on the Bus*."

At that point the door opened and a female who was about 5-feet 1-inch tall greeted them. She was certainly a stone overweight and wore a tee shirt with the caption 'Good girls go to heaven, bad girls go to Tenerife'. From her shape she wasn't wearing a bra and a very short denim skirt, which showed off too much cellulite on her thighs. She was twenty-four years old but looked another ten years on top of that. Her hair was bleached blonde at the front and pink at the back, with roots well overdue for touching up. She had a piercing through her right eyebrow; a stud in her nose, another piercing in her chin and a star was tattooed on the right side of her neck, just under her ear that carried various earrings and studs. She was obviously very fond of jewellery with three chains around her neck, one of which had a coin medallion on it. There were bracelets on both wrists, rings on every finger and on the little toe of her right foot.

"Mrs Linton," began the DS, "I am DS Laine and this is my boss, Detective Chief Inspector Hooper!" He had to shout above the music.

"I ain't his wife, no way, but I guess as you is the cops you need my name. I'm Andrea Brackley, but everyone calls me just A. I guess it's about Leroy. Have you found the dirty, stop out bastard? He ain't here."

"Do you think we could come in, Ms Brackley? And would you kindly turn the music off? We are investigating a serious case and have some very serious news for you."

She stopped in the hallway, turning to face them. "'Serious news' – what the fuck does that mean? Why, what's he done? He ain't done nuffin', he's a respectable businessman, an entrepreneur – we're decent. I got my kids, Jermain and Chrystal, to take care of; I don't want no bother from you lot."

"Andrea, calm down, you aren't being blamed for anything, we just need to ask you a few questions. Now, can we come in properly and sit down with you to talk?"

"Yea, but like I said, I ain't done nuffin', so talk, OK, but I ain't done nuffin', just remember that."

She led them into the front room. A baby was sat in a little bouncer chair just in a nappy and a little boy of about three was laying on his front on the floor, hands under his chin, watching a huge, flatscreen television.

Once she had sat down, Hooper spoke quietly to her. "I am very sorry to have to tell you this, Andrea, but Leroy was killed last night in a flat on the Millfield Estate." Her mouth dropped open for a couple of seconds, she was silent and then she let out a bloodcurdling scream.

"Noooooooooo, not my Leroy, it can't be. You must be mistaken; he knows what he is doing. He has Big Fitz with him, he can't be. You're fucking with me, get out of my fucking house, you evil pigs!" The outburst had also set off both children screaming. She reached down, picking them both up onto her lap.

Dan paused for a second, taking in the scene and then continued. "It's not a mistake and Fitzroy Livingstone is also dead. We are very aware of his business dealings and I am sorry, but we have a search warrant to search these premises. Have you any family or friends you can call to be with you at this time? In the meantime, please stay in this room until the rest of the house is searched." Andrea seemed to quieten and slowly nodded her head in agreement.

With that, Bronco went to the door and beckoned the search team, along with a dog van who had pulled up outside the house, to come and start. Still in shock, Andrea picked up her phone and called her mother.

The detectives waited while the search team split, some taking a ladder upstairs with them to get into the loft, while those downstairs made way for the drugs dog to begin in the kitchen. The first call came from upstairs in one of the four bedrooms. They both went up to see that a PC had found a machete under the bed and a pistol in the bedside drawer. In about a half-second, Dan took it in his gloved hand and removed the magazine from the grip to check there wasn't a bullet in the breach. "Wow, Chief!" exclaimed Bronco, "You've done that before."

"Yes – too many times," Dan replied. "This is a Baikal made in Russia to fire tear gas pellets. They get converted to fire bullets in various Eastern European countries before being smuggled into England. A few years ago one would have cost over a grand; now they are so common you would get one for one hundred and fifty pounds in a pub in the East End." He placed the gun and its contents into an evidence bag and then sealed and signed it.

It took the team just over two hours to complete the search. They found a wall safe in the back bedroom which they cut open with an angle grinder and found almost one hundred thousand pounds in notes, another pistol and ten various high end watches: Rolex, Patek Philippe, Hublot and Audemars Piguet, to name just a few. They also found two laptops and various hard drives; they were all bagged, logged and taken away for analysis. In the garage, the dog unearthed a holdall filled with drugs.

While this was going on, the mother, Mrs Brackley, arrived like an older caricature of her daughter, in very tight satin leggings, a crop top showing a few very old faded tattoos, a sleeveless fur waistcoat, purple and green spiky hair and enough piercings to set off a metal detector. She ran sobbing to her daughter and began to yell at the WPC with her. DCI Hooper immediately walked up to her, standing less than a foot away, and said in his most firm military voice, "Madam, I will not allow you to talk to one of my officers in that way. If you continue, I will have you arrested for breach of the peace. Your daughter's partner is a known drugs dealer and on these premises, we have found illegal weapons, firearms, cash and what we believe to be a large cache of class A drugs. So, as upsetting as his death must be for her, I will not have you taking it out on my officers, do you understand?"

She stood looking open-mouthed, as did a few of the officers, turned to her daughter and said, "I need a fucking drink, A, have you got any vodka?" and stormed red faced to the kitchen. With that, Dan and Laine left the officers to finish up and headed for the mortuary.

CHAPTER 21

Gareth Evans was just washing his hands as they arrived. "Ah, you timed that like a Jonathan Davies pass, you crafty pair – not that you missed too much. Come up to the office, I'll bring you up to date."

Dan was always impressed every time he came to Gareth's office; it was a proper old-style office with a huge bookcase down one wall filled with reference books, there were certificates on the wall and a picture of Rudolph Virchow, known as 'the father of modern pathology', the founder of social medicine and, to his colleagues, the 'Pope of medicine'. A distinguished-looking gentleman with a white beard and cod-like eyes. The doctor sat behind the desk while the detectives sat on two large, tan leather wingback chesterfield chairs. The room oozed class and history.

"Let's start with the easy one. As we thought, Mr Livingstone met his end with one snap of his neck, severing the cervical vertebrae at C2, something that you often see in films, but in life, is very difficult to achieve. In fact, I have never seen it before, unless it's in a road traffic collision, but research tells me that there is a move taught to students of Krav Maga, the Israeli martial art that can cause this. The other interesting point is that I found a small but deep bruise on his neck, directly on the carotid artery, which he received just before his neck was broken – this leaves me to believe that he was struck there, rendering him unconscious before his neck was broken."

Bronco gave a low whistle, shaking his head. "This sounds more and more like the special forces, don't you think?" Dan agreed, but asked the Doc to continue.

"Now, on to our Mr Linton. I can confirm the cut marks on his chest match the cut marks from the last victim. He was a mess, apart from the fact that he had an enlarged heart through excessive steroid abuse – that would have shortened his life by a good few years. He died of a huge overdose of heroin and cocaine; I won't bore you with the figures but it's there in my report if you need it. He had been injected with a substantial dose of heroin into the carotid artery where I found the needle mark, but he had even more drugs ingested via his mouth while unconscious. If that hadn't killed him he would no doubt have died from choking on his own vomit. I think most of this was obvious from my first look at the body in situ. What I *did* find, which fits your comment, dear Bronco, is that he had indeed been Tasered. I found two punctures on his lower chest that would fit in with the darts fired by the Taser, but these were larger and deeper than any I have seen before. He had suffered severe ventricular fibrillation four times in a few seconds. To have caused this much damage, coupled with the puncture marks, points to it being a very powerful Taser, possibly one used by special forces, but that, my dear friends, is *your* department – thankfully, it's not mine."

The doctor and the DC both turned and looked at Hooper, waiting for a comment.

He looked at them both, blew out his cheeks and shook his head saying, "What can I say? It certainly looks that way. I know a bit of Krav Maga and it's deadly and not just used by Israelis – many of our own guys use it. As far as the Taser, I do know for a fact that there are seriously powerful versions, which have been made just for special forces, and it's not unknown for them to be commandeered by troops when they leave the service. Thank you, Gareth. I do continue to be worried about where this is going to lead, but as you rightly say, it's *our* department, so we need to get back to the office and bring everyone up to date."

On the drive back to the nick, Dan and Bronco chatted over the day so far. "The fact that both killings are local, Guv, I think we need to see if there are any ex-SAS or similar living in the area. It's also interesting that it was only Linton's chest that had 'guilty' on it, not Big Fitz's."

"You're right, Dave," the DCI replied, "but it could just as easily be a foreign operative. If you link Goran Brdjanin to Bosnian war crimes and Linton with his drugs, there could be an Eastern European drugs gang behind it. We can't rule anything out other than the killer certainly has special forces skills." Dave asked to be dropped off at the post office so DCI Hooper continued to the station.

CHAPTER 22

Dan had been so engrossed in their conversation that he realised he hadn't eaten lunch, so he quickly made his way to the canteen. It was empty when he walked in and was greeted by a huge smile from Sue Thompson. "Hello, stranger, it's been a few days; you're either on a diet, which you obviously don't need," she said, looking him up and down, "or avoiding me, which I hope you're not," she chuckled.

"No, Sue, it's neither – just work getting to me. This case wasn't easy to start with and it's just got a lot worse."

"That's understandable, Dan. There isn't much you don't hear behind this counter, everyone is talking about the Millfield, but not eating won't help and if you don't mind me saying, you could do with a good night's sleep."

Dan stood to attention, smiled, saluted and said, "Yes, Ma'am."

She chuckled again, putting her hand to her mouth. "Sorry, I hope you don't think that that was too forward."

He shook his head. "No, not at all. I'm sure it's deserved. So, what do you suggest?"

"Well, first of all, some lunch. Have you time for the shepherd's pie? It's very good, if I do say so myself and then, while I am being this forward, you should let me cook you dinner one night. It will beat those Tesco cooked chickens you live on and I know Andy would love to meet you again. No pressure – just a meal between friends." He reached out and took her hand.

"Sue, that is so kind of you, I would love to. Please don't take this the wrong way, but I need to take a rain check on it for now as I think this case is going to have me flat out, but as soon as it's over, that's a date, or… well, it's a meal between friends," he quickly corrected and they both laughed. He continued, "In the meantime, I am afraid it's just a sandwich, please." He took the sandwich, paid for it and they both said goodbye. He really did like her but always in the back of his mind was the fear of going back into another relationship. He wondered if he would ever get over Catherine and not a day went by when he didn't think of her and what happened to her.

He ate his sandwich in his office whilst checking his e-mails and reading through Gareth's report in full. Bronco peered around the door and said, "I'm going to follow up on the special forces thing. I've sent an e-mail to the Director Special Forces at SAS RHQ in Hereford, asking for details of any member or former member either from or living in this area. I don't expect him to reply but I thought it worthwhile going direct to the top."

"That's good, let's hope it helps. Could you get everyone together? We will see what they have come up with."

CHAPTER 23

For Jimmy Edmunds it was only his 3rd week on the job. He had sailed through his 18-week residential training at the Peel Centre, Colindale, North West London, better known by its old name, the Hendon Police College. His great-grandfather and been a copper in the East End and it was all he ever wanted to do. He had been sent, with another new PC and two PCSOs, to search the area along the towpath at the side of the canal, over a half-mile stretch, where the anonymous phone call ping had happened. They spread out and slowly walked, by looking down all the time, hoping to find something. The uncut grass at the side of the path was filled with all sorts of waste from beer bottles and tops, Coke cans, used condoms and, more seriously, dirty hypodermic needles. The path itself had fag ends, ring pulls, even a broken CD of Simply Red – everything was bagged and labelled. They had spent well over an hour so far and hadn't even got halfway. Dog walkers and passers-by using the footpath didn't help their job. Jimmy could see the others were losing concentration. "Let's take a break for five minutes, guys, we need to concentrate on this." They stopped under some trees and the others sat on the grass, two of them lighting up a ciggy. Jimmy stood looking down at the canal. He used to fish as a young boy and wondered if there were fish in here. He saw a bubble break the surface near the edge and, as he looked down, something in the weeds at the side of the bank caught his eye. He bent down to get a closer look;

it was catching the sun and glinting so he laid down on the path and saw that it was a broken piece of SIM card. He rolled over, took out his phone to take a few pictures of it and then took an evidence bag out of his pocket. As he was already wearing gloves, he carefully reached down and lifted it from the weeds. He marked the exact spot where it had been found, took more pictures of the location and e-mailed them back to the nick. They then continued their search with more enthusiasm, but after another hour or more, nothing else of interest was found so they returned to Union Street.

CHAPTER 24

The Chief Super had been true to his word and they had moved to incident room 1, which was packed. More computer screens had been set up and extra phone lines added. There was a real buzz around the place.

Walking straight to the whiteboard, Dan turned to address the people in the room. "Good afternoon, everyone, and welcome to our additional staff. For those who don't know, I am DCI Dan Hooper and I am the CIO of this case and this is the 5th briefing of Operation Nightjar. Most of you will receive orders from our office manager, Brenda Shaw; the rest will be working directly with my team. HOLMES is up to date, so please input as soon as you get anything to keep it that way." He then brought everyone up to speed with the latest news from Julie Burton and filled in background details for the new arrivals. He also expressed his concerns that they were either dealing with a professional killer or former special services operative. Telling everyone they really had to get on top of this quickly, he handed over to Brenda.

She had been standing by her desk and turned to the room. "The latest piece of news is that, thanks to a sharp eyed young PC, only in his 3rd week here, the search of the footpath by the canal produced part of a SIM card. It was in weeds at the water's edge. There is a partial fingerprint on it and it's being checked as we speak." With that she turned back to Dan, who turned toward DI Roberts.

She stood up to say, "Not much joy from me, I'm afraid. I had a good chat with Dave Anthony and he said he has no knowledge of any possible drugs link with Linton and Brdjanin. He said, as far as they know, Linton is supplied direct from the Turks in Stoke Newington but, apart from intercepting a few couriers, they have no direct proof. He has never heard of Brdjanin. I did visit Bob Baker; he's the Deputy Assistant Commissioner and head of the LFB Eastern District in Barking. He was convinced that Linton had supplied the drugs and was pleased he was dead, but I don't think for one second he is a person of interest to us."

Dan thanked her and Stan Jones stood up. "Guv, I've been giving this some thought, in fact, I've been busier than a five bob prossie on 'buy one, get one free' day." He paused for the groans to die down. "Obviously, Chummy knows what he's doing, so it's fair to assume he will try to avoid all CCTV and ANPR cameras. The fact that the anonymous call came in from near the canal, which is to the east of the Millfield, I have tried to work out which would be the best routes to avoid cameras if you had to go that way." Pausing, while turning around the room for praise but only getting a few calls of "Come on, Joneses," he continued, "Why? You may ask. Why, as there won't be cameras there to see anything? Well, I shall tell you, I have been looking at cameras, not on the route, but ones which may catch bits of it in the distance, where perhaps there's a crossroads or a side road in view. I still have work to do on it, but with some extra help I'd like to continue looking, if that's OK."

The DCI smiled, raising his eyebrows. "Well done, Stan, a great idea. Why not get some officers to walk the routes you think might have been used, to look for private CCTV? That's good thinking though, I am impressed." With that, DC Jones took a bow and sat down to a few more jeers.

At that point, Brenda came back in. "Excuse me, Guv, but I've had the fingerprint report back and we have a match." Everyone turned and looked, "But sadly, it's for Linton – he must have put it in. Do you want a diving unit to check the water there? Young PC Edmunds marked the spot well and took lots of photographs."

"That's a real shame," Dan replied, "but to be expected. This guy is far too clever to not wear gloves; I'm amazed we even found the SIM, but I guess it *was* at night – he must have thought it had gone in the water. Yes, let's see what's down there and get the young PC to go with the diving unit – we need to cover every base."

He then turned to technical wiz, William Clark. Looking more nerdy than usual in sandals over striped socks, baggy cargo trousers and Desperate Dan tee shirt. His head had a couple of days' growth on it and he had a lot of stubble around his goatee. He stood up, yawning. "Sorry, I have tried everything but they have obviously used a very sophisticated voice changer and every time I get close to getting it right, it instantly reverts back to the original again. I am certain, though, that it's an English voice. I did check on the photographs of the young boy. Using Machine Identification Code (MIC), I can see it was printed on a basic HP LaserJet printer of which there are millions, so it would be almost impossible to trace it. It was easier to trace the boy from the picture of the house as it's typical of the Cranbrook area. I tracked the house with Google Street View and it's 31 Glebe Crescent. His name is Devan Regis, aged 15, living with foster parents, June and Arthur Goldman. He attends Fullcross Secondary. I hope that helps, but that's all I have."

Dan stood up again. "Thanks, Billy. Well done and try to get a good night's sleep tonight. DI Roberts, can I pass the kid's details on to you? I don't want to get bogged down with it, but just give him a pull and see if anything comes up.

Perhaps liaise with Drugs again, just in case. Any questions or thoughts? OK, well, in that case, let's get to it and the next briefing is at 8 am. Thanks, everyone."

Dan and Bronco both left the office just after eight and agreed they could do with a pint in The Mason Arms across the road from the nick. Dan went for a draught Guinness while the DS had a Doom Bar. At the bar, they both agreed they might as well eat there, so they both ordered the steak and kidney pie, which was that day's special. Sitting in the corner, away from a few of the other off-duty coppers who frequented The Mason Arms, they talked over the previous day. Bronco began. "I just don't get it – the only link to the victims is the fact they were both related to families of people in public service and the only link to the actual crime is the word carved on the body – but only on *one* of the two at the Millfield. We know it looks like a professional hit, but is it? And I hate to ask this, but you have to wonder, is it some crazed vigilante? Let's hope we hear something back from Hereford soon, that's at least one avenue."

Dan took a deep breath, replying, "I just don't know. The feedback Arthur got from the secret squirrels in Whitehall played down any foreign involvement, so I guess it could be some kind of vigilante. I was pleased with Stan's input about the CCTV though. Beneath all the jokes he's a good, solid copper and not much gets past him. If he weren't such a joker he would have gone much further in the job. But for now, all we can do is surely keep at it; we are due a break soon." Their meals arrived at the table and they ate them in hearty silence. Neither wanting another pint, they finished and left for home.

CHAPTER 25

Jimmy Edmunds had been well chuffed to be told to go back to the canal and meet with the Underwater Search Unit. By the time he got there they were already unpacking their equipment. He quickly introduced himself to the unit leader, Sergeant Terry Ellis, and showed him exactly where the SIM card had been found.

The unit of four set up a rig with large weights, buoys and ropes, dropping the first weight into the canal about ten metres upstream from the marker and then unwinding the rope joined to it and the other weight ten metres downstream, both a metre out from the bank.

When everything was set, the diver in wet suit, face mask and attached to a lifeline, climbed down the ladder and into the water. Jimmy was confused about what was happening, but the sergeant explained that when diving in a canal like this there would be nil visibility, so it had to be a fingertip search. The diver slowly made his way, inch by inch, along the rope tied to the weights, reaching each side as he went, while keeping in constant touch with Sergeant Ellis via the two-way radio. When he reached the other end of the rope, he moved the weight about a metre further away from the bank, swam back to the far end, moved that one and started again. He came across a car wheel, a traffic cone, assorted drinks cans and bottles. He had been searching for over half an hour when he let out a yell and a "For fuck's sake!"

"What's up?" the sergeant asked.

"A fucking eel swam up inside my rig; the bastard scared the shit out of me." Everyone on the bank burst into laughter and there were a few cheers. As the laughter died, they quickly settled back to concentrating on the job and, after a couple more moves of the weights, the diver was two thirds of the way across the canal when he called out, "I think I may have it!"

"OK, mark the spot and come out now; it's time you took a break. We will let someone else finish off," replied Sergeant Ellis before instructing the next diver to prepare. The first diver came up the ladder and removed the phone from his pouch belt, which the sergeant put into an evidence bag. The two divers then conferred before the second diver submerged in the water to continue.

Jimmy radioed the nick with the news about the phone and in just under half an hour the search was finished and they packed away. Thanking everyone, Jimmy made his way back to Union Street. The desk sergeant instructed him to report to Brenda who thanked him and informed him he needed to take the phone to Billy Clark in the technical department in the annexe at the back of the station. He was really pleased to have been doing this so soon into his career and wished he could do more to help the case.

He was renting a room in a B&B on Darwin Street only a couple of hundred metres from the nick. It was run by a lovely couple, Jean and Dave Reeves, both in their seventies. He was a retired station sergeant and they took a few new recruits in. Having stopped to eat at the local Toby Carvery, he was back home by just after eight and, as he opened the front door, Dave was coming down the stairs. "Hello, Jimmy lad, how you are doing?" Dave asked. Jimmy was keen to tell the ex-copper how pleased he was with his day. "Brilliant, son, that's the way to go – keep at it." Jimmy went to his room and couldn't stop thinking about the case, so much so that, later that night when he couldn't get to sleep, he had an idea to go back to the canal at about the same time the call had been made the previous night. He dressed, let himself out as quietly as possible and made his way back there.

It looked quite different at night but, fortunately, it was almost a full moon, so it wasn't very dark. He made his way along the towpath, looking all around to try and take in what looked different at night. He walked for a good half-mile before turning to walk back. As he was approaching some bushes, he heard panting noises and a loud moan, followed by coughing. He stopped and waited as two men walked out from behind the clump of bushes, lighting cigarettes. When they saw him, one man said, "Hello, son, are you looking for some action?" Jimmy then realised what the two of them had been doing and he swiftly removed his warrant card from his pocket.

"No, I am not. I am a police officer and I would like you both to answer a couple of questions."

"We don't want any problems, officer. Sorry, we thought you were cruising here. Neither of us wants it getting out and about what we were doing here."

"You don't need to worry about that, but I do need you to answer a few questions."

CHAPTER 26

He should have slept well after such a good result on the Millfield, but he didn't – the nightmare came back; the screams, the gunfire and the senseless horrors that had changed his life forever. How could he ever forget that night and what led up to it?

BAGHDAD, TWO YEARS AGO

It had started with a phone call from an old pal from the Regiment, Tommo, saying that a new PMC, Private Military Company, was recruiting operatives to work in the Green Zone in Baghdad and were paying top money – fifty grand to sign on, then ten grand a week plus unlimited expenses, all paid into a Swiss account. The work was secret but mainly close protection of high profile targets and escorting them when they had to leave the Green Zone, sometimes to other towns that were re-building after the war.

He had thanked Tommo, taken the details and, with nothing else on offer, e-mailed the company, Coeus, based in San Diego. Following a video call where everything was agreed, just four days later he was flying with Emirates, business class, from Heathrow to Baghdad. Landing at Baghdad International Airport is a strange experience; the airplane can't just make a normal landing. For security reasons, the pilots employ an old, trusted tactic, called a corkscrew landing, circling time and time again to avoid rocket fire.

He was met at the airport by Chris Zane. At around 40 years old, standing six-feet one-inch in a dark blue suit that could have come from Savile Row, over a Ralph Lauren white polo shirt, all topped off with a blond crewcut and tan, he was everyone's idea of an All American male. After shaking hands and introducing himself, he led the way to a black Hummer parked in the restricted zone directly out front and guarded by two men in full combat gear. He sat with Zane in the back with the two guards in the front. Having been to Baghdad before, both in the Regiment and for other private companies, he knew the route along Airport Street and onto Qadisaya Express Way well. Zane explained that he was a former SEAL Team Six DEVGRU, an elite special force that neither the White House nor the United States Department of Defense will confirm exist and had been in Baghdad for just over a year with Coeus.

In just over twenty minutes they had entered the Green Zone. With two identity checks of who was in the vehicle, they turned off the Express Way and drove into a guarded stockade, very close to the American Embassy in Kindi Street.

Once inside he was taken to an elevator, which took them down two of the eight floors below ground and into an office at the end of a long corridor. The room was well furnished with maps on the wall and, sat behind a large desk with the Stars and Stripes flag displayed, was the man he had seen on the video call a few days ago, Major General Grover J Buchanan – a retired fifty-something barrel-chested man with piercing green eyes, tanned skin with a shiny bald head, dressed in tan chinos and a long sleeved, light blue Guess shirt, open at the neck. His cuffs were rolled back to reveal a Panerai Luminor 493 special edition watch, worth well over twenty grand.

He was welcomed and thanked for his speedy arrival and briefed that he would be joining Unit E, the most elite group of men and women working in the field for Coeus. In a broad

Texan accent he said, "We do what the others can't or won't do; we pay the best and expect the best. Remember that and you will fit in here just fine." He was told his duties were to begin that night with a briefing at 20.00 hours and Lieutenant Colonel Zane would show him around.

They first travelled down two more floors in the elevator, which opened into a storeroom filled with equipment. They already had his sizes and everything was ready for him: full combat gear with Kevlar body armour, flak jacket and helmet, along with the latest night vision and intercom equipment. From there they travelled down to the next floor when he noticed that the bottom floor button could only be accessed by a fingerprint panel. The door opened on to the armoury where he was given an M4 carbine, manufactured exclusively for the United States Army Special Forces, made to fire the 5.56 NATO cartridge and fitted with laser and night vision sights and a Glock 19 sidearm. There were a wide range of knives and he chose a British Fairbairn–Sykes fighting knife and a Nepalese kukri favoured by the Gurkhas.

From there he was shown to a dormitory up on the 2nd floor containing twelve beds and lockers. Most of the beds had men all wearing combat gear, either lying or sitting on them, some smoking, some with earphones listening to music and some sleeping. Zane introduced him to everyone; they were an international group consisting of Americans, South Africans, Israelis, Bosnians and Chechens. There was a mixture of hellos and waves, but some were just ignorant. The first to walk towards him and speak was a slim Israeli holding out his hand. "Fishel Eshkol, but call me Fish. I'm the 1SG here. Welcome to the fun house; I guess you're a Brit or an Aussie," and was happy to know he was a Brit. They shook hands and he pointed him in the direction of his bed and locker.

Having spent the next hour sorting his kit and double-checking his weapons, they all moved up to the third floor *where there was a canteen, to eat before the night's briefing.*

Now dressed in full combat gear, Zane led the briefing standing in front of a live video screen. "Right, tonight's target is Ammar Al-Tikriti, a former captain in Directorate 9, which most of you will know was the Secret Operations wing of Saddam's IIS – Iraqi Intelligence Service. He has been missing and in hiding for a long time; we believe he has first-hand knowledge of, not only weapons dumps still being used by Daesh, but also where they have hoarded valuable artworks and possibly gold. We have also had good intel from a trusted informant, as trusted as they can be in this Godforsaken place, that he is in a farm about fifty Klicks north-east of here near Khan Bani Saad, very close to the Sirwan River". Turning to the screen he continued, "We had a UAV fly over today. As you can see from the VT, it's very isolated. We will travel in two vehicles to just over a mile from target and then deploy over rough terrain to grid 33.535069–44.556972, splitting into two groups of four men, Alpha and Beta, and two of two men, Charlie and Delta. Alpha and Beta will enter from the front, with Charlie and Delta at the rear, in case anyone gets out that way. As you can see, there is cover with various small wadis. I will lead Alpha; Saffa, you take Beta; Chech, you're Charlie and Fish, for this op you are Delta with English, as it's his first time with us." With that, they all got up and made their way out to the compound.

Splitting into two groups they climbed aboard two Stryker IAVs, Interim Armoured Vehicles, and began the journey, choosing to take the longer route to avoid Highway 2 and many of the main checkpoints. They then headed out to the east of Sadr City, then toward the north-east, past Al Baiueia and the Christian Cemetery, only slowing down twice to be waved through what appeared to be local militia checkpoints before going off-road across to the drop off point.

Leaving the vehicles, they split into their groups, locked on their night vision, turned on their Liberator III headsets and throat mics and set off for the target.

Following Fish, they quickly and silently made their way along a wadi and in fifteen minutes were in place behind the farm. Chat was kept to a minimum and once everyone was in place, Alpha One gave the order to move in. They watched through their telescopic night sights as Alpha and Beta slowly approached the entrance of the farm. A dog barked once but never again – one of the men set charges around the front door while the others waited back. Once the charge fired, four men ran forward, first throwing M84 stun grenades into the house before entering. As Charlie and Delta kept watch from the rear, they heard screams and then there were shots fired. It was easy to recognise it as the sound of the M4 carbine that was followed by some banging and crashing, then silence. Very shortly their earpieces crackled, "Alpha One to Charlie and Delta, target secured, proceed back to the IVAs and rendezvous back here." Both groups confirmed and within twenty minutes were back at the front of the farm. They stood guard by the front door and Alpha ordered Charlie to help bring four large trunks out, which they loaded into their vehicle, another carried out two laptops and then two of the men from Alpha dragged a shirtless man out. He had blood on his neck and chest, wearing traditional sirwal trousers, with bare feet, his hands secured with cable ties behind his back and a black hood over his head. It was obvious he was unconscious. He was placed in the other IVA along with Alpha and Beta, while Charlie joined Delta for the drive back. They had only gone less than a mile when they heard an explosion back at the farm, which shook the vehicle. He was shocked to hear it and asked Fish what had happened. "We don't leave any witnesses, English, that's the orders." He then enquired who else had been in there but Fish just repeated, "We don't leave any witnesses; I hope that's not a problem for you."

The rest of the journey was made in silence. He couldn't help but wonder who the witnesses had been – were it a wife and children he really didn't think this was what he had signed up for.

Once back in the compound the target was dragged from the first vehicle and into the building, still unconscious, along with Zane carrying the laptops. The rest followed, carrying the four large trunks between them to a storage room on the ground floor. The Saffa, Tinus, and one of the Chechens, Nezh, grabbed crowbars and carefully opened the first trunk. It was filled with jewellery and what looked like religious bowls and chalices. The next one contained very similar items, but when the third and fourth were opened the rest gave a cheer because one was filled with bundles of American dollars all wrapped in cellophane, and the other, bags of what looked like heroin. "We hit the jackpot, guys," said the American, Denver. All the men high- fived each other, but he just stood there, confused. Fish turned to him and said, "English, don't look so worried, this is part of the deal. The company gets the target and all high end booty – we get cash and drugs. We split the cash and sell the drugs to a contact in Basra and split the profit from that as well. We can double our pay this way." He nodded, smiled and walked away, leaving Denver to count the cash. There was over two hundred and fifty thousand dollars, which was divided by thirteen as he was told one share went to the Major General, leaving almost twenty grand for each of them. It would have taken him months to earn that in the Regiment.

Once they were back in the dormitory, they began to pack their gear away and clean their weapons. He turned to the man on the next bed, an African-American called Joel, and asked if tonight's sortie was the normal thing they did. "Well, brotha, I tell you, we never know from one day to the next what we are doing, it all depends on intel from on the ground and from Langley, but basically it's the same – hit, hit hard, take the target, the evidence and any bounty and leave no witnesses behind." Seeing his expression he added, "You don't look too happy about it, man, but that's the bottom line – take it or leave it."

He finished packing his gear, got into bed and soon the lights were out, but he didn't find sleep easy to come by. He kept going over the night's mission, time and time again, wondering who had been killed at the farm and what was happening to the target.

He woke early after a fitful night, had a shower and went to the canteen to get a coffee and breakfast. He wasn't hungry but knew he should eat. He was surprised that the only other person in there, apart from the cook, was a female, a very attractive Southeast Asian, IC5, mid-thirties, in casual dress. She looked up from her vegetable omelette with soy sauce, smiled and said, "Hi, you must be new." He replied saying that he had only arrived yesterday and introduced himself. "I'm Sun Mi, but everyone calls me Sunny. I assume you're part of Unit E?" He nodded and she continued, "I'm computer forensics, so not as exciting as your posting." He smiled, got his coffee and picked up some scrambled eggs with rye toast and took it to a table near her. They chatted for a while. She said that she was born in South Korea but moved with her parents to Palo Alto, California, when she was ten. Her father worked in Silicon Valley and she studied computer science at Berkeley and joined the LAPD before being recruited to Langley for the CIA and then on to here. She finished her smoothie and got up to leave, saying she would see him around.

As he was finishing his breakfast, Fish and Joel came in. They grabbed coffees and sat next to him. Fish patted him on his shoulder, saying, "Are you OK, buddy? You didn't seem too happy last night; you've had quite an eventful first day at work with us." He replied that he was fine. Fish then informed him that he had to report to the Major General in half an hour.

He made his way to Major General's office, knocked on the door and a voice from inside called "Enter." Grover J Buchanan sat behind his desk, tapping his laptop. After about thirty seconds he finished what he was doing before looking up. "Take a seat, son, we need to have a little talk... He just sat and looked at him first of all before continuing, "I hear you were confused over your duties here after last night's sortie. Let's set a few things clear – we have a very important job to do in this shithole of a country, with orders from way above yours or my pay grade. Last night we achieved our objective of detaining someone not too far off the most wanted list. He is being interrogated as we speak and has already given up crucial details that are being passed on to Langley, as will the info from the laptops. This is all high-level intel that will be very helpful to both your country and mine. As far as the spoils of war that was commandeered, if we hadn't taken it, within hours someone else would have and that isn't what we want to happen." He paused and took a swig from an Evian bottle before continuing. "You know the score better than most; I checked your record and even spoke to colleagues in Hereford before taking you on. People like last night's target have often committed genocide and mass murder. They have never kept to the Geneva Convention, so they don't deserve to benefit from it. Like it or not, as far as we are concerned, we are still at war with these bastards. I'm sure we have both lost good men and friends to them, so it's no surprise we don't leave witnesses. Have you anything to say?"

"No, sir."

"Right, well; get to it. You are leaving here at noon for your next mission."

With that he got up and returned to the dormitory.

Zane was already there as he walked in. "Ah, right, English, you're in a 4-man group with Fish, Joel and Tinus. Fish knows the details, it's only a basic escort and guard to Bub Al-Sham but, as always, watch out – there is a known active cell in the *area, linked to the Mahdi Army. Get kitted up and Fish will bring you all up to speed."*

The four of them took an M1114 Humvee with Joel driving. Fish explained they had to collect a contact from the Ministry of Planning before taking him to a factory a couple of miles north. They passed through two checkpoints and out on to 14th July Street, turning right and passing the Royal Tulip Al Rasheed Hotel before entering the car park of the Ministry, via another security checkpoint. Their passenger was an overweight, middle-aged Iraqi dressed in a lightweight suit but no tie, carrying a briefcase. Fish ushered him into the rear of the vehicle where Fish spoke quietly to him in Arabic. They continued their journey, crossing the Tigris on the Republic Bridge before turning left onto the Mohammed Al-Quasim Expressway and then cutting through to join Highway 2 to the left of Sadr City. They finally cut off to the left cross-country, before stopping at the gates of a large disused factory, very close to the building of the new Al Rusafa Stadium. Tinus jumped out and, with bolt cutters, he broke the padlocked chain on the gate and pushed it open. With Fish staying close to the passenger, they drove through before vacating the vehicle and scanning the area and then they walked towards what had been the reception area and office block. The bolt cutters were again used to enter the reception, which smelt of humidity and dust.

Once inside, Fish gave the order to search the offices while their guest opened his briefcase to remove what appeared to be a plan of the building, laying it on the reception counter. They split and took different offices, ensuring they were all vacant.

He was at the far end of the corridor in the final office when he heard gunfire. As he carefully made his way back down the corridor he could hear shouting in English with an Arab accent, saying, "This area is under our control, you have no jurisdiction here. If you value your lives you will leave now and let us deal with this traitor."

As he continued, he saw a stairway on his right and quickly made his way up to an open balcony on the mezzanine floor. Crawling out onto it he could see outside that there were two open-top old jeeps, both with machine-guns mounted on the back and each with a driver and passenger. Looking down to the reception there were four more armed men, all in black Mahdi Army uniforms. Fish was facing them with the rest of the unit stood behind him with their hands on their weapons.

"We do value our lives, sadiqi (my friend), and we are only doing our job, as you are. We want no trouble but we can't let you take our friend here."

The Arab lowered his head in a bow and yelled "Aistaeada!!" At the order of standby, his men all raised their guns and pointed them at the unit, a move that was matched instantly by the units. As this was unfolding, both passengers got out of the jeeps and climbed onto the back toward the machine-guns. "I don't think you have any choice, my friend, you are outnumbered and it matters nothing to me to leave you dead in the dirt here."

But Fish was still trying to calm the situation. "There is no need for this, what is this man to you?"

As they continued to talk, he quickly crawled away from the balcony and crept back down the stairs. At the end of the corridor was an emergency exit, which he used and slowly made his way around to the front of the building, crawling through the bushes that had overgrown the car park, until he came up behind the furthest jeep. Removing his Fairbairn-Sykes knife, he slipped silently onto the back of the jeep. The man on the gun was concentrating on what was going on in the reception; he didn't know a thing until a hand went over his mouth and the knife cut across his throat. He slithered silently onto the floor, when he slipped off the back and crawled to the left side of the jeep where he reached through the window and cut the driver's throat.

After, he climbed back to the machine-gun. Joel had seen what had happened and one of the Arabs turned to the car park to see what he was looking at. He yelled to the others who turned to see, while the unit kept their weapons aimed at the Mahdis. "Checkmate, my friend... I think. Now, drop your weapons and tell your men outside to come in!" Fish ordered.

But the leader turned, firing his gun at the Arab, the bullet hitting the centre of his chest. He was still turning when Fish fired a double tap into the man's forehead. Watching from outside, he saw what was happening and opened fire on the jeep in front, taking out the gunman and driver in seconds. The remaining gunmen dropped their guns and held their hands up, but to no avail – they were mowed down in a hail of bullets from the rest of the unit's guns.

Fish turned to their guest who was lying on the floor, blood pouring from his chest wound. Touching his neck for a pulse, he realised it was too late – he was dead. The rest of the team were collecting the Arab's weapons and dragging them out of the way.

He climbed down from the back of the jeep, checking that the two on the front jeep were indeed dead and jogged back into the reception. "Well done, English," Fish called out and the others patted him on his back or fist bumped him. That was all very well, he knew he had done what he had to do, but he had no time for those who shot the men with their hands in the air.

Joel was the first to talk. "What's the plan now, Fish? We shouldn't stay here too long, they may well have a backup nearby."

"I know, but at least we've got the plans – we'd best take them back to base, study them and then come out in force later to get what's here."

"What about these bodies and jeeps outside?" asked Tinus.

"We need to lose them and we have the dump site not far

from here. Load them into both jeeps – English drive one, Tinus the other – you know where to go, Tinus, but follow us, it will be safer, we will go cross–country."

Once loaded they cleared the area of any shell casings and set off in convoy across rough terrain. In roughly fifteen minutes they came to what looked like a deserted farmhouse in front of a steep hill. As they pulled in, four guards appeared, all in combat gear. Fish waved to them as they drove around the farmhouse where the guards opened two large doors in the side of the hill. As they drove in, he could see that a bunker had been dug out of the hill. It was huge, but dark and dirty and filled with rows of oil barrels. They dragged the bodies out of the jeeps into the outbuilding. "How many have you got?" asked one of the guards.

"Nine," replied Fish.

"Nine? For fuck's sake, who have you been fucking with, Fish?"

"It's a long story that I don't have time for. We need to do this quickly – best use the big tank."

With that the four guards took a handle each, lifted a large metal cover up from the ground and slid it over to expose a large tank in the ground. You could instantly smell the contained acid. They wasted no time in searching each of the bodies and dropped each one into the tank. They then replaced the cover and it was all done in minutes. The bodies would never be found.

The jeeps were left for another group to deal with and the four members of Unit E left to return to base. Once again, all he could think of was the killing of surrendering soldiers, then dumping them in acid. He had lost count of the people he had killed in combat over the years, but this was different. He still knew it wasn't what he signed up for and he rightly guessed it would only get worse – and it did.

CHAPTER 27

Dan and DS Laine were both back in the office just after 7.30. Neither having slept that well, they grabbed a coffee each and went to their desks. Brenda was already in and updating HOLMES. Over the next ten minutes the rest of the team arrived in the office before making their way to that day's briefing.

The room was full and fell quiet as soon as DCI Hooper entered. "Good morning, everyone. I hope you're all feeling bright and ready for another hard day. For the record, this is the 6th briefing for Operation Nightjar. Brenda has updated HOLMES, but let's hear what we have. So let's start with DC Jones."

Stan stood, cleared his throat in a theatrical way and turned to his boss. "We've had foot patrols out looking for cameras and, so far, we have seen six, with four in businesses and two in houses. A team will visit each of them today to look at the hard drives and bring anything in of interest. It's surprising how many vans are still out at that time of night, but thanks to the extra help, we think we may have narrowed it down to five or six vans, all travelling in the right direction at about the right time. We haven't got any reg numbers but, hopefully by the end of the day, we may be able to magic something up – just like that!" The last three words were delivered in his best Tommy Cooper voice.

"OK, thanks Stan, keep at it and update us as soon as you know more. Right, how about DI Roberts... anything from the lad in the pictures?"

She was one of the most organized officers Dan had ever met and he was always so impressed with her; there was no doubt she was on the way to the top, just like her father. She smiled and was about to speak when DS Laine rushed into the room.

"Sorry to interrupt, but we may have a breakthrough. I've just heard back from SAS HQ in Hereford and it would seem we have one of their former soldiers living in the area and not even half a mile from the area where the anonymous call was made. They are sending me through his record, which we will have shortly. His name is James Miller, born in Doncaster on seventeenth June 1975. The address I've been given is 42 Shakespeare House on the Dickens Estate. Let's get on our computers, I want to know everything about him in the next fifteen minutes: bank details, vehicles and health, etc."

"Inside leg measurement, Sarg?" Stan called out, but for once it was ignored.

Dan was elated; at last they had something to go on. He called for someone to get Google Street View up on the large plasma screen so they could view the address. Shakespeare House was a four-storey, dark red brick, 1930s tenement with walkways on each floor stretching the length of the building. It was generally in good order. The Dickens Estate wasn't anywhere near as depressed as the notorious Millfield. Within a minute one of the officers called out that the DVLA had confirmed he has a dark blue Ford Transit on an 06 plate, vehicle reg Alpha Victor 06 Lima Mike Papa, showing up as not insured. Dan called to DC Jones, "Stan, run that through ANPR for the last couple of days and see what comes up; we can do a proper search later. This is looking very promising."

The room was buzzing with excitement; this is what they worked for. Calls were being made to banks, the Police

National Computer was being scoured for information, as was social media and newspaper archives – even the HMRC was being contacted.

Bronco returned to the room and handed a printout to the DCI.

"Right, I have his military record from Hereford. Let me see... OK, the main bullet points are that he had been in the service since '93 and the Regiment since 2000, so he has more than likely served in Afghanistan, Iraq, Somalia and a few more very nasty places. He has been treated for PTSD and was retired, due to government cutbacks, just over a year ago and it would seem this wasn't very well received. What else have we got?"

A young WPC answered first. "He has a record, sir, one case of D & D last year. He was drunk in Wetherspoons in town, asked to leave and wouldn't. Fined one hundred and fifty quid."

Dan left DC Laine to co-ordinate things in the incident room while he ran up to the top floor to see the Chief Superintendent. He knocked on the door but went straight in. Arthur looked up. "Morning, Dan. What is it? Good or bad news?"

"Hopefully, it's good, sir," so he explained the latest news and they both agreed that they should bring in the Tactical Support team of the ARV. The Chief set about putting that in motion by contacting the head of the firearms unit and then arranging a search warrant for the address. Dan finished and made his way back to his office.

Over the next hour he spoke with Superintendent Alan Benson who would be the silver commander at HQ and Inspector Nunney who, again, would be the ground commander to formulate the TST's role and how they would approach things. It was agreed it would be safer doing it in the early hours of the morning, but as they didn't want to wait that long they planned it for 8 pm that night. In the meantime, Simon would get a specialist surveillance team to watch the flat and have a covert communications vehicle in the area, as well as oversee everything. He thought the best way to try and get in would be using a decoy fast food delivery company. They discussed this some more and agreed to meet at the nick at 6 pm.

The rest of the day was spent gathering as much information on Miller as possible. Dan did grab a sandwich from the canteen, but it was very busy, and he barely had time to exchange pleasantries with Sue.

CHAPTER 28

The first ARV arrived just before six, bringing Inspector Nunney and two more officers. They handed out specialised intercom sets to Dan, Bronco and Jane, so they could hear what TST were doing, along with bullet-proof vests for each of them.

By 6.30, incident room 1 was full. A dozen armed officers, looking like something from *RoboCop* with their Pro-Tec ballistic helmets and hard plate bullet-proof vests fitted with heavy titanium plates, were backed up by two dozen unarmed cops in full riot gear. To add to the scene was a man being used as the decoy in a blue Domino's Pizza puffer jacket over a bullet-proof vest. He would also be carrying a pistol inside the insulated delivery bag.

The Inspector led the briefing, first of all emphasizing how dangerous the target was, his military background and how he may well try to evade arrest and be armed. He kept going over each move they planned, time and time again. The plasma screen showed the front of the building and they also had a floor plan of the flat itself and of the building, showing staircases, planned entrances, exits and fall-back positions if they came under fire. He kept questioning his officers and requesting them to repeat the plan until he was sure everyone knew exactly what their part was. He was in constant touch with the observation unit who had set up in a boarded up flat in the opposite block of flats, which had been shut down after being used as a drug house. He had learned that the target hadn't left the flat, but they had seen the lights on and movement inside.

With the convoy of three ARVs, four VW Special Police Unit vans, the decoy on a genuine Domino's Honda motor scooter and Dan with his team in an unmarked BMW 5 Series, all set off and made their way across town, the men in the riot vans laughing and joking while both Simon's and Dan's teams were quiet, contemplating the night ahead.

The entire convoy pulled into in a car park a street away from Shakespeare House on the edge of the Dickens Estate, along with an ambulance. The AFOs took their weapons from their safes in the converted Beamers. Each man was armed with a 9mm Glock 17 and Heckler & Koch MP5 carbines. Good to go, under their helmets they pulled down their fireproof balaclavas and their darkened glasses that looked like the goggles you would wear to go skiing. All were wearing body cams and the team checked that all their communications were in order. Two of them carried ballistic shields while one carried 'the big red key', a very heavy iron battering ram, should they need to force entry.

A white Mercedes Sprinter pulled up next to them, which Inspector Nunney explained was the mobile communications vehicle, and a police helicopter arrived high above them. Meanwhile, the riot gear police remained inside their vans; Simon had a few final words with his men before taking Dan and his team into the communications van, which was manned by a team of two and looked like the inside of a space station. They sat down and could view the split screen showing feeds from all of the body cams, while there was a long shot and a close-up of the front of the flat being filmed from the stakeout.

CHAPTER 29

They checked communications again, with each man confirming he was live, as did the decoy and the two sergeants in charge of the riot unit. Superintendent Alan Benson, who was overseeing from headquarters as silver commander, also joined them on-line. At three minutes to eight, after checking with the Superintendent, Simon gave the order to move in. It was already dark and the streets were quiet. Quickly, but very quietly, they made their way to their start points. Four went to the rear of the flats and four to the stairwells on each end at the front. Once in place, the commander gave the order for the men at the front to move to the first floor landing, at the same time instructing the decoy to make his approach from just around the corner.

The men in the riot vans were out and moving closer to Shakespeare House.

From the van they watched on the screens as the men made their way to the first floor landings. It took Dan's mind back to many sorties during his time in the Paras. He knew those feelings – mixtures of excitement, fear, ego and 'Let's fucking do this!' that went through everyone's mind and body just before a mission.

The scooter pulled up by the left stairwell. He got off, taking the insulated bag from his storage box and made his way, whistling to himself up the stairs. On the landing the eight men had silently made their way, crouching low to each side of the front door at number 41. There was a light on in the hallway and they could hear the television. They all confirmed they were in place. The decoy made his way along the landing as if he hadn't a care in the world.

The atmosphere in the van was electric. The next few minutes were not only critical, but also extremely dangerous; the biggest risk was of course for the decoy, but everyone was holding their breath, on tenterhooks. Inspector Nunney stood up, looking at all the screens. "Stand-by. If the target opens the door, act immediately and don't wait for my command, but if not, I will give the order to enter."

The last few steps the decoy took seemed to take forever. As Dan and the rest watched, he knocked on the flat's door and called out, "Domino's delivery!" There was no response, so Nunney told him to knock again but louder this time, which he did. Another second or two passed, which felt like a minute and, then, on the close-up screen, they saw movement behind the curtain. At this, Nunney ordered, "There is movement inside – I confirm – movement inside. Be ready to strike."

A voice from inside called out, "What do you want?"

The decoy with one hand now inside the insulated bag holding his Glock 17, took a few steps back from the door, leaving space for the entry team and replied, "It's your Domino's Pizza delivery, mate."

The voice from inside replied, "Pizza? I've not ordered a fucking pizza."

"Well, the ticket says it's for number 41. I've got a large, deep pan Hawaiian and a large, deep crust Pepperoni Passion – it's all been paid for."

With that there was the sound of the door being unbolted and it slowly opened. As soon as the target looked around the door, all hell broke loose.

The decoy instantly dropped the bag behind him with his left hand, pointing the pistol in his right hand at the target, at the exact same time as the first two armed offices on each side stood pointing their carbines at the target, all shouting at the top of their voices several times, "Armed police! Armed police! Put your hands where we can see them."

The target yelled, "What the fuck's going on?"

The police responded with shouts of, "Armed police! Get down on the floor! Get down on the floor!"

He shouted yet again, "What the fuck is going on? What do you want?" and took a step forward out of the door.

"Get on the floor now, do not move, you will be shot." He still didn't move but the two officers grabbed his arms from each side and forced him to the ground. He cried out but didn't struggle as they put handcuffs on him and stood him up.

"Suspect in custody, no injuries," was relayed back to the vans and everyone there breathed a sigh of relief.

The lead, armed officer spoke to the target, "Are you James Miller?"

"Yes. Who the fuck do you think I am? What is this all about?" His voice was very croaky and his breath stank of booze.

"We are arresting you in connection with a series of murders. You do not have to say anything, but it may harm your defence if you do not mention when questioned, something which you later rely on in court. Anything you do say may be given in evidence. Do you understand?"

"No, I don't fucking understand. Murders? Who the fuck do you think I am? This is fucking out of order; I could take the lot of you on single-handedly if I wanted you bunch of jumped-up fucking amateurs. I'm fucking SAS!"

While he continued shouting, they led him, limping, along the landing and down the stairs.

Two of the special unit vans drove around to the front of the tenement block where the officers in riot gear had spread out, to cordon off the area.

Once he was locked in the cell at the back of the first special unit van, it set off, followed by a second van. A group of the riot gear officers then entered the flat with two AROs to search for weapons.

Dan, Bronco and Jane left the communications van and made their way with Simon Nunney to the flat, passing some of the AROs that were starting to stand down. They walked up the stairs but waited outside number 41, not wanting to contaminate the site any more than it was, by the search for weapons. After about five minutes the officers made their way out and one reported to the commander, "No sign of anything, Guv. We've given it a good going-over, but it might be worthwhile sending in a dog before SOCOs get here, just in case." Nunney nodded. "OK, well done. Let's get packed away and back to the nick. It's always good when we get our target and no shots were fired – it's a result. Good luck, Dan, I hope that puts this one to bed for you."

The crew made their way back to the cars. Dan thanked Simon and they travelled back to the nick.

CHAPTER 30

Miller was being checked in by the Custody Officer when they arrived. He was considerably quieter, but remained handcuffed. They emptied his pockets of a wallet, cigarette lighter and a bunch of keys, including door key and car key. Dan asked the sergeant to enquire about the keys, as they wanted to find his van. "I can't do that, Guv, sorry, but he is obviously drunk. We need to let him sober up before I can allow any questions. The last thing you want is any evidence to be excluded because we haven't kept to the book. He needs to be kept in overnight and questioned in the morning." Dan agreed and Miller was informed he was being detained and taken to the cells.

It was just after 9 pm and Dan, along with DS Laine and DI Roberts, made their way back up to the incident room. Everything was quiet and the room empty. They sat facing each other and Bronco was the first to speak. "That was intense, wasn't it? I must admit, at one point I wondered how that was going to go."

"Me too," admitted DI Roberts. "That's the biggest armed shout I've been involved in. I guess you were used to that in the forces, Guv?"

"I don't think you ever get used to it but I have had my fair share. To be honest, I was wishing I *were* on the front line with them tonight. Anyway, I want to get prepped for the interview in the morning, so let's hope he is sober by then. I have an hour or so to do, but you guys get off home, we can start again in the morning at 7 am."

Everyone was back in early the next day and all were very excited about the events of the previous night. Brenda, once again, had updated HOLMES and Dan had brought his policy book up to date before he had gone home last night. A special dog, trained to sniff guns and explosives, was being brought in that morning from another station to check out the flat. Dan gave a quick briefing but wanted to get on with the interview, which the Custody Officer had told him could take place at eight, once the prisoner had eaten breakfast.

Eight am couldn't come quick enough, it was agreed that with his extra experience, Bronco would lead the questioning with Dan stepping in if he felt it necessary. They would start out very friendly and see where that got them and slowly crank it up by using their judgement. They made their way to interview room 2, the smallest and most uncomfortable in the station, with its drab grey walls, four old chairs, a table and a distinctive stale smell of BO, farts and cigarette smoke. On top of the table was a double cassette recorder, which the police still used, as it was believed it was easier to detect tampering on a tape than a digital recording. Miller was brought in, limping, by two PCs. One stood behind him and one by the door. He looked tired, with bloodshot eyes and unkempt hair.

Bronco, looking directly at Miller, began the meeting. "This interview is being both audio and video recorded. I must remind you that you are still under caution. Will you state your full name, please."

"James Miller."

"State your address and date of birth, please."

"Forty-one Shakespeare House, Dickens Estate, 17.6.75."

"I am DS David Laine. Also present is DCI Dan Hooper." The other PCs in the room also provided their names. "There are no other persons present. Mr Miller has refused the offer to have a solicitor present. Will you please confirm that for the recording."

"I don't need a fucking solicitor, I've done now't wrong."

DS Laine continued on with the date and time. "We are in interview room 2 at Union Street Police Station. At the conclusion of the interview, I will give you a form, which will explain the procedure for dealing with this recording and how you can have access to it. Do you understand?" at which point, Miller nodded and grunted, "Yes."

"Right, Jimmy. I can call you Jimmy, can't I? That was what your pals called you in the Regiment, wasn't it? How are you feeling this morning?"

"Fucking rough, if you must know. I need more coffee and a fag."

"OK, Jimmy, we can do that. Black or white; any sugar?" He replied and the DS indicated to one of the PCs to sort it.

"So, Jimmy, how many years were you in the Regiment?"

"No comment."

"Now, come on, mate, there's no need for that, is there?"

"Get me my coffee and fags and I'll talk to you."

Bronco continued to try and get Miller to relax. "OK, Jimmy, we can do that. I only wanted to know what it was like to be in the Regiment, you must have seen some sights, had some fun, but we can wait if you wish, though I can't promise the coffee is up to even Costa's standard, but it will be hot and black for you."

They sat in silence for a couple of minutes before the PC returned with the coffee in a plastic cup. He took a packet of Benson's and a lighter out of his pocket, offered one to Miller and then lit it.

Miller took a large gulp of the hot coffee, coughed and drew on the cigarette, blowing smoke into the air. Although smoking indoors had been banned since 2007, it was often broken during interviews if they thought it helped.

DS Laine let Miller finish before continuing. "So, Jimmy, how many years were you in the Regiment?"

Miler looked directly at him. "No comment."

"Come on, Jimmy, this won't get us anywhere. How long have you lived at your current address?"

"No comment."

"You're doing yourself no favours like this, Jimmy."

"No comment."

This continued for some time, each question answered in the same way. Bronco was keeping calm, but Dan could sense it was getting to him, so felt it time to interrupt.

"Trooper Miller, as you have been told, I am Detective Chief Inspector Dan Hooper, but I am also Captain Daniel Hooper Paratrooper Regiment – retired."

Miller laughed out loud. "A fucking Para! Always going in after we've done the hard work, bunch of wankers. Am I meant to be impressed which Para were you in?"

"I was in 1 PARA which, as you well know, is attached to the Special Forces Support Group. I am a regular reservist, so am allowed to pull rank on you if I so wish. You should also know I still have good contacts with former comrades of yours in Hereford, so if you would rather, I can call my good friend, Captain George Sheppard, to fly down here now in a chopper and question you."

Miller stopped and looked at Dan for a moment or two. "OK. With respect, *SIR*, I don't give a monkey's about your rank or your history but I am getting pissed off with all this fucking about. Tell me what you want to know, I just want to get out of this fucking place. I'll answer you, but not him," he said, pointing to Bronco.

"OK, fine; let's start with something simple. Do you own a vehicle?"

"Why?"

"Because I am asking you, trooper, do you own a vehicle?"

"Yes, I do own a vehicle."

"OK, good. What is it and where is it kept?"

"What's it to you?"

"It's part of our enquiries, now please answer."

"In my garage; it's in the row of garages on the Dickens Estate. It's number 17; the keys to the garage and the van are on my key ring you've got. Why are you asking?"

Dan turned to Bronco and nodded. The DS got up and made his way to the door.

"OK, we will take a break. Interview suspended at 8.57 am," and he pressed *Stop* on the recorder. "Take Mr Miller back to his cell, please," he asked the PCs. Miller wasn't happy. "I'll ask again – what the fuck is going on?"

"You will find out soon enough, trooper," Dan replied.

CHAPTER 31

Bronco was waiting in the car as Dan came out. They drove with blues and twos towards the flat. "What do you make of it, Dave?"

"Well, he certainly had a chip on his shoulder, but you soon sorted him out. He has loads of bravado, but I expect he needed that in the Regiment. I didn't realise you had contacts at Hereford."

"I don't, it was a bluff, but I had heard of George Sheppard back in the day, so chanced it and it worked."

As they pulled up there was still one police van along with Forensics and a dog van. As they got to the flat the dog handler was just coming out with a SOCO who Dan recognised. "Ah, good morning, Chief, we're just about finished here, nothing special to report to far. We have bagged all his clothes and shoes in case we can find anything on them. This is Doug Finn; he and Apache here had a good sniff around, but couldn't find anything." Dan had a chat with PC Finn and they went to find the garage. It was located just at the rear of the tenement block and number 17 was halfway along. They let the crime scene officer unlock it and let the dog go in first. It was just a very basic garage with not much more room than the van. The dog looked and sniffed all around and PC Finn lifted him up on a small bench at the back with some boxes on it, but they got no signal from the dog and so they decided to come out. The van was driven out by the CSO and, again, the dog searched while the CSO checked inside the garage. When the dog had finished, they searched the van but there was no sign of any weapons.

Dan thanked them and Bronco drove him back to the nick. "Just because we didn't find anything there, doesn't mean he doesn't have somewhere else that he's keeping quiet about, does it, Guv?"

"No, we need to get back to put some pressure on him. We know he had to be clever to pull these killings off."

By just after ten they were back in interview room 2. Once again, DS Laine went through all the introductions for the tape. Miller was looking slightly better than he had earlier.

Dan began. "Mr Miller, do you have any other vehicles that you have forgotten to mention?"

"No, I don't. Again, why are you asking these silly questions?"

"When was the last time you went to the Millfield Estate?"

"I don't think I've ever been there, not even sure where it is."

"Have you ever been to or near The George pub on Moor Lane?"

"Never heard of it. Why, oh for fuck's sake, why don't you tell me what this is all about?"

"Can you tell me your movements over the past week or so?"

"Yes, fucking easily. Six weeks ago I broke my leg falling over pissed, coming down the stairs from my flat. I have been in plaster up until yesterday morning when it was removed. If you don't believe me, check with the hospital."

Both Dan and Bronco looked stunned. "Please take Mr Miller back to his cell. Interview terminated at 10.35."

As soon as they had taken him out, Dan shook his head. "I don't believe it. It can't be him, can it? There is no way anyone could carry those murders out with their leg in plaster, could they?"

"Hang on, Chief," Bronco replied. "We can't jump to conclusions, we only have his word for it. Let's get on to the hospital first and check the discharges; I don't know why it didn't show up on our search. We need to get back upstairs and sort this."

Bronco made the call to the local hospital. It took fifteen minutes to get through to the right person to authorise the information being released. As he put the phone down, he turned to Dan, shaking his head. The room was silent. Everyone was waiting to hear. In an almost-whisper, he said, "We didn't see it in his medical records because they haven't caught up yet from the hack they had two months ago. He's telling the truth. It's not him!"

CHAPTER 32

After the bad night he'd had he was up early and needed a good long run to get his head straight again. He had plans to make so he could move on to the next chapter of his mission. He was out before sunrise, running through the empty streets of the town until he got into the countryside. Turning down Forest Road, he ran into the old, disused gravel pits as the sun was rising, running up and down the hills now used for BMX bikes, pushing hard but all the time going over in his mind what lay ahead. Turning at the far end just before the pit, he ran over them again as fast as he could. By the time he got back, his head was clear and everything was going to plan and it wouldn't be long before his next target was dead. Back in the flat he showered, dressed and ate breakfast. He then made his way to another Internet café; he had important details to confirm with the help of Mr Google, after which it would be time to go to church.

St Augustine's was a relatively new church, built in 1954, standing proudly on Larks Lane and Wren Crescent, with the rectory situated to the rear. The early spring sun was shining as he walked towards it and people were making their way in for the wedding that was about to start. Onlookers stood on the pavement waiting for the bride to arrive. He made his way in and moved into a pew on the back row, kneeling with his head bowed. The church filled and as the choir began to sing, the congregation stood. The bride, with her father and four bridesmaids followed a young flower girl down the centre aisle to the altar. The priest greeted the assembly and the guest replied in the traditional Catholic way. The service, with Communion, lasted almost an hour, but he quietly slipped out as the register was being signed in the vestry. He had seen all he needed and had seen in person, for the first time, his next victim.

He was back in his flat in fifteen minutes and sat running his plans over in his head. At times he had to stop and think what had led to all of this, what road he had taken to be doing what he was doing, but he kept forcing his mind back onto the task ahead. He napped for an hour, but when he woke he wanted to clear his head once again so he got changed back into his running gear and set out for a short, sharp run.

As he came around the corner to the estate, he was shocked to see so many police cars and vans in the car park. He got an instant hit of adrenaline but slowed down to a jog and then stopped as if he were out of breath, with his hands on his knees. He watched the AROs load their weapons, wondering if they had come for him. It was something he had always prepared for. He had paid cash in advance for the flat for three months to someone who was obviously subletting it and had barely looked at his fake ID. He had a go-bag stored in a locker at the sports centre with everything he needed if he had to make a quick getaway.

He jogged on the spot, continuing to watch the goings-on and then slowly made his way over to the ambulance where one paramedic was stood watching, while the other still sat behind the wheel. He asked what was going on, saying it looked exciting. "It's an ongoing police incident from what I can make out. It's about a couple of murders." He acted shocked, but excited. The medic continued, "They think the murderer is holed up in Shakespeare House, they are about to go in." Shakespeare House, he thought, what a relief, it was directly on the other side of the square from his flat in Orwell House. With that, he made his way back to his flat. He could see part of

Shakespeare House from his flat and watched the tactical units approach the building, but couldn't see the target flat. He felt relieved that they weren't there for him but was confused about who their target was. He changed clothes swiftly and went out again towards the car park to see if he could find anything else out. There were now lots of onlookers and a cordon of barricade tape had been set up, keeping everyone away from the car park. He stood at the back of the crowd and waited until he saw them bring the handcuffed man around. He was shocked, because he recognised the man as a soldier who had joined the Regiment just as he was leaving. He turned and went back to his flat. The first thing he did was to pour a large whiskey. Over the next hour or so he went back and forth in his head, wondering if he should move out of the flat or stay. The police had obviously thought that the SAS was a link, which, with today's modern forensics, he had expected. Finally, he made his mind up to stay where he was for now and complete the next stage of his plan. Someone would die tomorrow.

CHAPTER 33

The fact that Miller wasn't their man hit the room like a sledgehammer. It was as if all the oxygen had been sucked out of the room.

Dan walked to the whiteboard and took down Miller's picture. "OK, so we got it wrong and we are all disappointed, but we still have a job to do. It's very late now; I have to update the boss, so all of you get home and try to get a good night's sleep. We start again in the morning at eight. We will find him, thanks to all your hard work. Now, go home."

Bronco walked over as the others left. "Guv, it looked good. Don't take it to heart, we will find this bastard."

"I know, Dave, we just have to keep at it. I want to see him myself before he's released, but I must call the Chief Super first."

DS Laine patted the DCI on his back and left.

It wasn't an easy call to make but Arthur Jackson was very understanding. "We've all been there, Dan. I will square it with the top brass – just get back to it in the morning and let's hope we get another lead soon."

Dan noted a couple of things on Google then left his office and made his way down to the cells. The duty sergeant accompanied him and unlocked the cell. Miller was just sitting there.

"Mr Miller, I am happy to tell you that your alibi has been confirmed. I am very sorry for the trouble you have been caused. I could have got one of my officers to do this but

I wanted, solider to soldier, veteran to veteran, to tell you and say that I can see you're not going through the best of times and I have met many good men who have had to deal with PTSD. In fact, you're the second one I have met on this case alone, but there *is* help out there, so please don't be too proud to accept it. Here is my card. Feel free to call me at any time if you need help and here is the number of a place you will get help – please use it."

Miller stood up and looked the DCI straight in the eye. He paused, not moving – just staring. Dan wondered what he was going to do, but then Miller saluted and said, "Thank you, sir." Dan shook his hand, saying, "I wish you well, trooper," and with that he turned and left.

He went back to his office, switched his computer off and made his way home, feeling extremely low. He felt responsible for the events of the night and he felt for the first time in his life, a failure. From an early age, through hard work and determination, he had always succeeded, be it in sport, as captain of both the rugby and cricket teams, in exams, through school and university, in the forces and, so far, in the police force. But this was different; it wasn't just what it might do to his career, but the feeling that he was letting his team down. He sat with a glass of Merlot, flicking through his Toughpad, going over pictures and statements, looking for something – anything. He made copious notes and, although no further forward, at least he knew exactly how he would start business the next day.

CHAPTER 34

The incident room was once again full by eight the next morning. Brenda had taken all the information regarding Miller down and filed it away. Dan was awake early and had taken a workout in his home gym, set up in his garage. He strode to the front of the room and in a commanding voice welcomed everyone. "We will not be looking back at what happened yesterday and we won't be starting with a clean sheet today; it was just one avenue of investigation, but we have others to follow. Stan, bring us up to date on the search for the van.

Stan stood up and, understanding the mood of the room, refrained from any jokes. "As I reported yesterday, our search for cameras found four in businesses and two in private houses. On visiting them, we found that one of the private house ones was a fake and the other isn't focused onto the road enough to see anything worthwhile. Of the four businesses, two haven't been working for ages, one is only on their car park, but one catches a small part of the road, which may help. I have narrowed it down to three vehicles and I will be analysing that more today."

"Well done, Stan, that's good work. Jane, we cut you short when it all hit the fan yesterday morning, so bring us up to speed."

DI Roberts then stood. "Well, I didn't think it was of much use yesterday, but now it might be. I paid a visit to Glebe Crescent. Mr and Mrs Goldman are experienced foster parents who specialise in problem cases. Fifteen-year-old Devan Regis fits into that category. He has been in and out of care all his life and has been with the Goldmans for two years and likes it there. He's a very bright kid but really didn't want to talk to me. I showed the pictures to him and the Goldmans and said they were found at Linton's. He denied it at first, but they really read him the riot act, threatening to have nothing more to do with him. When I told him that Linton had been murdered, it finally did the trick. I asked him if he had seen anyone at Linton's place. He didn't want to comment at first, but in the end he said that, apart from the usual druggies, there was one guy who he described as being an IC-1 male, about six-feet tall, roughly forty years old and wearing a beanie hat, which is almost an identical description I got from the lady at the first murder."

"That may well be our man; thanks, Jane. I think we need more before releasing that info to the press, but it helps."

She continued. "Just to bring you up to date on the pensioners' muggings, there has been another one – a 94-year-old male tried to fight them off and was severely beaten. He is in intensive care and it isn't looking good for him. If he doesn't pull through that's another murder on our patch to deal with."

At that point, the desk sergeant came in. "Excuse me, Guv, but young PC Jimmy Edmunds would like a word with you. Can I send him up?"

"Yes, of course."

Jimmy came in, looking a tad nervous. Dan smiled. "Good morning, PC Edmunds, I believe we have you to thank for finding the SIM card and phone – well done. What can I do for you?"

Aware all eyes were on him, he nervously looked around the room, took a deep breath and began. "Well, sir, after finding the phone, I went back to my digs and couldn't stop thinking about the case. I wondered what the towpath would be like at the time of the phone call, so I went back last night and it turns out that at night it's a bit of a gay cruising area. I encountered two men who had just finished their fun, stepping out from the bushes about thirty metres along from where the phone was found. I questioned them and it turns out one, who is a regular, was down there the night before. He was waiting in the bushes and heard someone talking in the distance, but couldn't hear what was being said. When he peered out he saw a man throw something into the canal and walk away. He says he wondered if he was cruising but didn't know the right place to be, so, after thinking it over, thought he would take a chance and follow him. But the man, who was by now a long way away, kept walking. He soon realised he wasn't cruising after all, but he did see him turn and go in the direction of the Dickens Estate. Both men were reluctant to give me their details and I know the guidelines for questioning anyone cruising, so didn't think I should push it."

Stan couldn't help himself calling out, "That's a good lesson, son! Don't ever push it if you're cruising a gay area." It got a few laughs but the DCI interrupted with, "Thank you, DC Jones, we'll have no more of that."

And then to Jimmy, "Jimmy, well done, that's good police work, although I wouldn't advise you doing things on your own like that again, but if you think of anything, let me know."

"Yes, sir, I will, thank you, sir," and with that, he left with a huge smile on his face.

Dan turned back to the room. "Well, where does that leave us? Could it be that the person we are looking for also lives on the Dickens? Bronco, what do you think?"

"We just don't know, Guv, there is no reason why not. The fact that the phone was dumped there and this guy obviously saw where the chappie was going, why don't we get some more feet on the ground and go door-to-door?"

"Yes, but let's also look to see if there's any CCTV on the route to and from the canal and the Dickens Estate." Dan and Bronco split the work to be done between every department, reminding everyone to keep HOLMES updated.

Over thirty officers and PCSOs worked throughout the day knocking door-to-door but with no real success. Stan, with the help of two PCs, studied more and more shots from the various cameras and, although they think they had narrowed it down to two vans, had no reg numbers.

Dan advised everyone to get an early night because they would start again in the morning, although he wasn't sure where they would start. He updated his policy book and thought it would do him good to get home as well.

He was walking down the stairs when a voice called out from higher up.

"Hello, handsome." He turned and looked to see Sue coming down the stairs. He asked how she was. After she had caught up with him they turned and faced each other. "I'm fine, thanks, Dan, but how are you? It must be a nightmare for you."

"You're not wrong, Sue, I've had easier cases and we just aren't getting anywhere. We thought we had him but we got it wrong. I have no idea where the next lead will come from so I thought I would call it a night and see if some relaxation helps to clear my mind."

Sue smiled and said, "Well, if it's relaxation you need, I'm your girl. How about we grab a pint before we go home? Andy is at his mate's for tea so I don't need to be home for a while and it would be nice to catch up. I know you're unsure but just as pals; what harm can it do?"

"You're right," he replied. "Why not? I'd love to," and so they made their way down and across to The Mason Arms.

Sue found a quiet table while Dan got her a white wine spritzer and a pint of Guinness for himself. They sat facing each other and Sue's eyes were sparkling, it was obvious she was enjoying being with him. They both said, "Cheers," and after taking a sip, Dan said, "So, to take my mind off of work, why don't you tell me all about you."

"There's not much to tell."

"I really don't believe that; come on, you don't want me to interrogate you, do you?"

"Well, if it involves you handcuffing me in a darkened room, it sounds like fun," she laughed. "OK, well, I was born in Grantham. Mum and Dad have both passed away. I went to the UEA in Norwich where I met Carl who was studying economics and I was doing catering and hospitality, which is obviously why I can cook and am so hospitable." They both laughed. "When we graduated, Carl got a job as a junior actuarial analyst for that big insurance company here in town. So, we moved here, I got a job at the Hilton and finished up as head of events there. Then Andy came along and while I was pregnant, Carl was transferred to their offices in Leamington Spa. He only came home at weekends and then, after a couple of months he'd missed some weekends because he said he was busy; when he *did* come home I felt something had changed. I was getting bigger and bigger and feeling very low and he just had no interest in me. He wasn't even there for the birth but got back the day after. I just knew something was wrong as he was meant to have taken two weeks off work but after about five days it all came out. He had found someone else at work and was in love with her. He didn't love me any more, packed his bags and left me with a week-old baby to care for. The last I heard he had a kid with her and then pissed off to New Zealand. Good riddance to him."

Dan was shocked. "Sue, I am so sorry, I had no idea and

certainly wouldn't have asked if I knew that – I really am so sorry," and he reached across and took her hand.

"Hey, its fine; that was ten years ago and that's why I am serving hungry police officers in a canteen and not running a 4-star hotel or cooking Cordon Bleu in a classy restaurant. But the hours suit me and I get to meet nice DCIs once in a while, for a drink." She looked down at them holding hands and smiled. Dan smiled as well but took his hand away.

"Sue, you are amazing. I really think the world of you and would love to spend more time with you, it's just that I am still–"

Sue lifted her hand up and put her finger onto his lips.

"Shush, you don't need to say anything, Dan. I know what happened to Catherine, it was awful. Everyone at the nick knows and what you went through is far more traumatic than what Carl did to me. Just know that I think the world of you too and I am in no rush, you know where I am if you need me." And with that she took his hand and squeezed it.

They chatted for another half-hour about Andy and his school. They laughed at some of the things kids come out with and they exchanged mobile numbers. The pair finished their drinks and walked back to the station car park. Dan walked Sue to her car and said he had enjoyed the drink and hoped they could do it again sometime. Sue agreed. Putting her hands on Dan's shoulders she reached up and kissed him on his cheek. They held each other for a moment before Dan turned and walked away. Returning to his car he watched her wave as she drove away. He drove home feeling happy; he really hadn't felt like this for a long time, but instantly his thoughts went back to Catherine and what happened to her. His mind wandered between these two lovely women all evening.

CHAPTER 35

After another fitful night he knew that he would soon have to move his base. As part of his plan he had a backup place to go – again, cash paid for three months to another unscrupulous landlord. He set about packing everything including rubbish; he didn't want to leave anything that might have his DNA on. He kept to one side everything he would need for his mission that night and began to take it to his van, which he kept in a lockup garage in the next street. He could see there were a lot of police in the area, but none seemed to be searching for anyone in particular. He walked past a group of young lads stood on the corner, talking and looking dodgy with their hoodies up and some with bandanas on their faces. "What's with the pigs, guys?" he asked them. They all looked at him and one just said, "Yo, man, they fuckin' doin' door-to-door after some murderer geez, innit." He just nodded and walked toward his garage. Walking back, what he had seen definitely confirmed it was time to move on. He got back and made a final sweep of the flat, wiping down everywhere with bleach. He loaded the van and drove away, taking a final look over the area. He knew he was doing the right thing when he saw some PCSOs making their way to the block he had just left. He only had to drive about a mile across town, this time to a terraced house, which he had previously kitted out. He unpacked and prepared for the night ahead.

He waited two hours after dark before leaving, taking with him his backpack and everything he would need for the night ahead. Rather than walking directly the half-hour, two-mile journey to his destination, he used side streets and back alleyways to avoid any cameras or police patrols. It was a quiet Sunday night and the streets were deserted. He could see the large, detached Victorian house from across the road, with a grey, stone wall and gates that possibly hadn't been closed in a half-century. He swiftly entered the gates, turned into the bushes behind the wall and slowly made his way to the rear of the imposing, five bedroomed house. The only light visible to him was from an upstairs bedroom. He pulled on an over suit and gloves before silently approaching the French doors. Retrieving a chisel from his backpack, he expertly forced the doors open. He stood, taking in the surroundings of the lounge before moving carefully and silently across to the door. After hearing faint noises from upstairs and checking the downstairs was empty, he slowly but surely stepped on the outside of the treads only, to make his way up to the back bedroom. Standing outside the door he could hear that the sounds were moans and grunts of a sexual nature. He wondered how many people were in the room, but that wouldn't make any difference. Taking out his Glock 19, he placed his gloved left hand on the door handle, took a deep breath, opened the door and stepped in, brandishing the pistol in front of him.

He really wasn't sure what he would see but he was taken aback by the sight of Father Cahal O'Donnell, Catholic priest of the parish, lying almost naked on the bed, wearing black stockings and suspenders with a pair of French knickers over his face and his eyes were shut, showing through the leg holes. He was masturbating furiously with the television on. It took him a second to realise something was wrong; opening his eyes and letting go of his penis he yelled, "Holy Mother of God! Who in God's name are you and what do you want?"

Crossing to the bed in two steps, he replied, "I want you, you dirty, evil bastard," and with that, he smashed him across his head with the gun. The priest twitched and laid back unconscious, a trickle of blood starting to run down his face. He took gaffer tape from his bag, put three strips over the priest's mouth and used more to tape him, spread-eagled, to the bed. As he waited for the priest to come round, he saw what he had been watching. It was a video of the priest sodomizing a young boy; the images sickened him, but he left it running. The video was playing through a video camera adjacent to the television and next to that was an attaché case filled with Sony Mini DVD tapes. It took no working out to guess what they were.

The next fifteen minutes were spent trying to awaken the priest so he could carry out the rest of his mission.

Once he had finished, he turned up the television, lifted the phone and dialed 999, placing it on the bedside table. He left quickly – down the stairs and out the front door. After changing out of the over suit and placing it in his backpack, he made his way back home. It was a very similar route to the one he arrived on and, seeing no one, he returned to his new house.

CHAPTER 36

It was just after eleven and Dan was about to get ready for bed when the phone rang. It was DS Laine. "We've got another one, Guv, it's The Rectory at the back of St Augustine's Church on Larks Lane."

The DCI arrived there within a few minutes; he was greeted by a couple of police cars and the Crime Scene van. Bronco was talking to a PC at the gateway and turned to meet Dan. "What is it this time, Dave?"

"I've not been in yet but have been told; I think I'll let you see for yourself, Guv," he replied as they put on their forensic suits and made their way in. Dan followed the DS up the stairs while the SOCOs were busy photographing everywhere. Julie Burton was by the bedroom door; she looked up and welcomed Dan. "I hear you've been two-timing me, DCI Hooper," she said with a smile. Dan looked surprised and she continued, "You were seen in The Mason Arms last night with Sue. Good for you, she's lovely."

Bronco smiled, said, "Really?" and Dan just said, "OK, so we did. There's nothing wrong with that. Obviously you can't keep anything quiet around here." He smiled again to show he didn't mind, and said, "Now to work – what have we got?"

Julie raised her eyebrows. "Get ready for a shock – the victim is the local Catholic priest."

The scene that greeted them when they walked into the bedroom was Father O'Donnell still spread-eagled on the bed held down by gaffer tape, the French knickers still on his head but pulled to one side. The gaffer tape had been removed from his mouth, his cock and balls had been cut off and stuffed into his mouth and the word 'GUILTY' was carved across his chest.

Bronco slowly shook his head. "For fuck's sake, that *is* a sight for sore eyes. What do you think, Guv?"

"Well, if the other killings are anything to go by, I would say that the Father might have had it coming to him. Who informed us?"

Julie answered, "It was a 999 call from this number. No one spoke but the operator could hear sexual noises in the background and a car was dispatched. As you can see, he has had his bits removed and placed in his mouth. The video was playing of the priest performing an unlawful sexual act on what is most definitely a young boy. There is a case filled with what I assume are other videos tapes of a similar nature. There are loads of them and it will need to be passed on to the Child Abuse Investigation Unit to try to identify them, but that could be a long job. After a quick look around the place it appears that he came in through the French windows, which have been forced. It's a big house, we could really do with some more help on this."

"OK, Julie – thanks. I'll see what we can do."

At that point, the large figure of Gareth Hew Evans, the Home Office pathologist, entered the room. Stopping just inside the door to take it all in, he said, "Ms Burton, Detective Chief Inspector and Detective Sergeant, I bid you all welcome on this Sunday evening. I always say 'sexually each to his own', but this is very extreme." He moved closer for a better look at the body. The blood from between the priest's legs had soaked into the bedding and his eyes were now wide open. "It would appear he received a blow to the head which rendered him unconscious, giving the murderer time to attach him to the bed and then castrate him. I would surmise that he, in fact, died of a heart attack and not through bleeding out. Death from penile amputation can arise not simply from blood loss but also from related issues such as overall stress and pain. Stress hormones and an inflammatory chemical cascade following such a traumatic injury can overwhelm the heart. I will know much more once we get him back and I will start at eight in the morning."

Dan thanked him and said he didn't think he and Bronco could achieve anything there tonight so they would leave Julie's team to continue their work. Like Evans, they would start again at the nick at eight. He called the Chief to briefly bring him up to speed and asked for more crime scene help. They agreed that they would chat first thing and Dan was to call him again at seven before going in.

He drove home slowly, picturing the scene. It was obvious the priest was a paedophile and, judging by the amount of videotapes, he had been for a long time. With the two previous murders being linked to family in public service, he had to wonder what the link might be this time, which also made him think for the first time how this person was getting the info on these people. Is he working alone? Is he just a hit man getting told who to kill? Is he, perhaps, a vigilante with special training, not only in killing, but also in researching targets? He doubted sleep would come easy tonight, but then he thought of Sue and smiled to himself.

He woke early again. He still had bad dreams, but he had had worse in the past. He had decided to lay low today after the closeness of the police at Orwell House, so instead of going for his run, he did his exercise going through the deck of cards, a workout many use if you have no equipment. Shuffling the cards first, for every heart he turned over he would do push-ups, diamonds were free squats, clubs, star jumps and spades, sit-ups. The number of the card represented the number of reps, with jacks being eleven, queens – twelve, kings – fifteen, aces – twenty and jokers giving a twenty-second rest. He went through the deck three times, the sweat leaving a huge pool on the floor. He felt better and, after showering and eating a full breakfast, he set about finalising his plans for his next mission. He was on a roll, with the most important names on his 'guilty' list to deal with.

CHAPTER 37

Dan was up at six, did a very quick cardio workout and had had breakfast by the time he called the Chief Super at seven. It wasn't the best of phone calls. "I am really sorry, Dan, but we are now looking for a serial killer. With so many murders in such a short space of time, I can see the Home Office sending someone more senior to take over the investigation. It's not your fault, but there is no way the politicians will let a DCI head a case like this now. You will always have my backing and I will insist that you continue to work the case. For now, continue as normal but be prepared for intervention from above. To add to our troubles, you know DI Roberts had been dealing with the attacks on senior citizens? Well, the last victim, an 80-year-old female who sustained a broken hip in a fall as she was mugged, has died in hospital from injuries received, so it puts a different importance on the case. I have put DI Wheeler on it for the time being, but he may need more help – I'll let you know."

Dan agreed and said he would check in with the Chief Super later in the day.

Dan went straight to the nick and swiftly went over his policy book to ensure everything was correct and in order. He felt disappointed but was used to taking orders – he knew it was the right thing to happen and that he would give whoever took charge his best.

Bronco and Brenda were among the first to come in. Dan called them into his office to tell them the news. They both commiserated with Dan but completely understood and said they would give their all to help close the case.

By the time everyone else had arrived, Brenda had given Dan the photographs taken from the previous night's crime scene, along with a basic report from Julie Burton. As Dan made his way to the front of the room he paused for silence before commencing.

"Good morning, this is the 9th briefing of Operation Nightjar and, following last night's incident, we are now officially looking for a serial killer. Because of this there will be a higher-ranking officer coming in to take over SIO. Please don't take it as a complaint about what you have done, as we all know it is a very difficult case and, with four murders now, the powers that be have rightly felt that someone with more experience should head the case. I hope you will all give whoever it is your utmost help." He went on to explain briefly what had happened the night before. "I am about to show you crime scene pictures but would remind you all, especially you, DC Jones, that this is a serious murder enquiry."

With that, he placed four pictures of Father O'Donnell onto the whiteboard; two were full-length, one of between his legs and one of his face. There was an audible intake of breath from the room. Dan went on to explain about the videotapes and the expected contents, at which point DC Stan Jones couldn't help himself and said in a high voice, "Well, live by the pork sword, die by the pork sword." There was scattered laughing and Dan just shook his head and smiled. "Enough. This is very serious and no matter what we think, we need to put that to one side and concentrate on finding the killer."

DI Roberts looked at Dan who indicated for her to speak. "PC Segon has been trawling through the feedback from the door-to-door and passed this on to me. Someone in Orwell House, which is just over the road from Shakespeare House, told a PC that a neighbour in number 27 who has only been there a couple of weeks, was carrying bags out today as if he was leaving. Described as IC-1 male, in his forties, about 6-feet tall, fit, runs once or twice a day and wears a beanie hat. The PC knocked but no answer. A Whitechapel-based company called SA Holdings owns it. Company records show they own over two hundred premises throughout London and the home counties. Sadiq Ali is the owner and we spoke to his secretary. She said he is on holiday in Bangalore, but the records show the tenant as Deepak Bhatt, a student aged 28. Obviously not the man living there, it being more likely a sublet, but it is a very common thing with the Asian community. It must be worth a look, Guv."

"Yes, I agree, but after last time we won't jump the gun. Right, then, DC Jones, what have we got regarding cameras and vehicles?"

Stan stood up with a huge grin on his face. "Sorry, Guv, it was too good to miss. Right, well… to recap, what we have been searching for from day one is to see if any similar vehicles that pass both ways in the right time frame from the first murder, match any that pass either way from the Millfield towards the Dickens. Well, for what it's worth, I have identified a grey Vauxhall Vivaro and a dark blue Ford Transit, but we don't have any registration numbers. I have left some PCSOs to search more but can go back if you want me to."

"No, let them continue. Could you get over to Orwell House, take a couple of PCs with you, just in case, to see what you can find?"

At that point Brenda returned from taking a phone call. "Guv, I have just had Sergeant Hicks from the Child Abuse Investigation Unit. They began on the tapes first thing and one of his team immediately recognised a boy in the second tape he looked at, as the grandson of Assistant

Chief Constable Michael Brady, from the Hertfordshire Constabulary. If you remember this time last year, he was in the news; his name was Jordan Brady and he committed suicide aged 13. They said they thought you knew ACC Brady and that you would want to inform him."

Those in the room were once again shocked and Dan agreed he would contact the ACC. "Yes, we have met a few times – I'll call him shortly. This is getting more and more confusing. How can the suspect be finding out all these things? There must be some Internet trail or something. Could we ask Billy Clark to look into that?"

"Excuse me, sir," a voice called out from one of the desks. It was one of the PCSOs who had been drafted in to help with desk work. "I have just run Father O'Donnell's details in NPC and it would appear he was questioned four years ago for soliciting in a public convenience in Hampstead and approaching a minor, then for indecency in the gents at the end of Carnaby Street when it would appear he was bang to rights, but with pressure from above, the CPS wouldn't follow it through."

"How many times will we hear that?" Bronco exclaimed. "What with them and namby-pamby, so-called do-gooders, the magistrates are making this job a joke!" A sentiment agreed by the rest of the room.

Dan set the tasks for the day, then returned to his office when his phone rang. It was Megan Barrett from the press office. "Sorry to bother you, sir, but the Chief has scheduled a press conference for 1 pm and it's going to be a big one – he wants you there for it."

That's all I need, thought Dan, but realised his next job was to call ACC Brady who was based at the Hertfordshire Police HQ in Welwyn Garden City, just off the A1.

"DCI Hooper, how are you? What can I do for you, Dan?" he

asked in a bright voice.

"This is not an easy subject, sir, but last night a priest was murdered on our patch. He was in a sexually compromising situation and in his bedroom was a large quantity of mini videotapes of him having sex with young boys. I am very sorry to have to tell you that a boy on one of those tapes has been identified as your late grandson, Jordan."

There was a silent pause before he replied, "How in God's name would anyone know that? Are you sure?"

"Well, sir, it would appear that one of the Child Abuse Investigation Unit knows you and remembers seeing his picture in the paper when he died – he could be wrong but I thought it better to speak to you than his parents. I would point out that there were lots of these tapes and they are still being examined."

"Yes, of course, Dan, thank you. Could you arrange for an image to be sent to me? I will identify him. This will break my son and daughter-in-law's hearts but will perhaps give them closure on why young Jordan tragically took his own life."

"There is something else that you should know, sir. The murder of the priest is the same MO of two previous murders in the last week or so; one was a Bosnian war criminal who had killed the wife and unborn son of a serving army sergeant, the other a drugs dealer, who we were fairly sure had supplied ecstasy that had killed the daughter of a fire chief. We haven't released this fact, but in each case the word 'guilty' was carved on the victims' chests. It would appear to be someone targeting those responsible for the deaths of family members in public service."

"Really, how close are you to catching him?"

"I am afraid not close at all; it would appear to be someone with a special forces background – they are like professional hits. I have been CIO as our Super was away on holiday and he then had a heart attack, but it looks like a more senior officer is coming in to take charge now."

"So, a vigilante, perhaps – one could almost wish for him to *not* get caught with so much shit out there and so many getting let off by – we all know who – he is almost doing us all a favour. It makes me sick; it's not how the job *used* to be or *should* be today – we should be here to protect the public, not let them down. But don't you dare quote me on that."

"It's something that we hear all the time, sir, and I can't disagree." Dan went on to explain more about the case.

"OK, Dan, well, if you can get the image over to me, that'd be great and please keep in touch to update me on how it's going," and with that, he ended the call.

CHAPTER 38

The morning flew by and, at just after midday, Megan Barrett arrived and spoke with the Chief Superintendent and Dan about how the press conference would go. They all agreed that, apart from confirming the latest murder, they would have to finally take questions from the press.

From 12.30 the room was rapidly filling with camera crews setting up and the car park outside was filled with broadcasting vans of various sizes, all with huge dishes on their roofs.

Dan was about to grab a sandwich when his phone rang; it was Stan Jones. "Guv, the flat is as clean as a pair of nun's knickers; it's all been well wiped down with bleach and emptied of anything apart from the old furniture that's there. SOCOs may find something, but again, it looks like a professional job. I did talk to the neighbours and got a brief description similar to the previous one of about 6-feet 4-ish inches, wearing a beanie hat and going for runs. It can't be a coincidence, can it?"

"No, Stan, it can't. I am about to go into the press conference, so can you arrange to get the sketch artist down there? Let's see if we can come up with an image."

"OK, Chief, will do. Good luck with the press, you know what a lot of two-faced bastards they are."

By the time Dan entered with the Chief Super and Megan there must have been close to one hundred reporters there.

They took their seats behind the table, which was filled

with more microphones and voice recorders than ever. It had been agreed that Megan would open the conference but that the CS would lead it.

"Ladies and gentlemen, thank you for attending here this afternoon. You will hear from both Chief Superintendent Jackson and Detective Chief Inspector Hooper and after that they will answer as many of your questions as possible, but please remember this is a very urgent ongoing case and time spent here isn't time spent investigating, so with that I will hand you over to Chief Superintendent Arthur Jackson."

The Chief paused for a second to look at his notes and slowly looked up. "Good afternoon. At 10.38 pm last night, a 999 operator received a call where no one spoke, but she could hear certain unexplained noises in the background. She felt this was urgent, so the number was traced and a police car sent urgently to the Vicarage at the rear of St Augustine's Church in Larks Lane. The front door was wide open and at approximately 10.48 pm the officers entered the property and on searching the empty downstairs made their way to the first floor, where in the master bedroom they found a body we now know to be of Father Cahal O'Donnell. Evidence at the scene has led us to believe that the murder of Father O'Donnell is linked to the three previous murders in Operation Nightjar. At this moment in time we won't be releasing the cause of death. I will now hand you over to DCI Hooper for his update and then we will take questions."

Dan took a deep breath and began. "As you have just been informed, the murder of Father O'Donnell is being linked to the previous three murders. Our investigation has been widespread and intensive; my team have scoured through hundreds of hours of CCTV and we would like anyone to come forward who has seen a grey Vauxhall Vivaro and a dark blue Ford Transit parked in the area. We believe a person of interest may have a military background and may have been recently living on the Dickens Estate. As we speak, my officers are endeavoring to get an artist's impression and description of this person. Our investigations are continuing at pace. We don't at this moment think members of the general public are in danger but ask them to remain vigilant at all times. I will now take questions."

"Dominic East, BBC. Is your investigation being hampered by government cutbacks and staff shortages?"

"It's no secret that cutbacks have hit the force hard, but we are dealing with it and, certainly in a case such as this, all the resources we need are in place to investigate properly and thoroughly. Next."

"Rebecca Bewley, *Daily Mail*. Detective Chief Inspector, is it unusual that someone of your rank would be CIO on such a big case as this? And is it only the fact the Superintendent Ward, who I believe was on holiday in Italy at the time of the first murder and has subsequently suffered a heart attack, and so is on sick leave, that you are in charge of this case? Are you sure you are up to the job? Should someone more senior replace you? And again, is this not a sign of the government's cutbacks?"

"I think I should answer that," interrupted CS Jackson. "Yes, CS Ward is convalescing after a heart attack, but we have every faith in DCI Hooper, a fine police officer with a first-class record, not only in the police force, but also as a former officer in the army. I think I should point out that this press conference is to try and move this very serious investigation forward, not to waste time with negative comments about officers who are working tirelessly to find the culprit, or what this or any previous government's actions have been in relation to the Police Force." With that he nodded to Dan to continue.

Dan pointed to the reporter he recognised from Sky News, who stood. "Martin Timpson, Sky News. Detective Chief

Inspector, can you tell us what makes you so sure that these murders are linked?"

"Certain similarities that, at this moment in time, for investigative reasons I am unable to reveal."

Timpson nodded and continued, "While I respect your reasons for confidentiality, there are now four murders which would mean, if linked, you are now looking for a serial killer. Do you not think the public has the right to know more?"

Dan turned to look at his CS who gave an almost missable shake of his head. Dan replied, "I understand your comment but am unable to say anything else at this moment as it may compromise the case. I am sure we will be able to reveal more at a later date."

"In that case, DCI Hooper, what would you say if I told you that information has come to us at Sky News that, with the exception of one of the murders, three of the bodies had the word 'guilty' carved on their chests? One had been decapitated, one had been castrated and all of those three had links to the deaths of family members in public service. Detective Chief Inspector Hooper and Chief Superintendent Jackson, are you not looking for a vigilante who appears to be settling scores with those who have beaten the justice system?"

At that the room erupted with calls from all the assembled reporters. Megan Barrett called for quiet and CS Jackson leant forward and said, "Ladies and gentlemen, this is an ongoing quadruple murder investigation and I will not, and ask *you* to not, do anything to hinder our investigation in bringing the murderer to justice."

He nodded to Megan, who said, "OK, that ends this press conference, thank you for your time, but please bear in mind what Chief Superintendent Jackson has just said."

The room filled again with shouts of questions, but they

all stood from the table and left the room.

Once outside, CS Jackson said, "Right, both to my office now and, Dan, get Bronco and DI Roberts there as well."

The Chief Super looked angry. "Right, we really didn't need that, did we? The press these days are far more concerned with trying to score political points than reporting the truth and it's a known fact that Timpson loves nothing more than making the force look stupid. Megan, talk to Timpson now, see what you can find out." Turning to the others he said, "With so much going on and so many officers and PCSOs involved, something was bound to get out. But do you think it could have come from any of your close team, Dan?"

"I really doubt that, sir; obviously we can't be sure but I think if it was from the close team there would have been a leak sooner."

The Chief agreed. "Jane, your thoughts?"

"I agree, sir – not from the main team."

"Bronco?"

"I also agree, sir, but the fact is, so many of the force are pissed off with how hard the job is through no fault of our own – how often we get let down by courts, councils and the CPS. Morale is very low, especially on the ground where no respect is shown to the job any more, even from young teens. Sky may well have paid a few grand for that info and they may even have leaked it, thinking it might help."

"Thank you, Dave, I don't disagree, but what we don't want is to let it derail the investigation." At that point his phone rang. He listened to the conversation, looking at Dan and just replied with, "Thank you, sir."

"Not the news you wanted to hear but that was a warning that the CIO's post is being taken over this afternoon by Detective Superintendent Henry Cornelius. I have met him, he has a good record, but upsets a lot of people in doing so."

"I know him too," Laine replied. "We were both PCs

together. I have to say though, he has never been on my Christmas card list."

"OK, well, Dan, I know you will give him all the help you can, but let me know how things go."

With that they all left and made their way back down to the incident room. "You will need to watch him, Guv, he isn't the nicest of men. He will step on anyone to get what he wants," Bronco warned.

"How well do you know him?"

"Well, it was obvious from my PC days that he was an arsehole and he never seemed to worry too much if anyone got hurt in an arrest. Once he was in CID the word was he was happy to find evidence when it wasn't always there; the fact is, most of his kind left the job years ago but every time he looked like getting the boot he would crack a big case one way or another."

"Thanks Dave, I will bear that in mind, but let's hope we can all just get the job done."

CHAPTER 39

They hadn't been back in the incident room five minutes when the door burst open and two men entered. The first one was a barrel of a man, standing about 5-feet 10-inches tall, with a large beer gut that spilled over his belted trousers with a shirt-tail half out. His tie was pulled down and his top shirt button was undone. His nose and cheeks were covered in spider veins; the sign of excess alcohol and this was all topped off with a bad comb over.

His loud Cockney voice boomed, "Right, all of you, pay attention! I am Superintendent Henry Cornelius and I have been appointed to take over this cluster fuck of an investigation. Who is DCI Hooper?"

"I am, sir," Dan replied, walking forward to greet him with a handshake.

"No need to shake my hand, solider boy, I am here to sort the fuck out of this mess you've helped create. Bloody soldiers coming into the force – what a fucking waste of time."

All the occupants of the room were in shock. Dan just stood there, amazed.

"Don't just stand there – out of my way! Who is second-in-command here?"

"I am, sir, DI Jane Roberts."

"Ah yes, the posh bird whose dad's in the job. Right, you will work with DI Churchill from my team. He will tell you what I want done and I don't care who your old man is, I expect you to do as you're told."

He looked around the room. "Well, fuck me, if it isn't Dave--never-got-any-fucking-where Laine. No wonder it's a fucking failure if you are involved. Right, there will be changes starting now and we will catch this fucker. Hooper, I will take your office – let's sort that now. I've read HOLMES on the way over, but you can bring me up to speed if you have anything at all that might help, but I doubt you have."

Dan led him to his office. Cornelius looked around and exclaimed, "What a shithole! Right, son, where's your policy book? It had better be up to date, then you can clear the fuck out of here and leave me to sort this shit out." Dan walked over to pick up his book when CS Jackson walked in.

"Superintendent Cornelius, I think we need to get one thing clear if you are going to work under this roof. While I may respect your record for solving cases, I will not have any of my officers spoken to in such a foul-mouthed, derogatory and unprofessional way. Unless you address this, I will have no alternative to not only report you to Professional Standards and have you removed from this case, I already have an alternative office ready for you, so there is no need to move DCI Hooper from his. Had you have reported to me upon your arrival here, as is customary, and not steamed in like a bull in a china shop, I would have told you so. You can use Terry Ward's office; I'm sure someone will be only too pleased to show you where it is. Now, can we please get on with the job in hand and do what we do best in a professional manner – do I make myself clear?"

Cornelius looked shocked and angry but could do no more than nod and say, "Yes, sir, I understand."

The Chief Superintendent just turned and walked away.

When he was out of earshot, Cornelius looked at Dan and said, "If you think I give a flying fuck about what I have just been told, you're mistaken. Do I make myself clear, soldier boy?"

Dan had been in similar situations in the army and knew there was only one way to deal with bullies, else it would just spiral out of control. He closed his office door, moved to within a few inches of the Superintendent towering above him and looked straight into his bloodshot eyes. "I am here to do all I can to catch this murderer and will work night and day if you need me to, as will all of my team, but if you ever, ever, speak to me or any of my team like that again, you have my word that when you least expect it I will personally put you in hospital for a very long time and you will never be able to prove it was me. I totally abhor bullies and that's what you are. Do I make myself clear, Superintendent?"

At which point, Cornelius turned and walked out of Dan's office, calling out, "Would someone show me where Superintendent Ward's office is?" and, after looking back to Dan, finished the sentence with, "please."

CHAPTER 40

He had spent most of the day going over the planning. It was exactly how he wanted it to be: he knew when and where the targets would be, he had recced the site and would put the plan into action in a couple of days.

There were a few items he needed to get so he left to go to the shops. Walking wherever possible, through back streets and alleys to avoid cameras, he came out by a small parade of shops and the first thing he saw was a newspaper placard with the headline 'THE GUILTY VIGILANTE KILLER STRIKES'. He was shocked; he knew that it would all come out in the news sooner or later, but thought that the police would have kept some details quiet. He wanted to buy a paper, but thought it better to check on the Internet back at the flat, so, without stopping to shop, he made his way back. After reading the headlines he watched a recording of the press conference on the news and it would seem the police had a very vague description of him. He would need to change that as quickly as he could, dressing differently and certainly losing the beanie.

He wasn't scared of being caught; he was prepared to accept his fate, he had known that from the start. It could either end in prison or death, but he didn't want that to happen yet. He had at least one more mission to complete here before moving on. But to complete them he needed to take extra care and, with that in mind, he knew the right thing to do was to put the next mission on hold at least for a few days.

He went on-line and ordered some new clothes; a pair of

chinos, a smart Ralph Lauren windcheater and a couple of Ralph Lauren polo shirts, an upmarket tracksuit, a couple of baseball caps and an expensive pair of trainers. He wanted to look wealthy, not like an ex-service man. He also ordered some fake tan lotion and then shaved his stubble and head, deciding to stay indoors until the new clothes arrived.

CHAPTER 41

Dan was feeling very low, it had been a shit day and it was bad enough that they were no further in finding the killer. He now accepted that someone more experienced should take over as CIO but, for God's sake, what was this Henry Cornelius all about? He was also angry for losing his temper, but as he had said, nothing got to him more than a bully – he had seen far too many of them in the forces and didn't intend to let one bully him in this job. Everyone in the station was upset and, for the first time in his life, Dan questioned if he wanted to stay in the force. Bronco was equally as pissed off with it all so they decided to call it a night and go for a beer.

The Mason Arms was very busy with more than a fair share of coppers talking about the events at the nick, as well as a few journalists hanging around looking for a titbit of news. As they got to the bar, Dan spotted Sue with Julie Burton sat at a corner table. Bronco was looking for somewhere to sit but everywhere was full and Julie, seeing this, waved them over.

"I think we're all in need of some liquid refreshment tonight after that fiasco this afternoon. Do join us; I think you know Sue, don't you, Dan?" Julie enquired with a grin.

"Yes, indeed I do. Hello, Sue, are you sure you don't mind us jumping in?"

Sue gave a naughty laugh. "What kind of jump are we talking about here, Detective Chief Inspector?"

All four roared with laughter and at least the dark

cloud hanging over them from the afternoon, lifted for a little while. After chatting for the next half-hour and Sue mentioning that her son Andy was staying with a friend that night, they all agreed to eat there. It was a good way for them all to unwind and, by just before ten, they decided to call it a night. They all said their goodbyes in the bar. Dan had to visit the gents, but when he came out Sue was still there.

"I thought, being the gentleman you are, you might escort me to my car, kind sir."

"How could I refuse?" he replied, and Sue took his arm as they walked out.

"I know you must be so pissed off with what's happened today, Dan, but you must know that everyone at the nick is on your side and they know you're a good copper. Keep your chin up and you know where I am if you need a hug, or perhaps, as you said earlier, a jump," and again, they both laughed.

"Thanks, Sue, you are very special and I know I will get through this; above all, I want to catch the killer before anyone else is murdered."

By the time they had finished speaking they had reached her car. She turned and put both hands on his shoulders. They stood for a second looking at each other and, at exactly the same moment they both moved together and kissed properly for the first time. They held each other so tightly, their lips slowly parting and their tongues flicking each other. Sue let out a little whimper and they finally broke away.

"Well, I didn't expect that tonight, Detective Hooper. You're welcome to come back to mine if you want to continue this."

"Sue, you know I want to and you know why I can't give what I want to at the moment – please bear with me."

She smiled and gave him a peck on the cheek before opening her car. Again, Dan was left watching her drive away, his emotions in turmoil.

CHAPTER 42

Two days had passed since he ordered the new clothes and he was still waiting; two days that were making him go stir-crazy again. He needed to get out but he also knew he had to be careful. He had seen the police facial recognition picture that was meant to be of him but was sure that once he had the new clothes and fake tan he wouldn't be recognised. He had been working out on the deck of cards a few times each day, but still found it hard to sleep at night, even after a few whiskeys. It was inevitable that the black cloud would envelope his mind and his thoughts would drift back to the bad times again.

BAGHDAD, ONE-AND-A-HALF YEARS AGO

The Beginning of the End

The past six months had been a downhill spiral for him; he had lost count of the unarmed civilians that he had seen murdered by the men he was working with. Yes, he had killed enemy soldiers while in the Regiment and terrorists while he was there, but that was to protect his or his own comrades' lives, not because "We don't leave any witnesses".

Two months ago, Major General Buchanan had been recalled to the States leaving Zane in charge, but discipline had fallen, as quickly as the drug-taking had increased. They regularly found drug hauls along with cash, which was still split amongst everyone, but the majority of the drugs were *kept and used by most of the men, some slowly drifting into addicts. This, in turn, led to a more outrageous behaviour that was getting increasingly dangerous.*

His only saviour had been getting closer to Sunny. Over their regular breakfast meetings they had built a friendship and respect for each other and they had even travelled out of the compound to eat a few times at Dojos, one of the few restaurants in the Green Zone, situated just off 14th July Street. Although she was unaware of the murders that took place, and he didn't want to mention it, she was getting more worried about the drugs and discipline and had told him that she was thinking of leaving to go back to America. He, too, had thought of leaving, but had heard rumours that if anyone in the unit tried to leave, they would be stopped, ending up in a barrel filled with acid. He knew then that he had to bide his time.

They had been quiet for almost a week and he was getting stir-crazy, so was pleased when Zane told him he would be joining him, along with Joel and Fish for an easy pick-up mission that evening, leaving at 20.00 hours. They were all dressed in full combat gear by 19.45 and climbed aboard the Humvee. Zane informed them that they had to pick up a contact at the Karkh Cemetery near the infamous prison at Abu Ghraib and take him to a site just north of there. Joel was driving as usual, taking them out of the Green Zone on to Airport Street before turning right, heading up through the suburb of Khadra, then onto the road to Fallujah, past the edge of the Baghdad Airport and on to the cemetery. It was dusk as they arrived, turning right, just past the entrance following the high wall on a dirt track around to the back.

As they arrived at the back a large truck was stopped about 30 metres in front of them, blocking the way. With a fence on the left-hand side and a ditch on the right by the cemetery back wall, he couldn't drive around it. The very next second a battery of lights came on from the truck, blinding Joel and

Zane sat in the front. At the same time, heavy machine-gunfire started hitting their vehicle. Joel reversed as bullets riddled the front of the Humvee, bouncing off its armour-plating. They were still reversing when a rocket-propelled grenade hit them and the explosion sent the Humvee spinning onto its side. Smoke and flames were shooting everywhere.

Sitting in the back as the gunfire began, he was instantly ready to exit the vehicle if needed, but the hit of the RPG sent him flying out of the door, somersaulting into the filthy water of the ditch. Fish was returning fire from the back, until a second and third RPG hit the wreck. Laying in the dirty, stinking mess of what was obviously a sewage ditch covered with bullrushes, he could do nothing to help and so he edged himself deeper into the reeds.

Dark smoke from the wreckage began to swirl around, giving him a bit more cover. Through the reeds he watched as two men walked to the wreck, firing a volley of bullets into the wrecked remains, making sure no one survived. He realised they couldn't have known how many had been in the vehicle and the explosion of the first hit must have obscured them from seeing him being thrown out. Creeping further down the ditch towards the truck, he saw one man still holding the RPG launcher standing next to the truck, while the other two were still looking into the wreck.

He had been separated from his M4 Carbine when he was thrown into the ditch, but he still had his Glock 17 and both knives. He needed to wait for the three to get closer together before he tried to take them out. Keeping as low as he could in the ditch, he watched the two laughing as they walked back towards the truck – and the third man. It couldn't have been better for him as they stood and hugged. He was firing as he raised himself from the ditch, hitting two in the back of their heads and the third dropped the launcher, going for a gun on his belt, but was too slow as the next bullet hit him in his throat before another hit his chest. Climbing quickly out of the ditch, he fired two more shots at each of them, leaving nothing to chance. He quickly checked in the truck to make sure it was empty before heading straight to the wreckage of the Humvee. Joel and Zane had taken the biggest hit from the RPGs; they must have died instantly. Fish was in the back next to where he had been sitting; a large piece of metal, blown off from the door, had sliced the side of his neck and blood was everywhere. All three were riddled with bullet holes.

He wouldn't leave their bodies there, so he had to load them into the back of the truck. By the time he had done that he was covered in blood but had no time to worry, he had to get back to base as soon as he could. Unable to get past the wreck, he had no choice but to reverse for about three hundred metres before he could turn around. He was aware he couldn't take the truck all the way and, while he was in it, he was in danger of being seen by other paramilitaries. He drove around and onto the main road, but quickly pulled off into an industrial area. Spotting a delivery van, obviously left for the night, he easily broke into it and transferred his dead friends' bodies into the back. There was a water tap on the wall that he used to clean himself as best he could. Still dripping wet, he began to make his way back to base.

The guards at the checkpoint into the Green Zone checked his pass and queried why he was in the van. He swiftly explained it was cover for a surveillance operation, which fortunately convinced them. In a few minutes he was pulling back into the compound.

Rushing to get in to inform the others, as he got to the door, he was taken aback by the very strong smell of marijuana and then he heard screaming followed by a gunshot.

That was the moment his life changed forever.

CHAPTER 43

Three days had passed since the incident in his office. The press was virtually camped outside the nick and any time anyone arrived or left they were subjected to a barrage of questions. To be fair, the Super quietened down and was getting wider searches of CCTV and more door-to-door enquiries made, but so far, all to no avail. More police officers had been drafted in to help and the budget approved for extra overtime where needed, which, in this day and age, was a miracle. The artist's impression of the description, given by people on the Dickens Estate, had been given wide coverage in the press. Many calls had been received with every single one being prioritized and dealt with and all this took a lot of extra man-hours, but, so far, none forthcoming with any further leads.

The press was having a field day, their front pages filled with hysterical and irresponsible headlines such as 'Vigilante Killer Runs Wild', 'Guilty or Hero – You Vote on Vigilante' and many more. Social media was full of it and someone had even created a Facebook page in support of him that, in just three days had over five thousand likes. Cornelius was getting more frustrated and an air of failure was spreading throughout the station.

The Chief Super called Cornelius, Dan and DI Roberts into his office. "Sorry to take you away from Operation Nightjar for a minute or two, but we are also receiving pressure from above to deal with the pensioners' muggings and death of one of the pensioners. I don't want to do anything to slow down your progress, Superintendent, but could you let DI Roberts spend some time on it? DI Wheeler isn't experienced in a case like this, although it's kids – they're very savvy these days but even he has come up against a brick wall. To make it easier on you, Henry, let Jane report back to Dan if she needs anything, leaving you free to continue on with your case. Is that OK?"

"Yes, sir, that's fine," he replied in a stern voice, obviously not happy with the situation, and then he turned and left the office.

Both Dan and the Chief Super looked at each other with raised eyebrows. "OK, Dan, well… do your best to keep him happy and, Jane, let's get this one tied up quickly. OK, get to it but keep me up to date, both of you."

Jane followed Dan back to his office where he said, "Well, at least that gets you away from Cornelius for a while, that's a blessing."

Jane laughed. "Yes, but to be honest I'd rather be working with you on Nightjar."

"Why don't you get yourself up to date with Wheeler and then come back and we can try to come up with a plan?"

With a smile she replied, "Will do and thanks," leaving him sat at his desk.

The rest of day had dragged and, just before 5 pm when he was planning to call it a day, Jane appeared at his office door. "Sorry to bother you, Guv, but I've just had a call to say we've another mugging, this time near the Millfield and the victim is dead. Do you want to come along?"

CHAPTER 44

They travelled in separate cars as Dan was unsure if he would be staying or leaving it all to DI Roberts. Driving to the Millfield once again, he couldn't help but think how both the council and the police had let the good law-abiding residents here down and let villains, drug dealers and now it seemed, murderers, take over the place.

The incident was on the edge of the estate, where the main walkway from the town centre passed under the main road via a dirty subway. Patrol cars were parked on each side and both entrances taped off; two more patrol cars were parked on the Millfield side, their lights flashing. Julie Burton's Crime Scene van was already there and floodlights were being taken into the under road pathway.

DI Roberts pulled up just behind him and, like Dan, always chose to use her own car – a black Audi A4. They walked together towards the tape and Dan was surprised to see PC Edmunds there.

"PC Edmunds, we meet again. How are you getting on?"

"Fine, sir, thank you. I wish I had been more help to you on the Nightjar case though."

"You did very well, so don't worry, we are all banging our heads with that one. Any idea what we have here?"

"Yes, sir, I was the first to answer the call. A mugging again – an old gentleman who appears to have put up a fight and got seven bells knocked out of him."

With that, he gave both officers the sheet to sign in and

they made their way to the entrance.

Julie saw them and as soon as they had both suited up they made their way to her, avoiding a row of markers on the floor. The body was lying twisted on its side on the floor and while one SOCO took photos, another was on his knees doing a fingertip search.

"Dan, Jane, this is sad. The victim is 96-year-old Ernie Gray. Less than an hour ago the lady over there found the body – she is talking to that PC. She is Doris Murray who also lives on the Millfield and knew the victim well. She is quite shocked. By the look of it he was mugged but, bless him, he must have put up a fight and has taken what looks like, not only a beating, but a kicking as well. He has no wallet or money on him, his Tesco bag-for-life is over there with a few groceries in and, by the cut on his wrist, I would guess he has had his watch cut off. There's blood on the end of his walking-stick where he may have hit the attacker and there are a few drops of blood under the markers, which I doubt came from the victim."

"OK, thanks, Julie. Jane, shall we to chat to Mrs Murray?"

Doris Murray was well into her eighties. She was smartly dressed in a red coat and hat with a metallic remembrance poppy, a Marie Curie pin and a pink breast cancer awareness pin, all on the lapel. She was obviously very shaken; the PC had found a seat for her and a cup of tea.

Dan let Jane go forward to lead the questions. She introduced Dan and herself and said, "Mrs Murray, I am sure you are very upset. I'm told you were friends with the gentleman. This is a nasty crime and I am sorry to trouble you, but can I ask you a few questions?"

She took another sip of her tea, wiping her mouth with a handkerchief. "Don't be sorry, love, I want the evil little bastards caught for doing this, so ask away and no need for Mrs Murray, it's Doris – everyone calls me that."

"Thank you Mrs, ah, sorry... Doris. Could you tell me how you knew the victim?"

"Please don't call him a victim, love. Ernie was a hero, not a victim. I've known him for thirty-odd years. We both went to The Legion club and he was a paratrooper in the Second World War, a D-Day veteran. He's told me all about it; you know, he was dropped in behind the enemy lines the night before, lots of his comrades died that night and the next day, but Ernie was a survivor, at least until this. We went back to Gold Beach, at Arromanches in Normandy three years ago with a coach party from the club and he was treated like the hero he was. When we visited they took us to Bayeux where he was awarded the French Legion of Honour by the local mayor. Like I said, love – a hero, never a victim. He hated the way the world was going, youngsters with no respect, and we had heard about the muggings and the poor dear dying in hospital – we were only talking about them at the club Sunday lunchtime – there's no way he would have let those yobs get away without a fight, bless him."

"Doris, I'm DCI Dan Hooper, but I am also a retired captain from the Parachute Regiment and no matter how old, anyone from the Regiment is a brother, so I feel for your loss and can assure you I will do all in my power to bring the killer or killers to justice."

Dan had seen Gareth Evans, the Home Office pathologist arrive, so he left Jane to finish up with Mrs Murray.

They shook hands. "Dan, what a sorry sight this is, my friend. What is this country coming to? It beggars belief that someone would do this to a fine, old gentleman and I bet that's what he was – look how smart he is," he observed, while turning him over from his side. "Look – a blazer, shirt and tie, just to pop to the shops."

"Not just any tie, Gareth, a Paratroop Regiment tie," and Dan went on to explain what had been relayed to him.

Gareth went to work, carefully looking the body over. "Well, he certainly took a beating. I will need to get him back to find the exact cause but it may well be heart failure due to the attack. If it weren't for men like this none of us would be here today, or if we were, we would be eating sauerkraut. You don't often hear me swear, but this is a fucking disgrace, Dan. You need to nail this one."

Dan was about to comment when PC Edmunds called him. "Excuse me, sir, but I was just chatting to a young lady. She didn't want to give me her name but said the muggings have been going on for more than a few weeks. It's a gang thing apparently and there are a lot of them but they normally strike in pairs on bikes. They've been stealing phones and handbags, anything they can get their hands on. She said people don't bother to report it as most of them are scared of the gang culture on the estate. They call themselves the Green Street Crew; they've got their tags all over the estate. Most of the time they keep their faces covered with green bandanas. I hope that helps, sir."

"Yes, it does. Well done again, Jimmy, you're going to go a long way in this job. If you hear anything else, let me know but don't go off on your own again, it's too dangerous."

By now the press had arrived, some still in town looking for titbits about the 'Vigilante Killer'. He told Jane he was heading back to the nick and as he walked to his car he was stopped by two reporters, one of them asking, "DCI, has the vigilante struck again?"

"No, this certainly has nothing to do with it, but I hope you give it the coverage it deserves. Detective Inspector Roberts will answer any questions when she finishes there and we will issue a statement shortly."

He made his way back to the nick calling the Chief Super on the way who agreed that, for now, he should work with Jane on the muggings and could take Bronco as well and DI

Wheeler could assist Cornelius.

As he got back, he bumped into Sue as she was leaving and they hugged in the car park. "What a lovely surprise. How are you, Dan?" she asked. When he explained where he had been, she also questioned what was wrong with people these days. They stood chatting, laughing and holding hands for a couple of minutes and then Dan made his excuses to leave. They kissed on the cheeks, agreeing they would catch up soon.

He made his way back to his office, called Jane Roberts to tell her what the Chief had said and asked her to come back to the nick once she was done at the site. Bronco was still there working on follow-ups from phone calls when Dan called him into his office and brought him up to speed. As they were chatting, his phone rang. It was Megan Barrett, the press officer. He was about to fill her in with the details when DI Roberts arrived back, so he handed the phone to Jane. She gave Megan all the details and explained that they had a team doing door-to-door through the estate. When she finished the call she turned to Dan and said, "It turns out he has a daughter in Bishop's Stortford; I'll get the local nick to inform her."

"OK, thanks, Jane. I think it's time to give the Millfield a thorough going-over; the place has been a no-go area for far too long. I'll speak to the Chief and see if he can talk the powers that be to bring in a team so we can seal it off for a day to slowly work through the entire estate and sort this gang out."

Bronco shook his head. "Good luck, Guv, but with so much going on with Nightjar I think you'll be lucky to get a handful of PCSOs. Cornelius has got men running around in circles following every single call, no matter how stupid – there just aren't the numbers any more since the cutbacks of the past few years."

"Well, I have to try; we can't let the man's death mean

nothing. Let's call it a night for now and start at seven in the morning. If we have to bring in every yob from ten to twenty-five on the estate for questioning then that's what we'll do."

CHAPTER 45

It had been a better day; the clothes finally arrived along with the fake tan, which he quickly applied and, although he didn't like the sweet smell from it, there was no doubt it helped change his appearance. Dressing in the tracksuit, trainers and cap, he couldn't wait to get out for his first run in four days. It was a cold, crisp day; he took it very slowly, at first not wanting to draw attention to himself, but once he got on to Forest Road and the gravel pits he sped up, pushing himself over the hills and bumps, getting a good sweat on and clearing his head. He started to jog back down Forest Road, keeping his head down, passing a cyclist coming the other way and made his way back to the flat. After a shower he changed into the new chinos, polo shirt and windcheater, going out to get food. Walking back from the supermarket as he passed the newsagents, he looked at the placard where he had seen the vigilante comment days before. This time it read '96-YEAR-OLD WAR HERO BEATEN TO DEATH'. He stopped and bought a paper. Reading it he couldn't have been angrier at what he saw. His mission list had just got longer. Once he was back in his flat, he Googled a few things on his phone and started making new plans. He knew the Millfield well from his stakeout and dealings with Linton; he had seen the gangs on their bikes and standing on corners many times, but had always kept well away from them with his head down. He thought he was too big for them to want to bother with, when there were pensioners they could mug. He didn't like to rush his plans but wanted to get to whoever had done this before the police did. Again, his thoughts went back to what had brought his life to where he now was.

BAGHDAD, ONE-AND-A-HALF YEARS AGO

The Start of the Nightmares!

The scream and gunshot shocked him, which was followed by yelling. He swiftly drew his pistol and silently made his way up to the second floor. The door to the dormitory was closed but he could hear lots of noise from inside. He slowly opened the door and was stunned at what he saw.

Sunny was naked and tied to a bed. There was a bullet hole in the centre of her forehead, looking like a bindi on a Hindu. Denver was naked from the waist down, violently fucking her, while Nezh and Tinus had their combat trousers around their ankles, wanking over her dead body. All three were far too gone to even notice him enter the room, which was thick with pot-smelling smoke. A two-kilo bag of coke was split open on another bed and four more men were either unconscious or in a drug-induced haze.

Taking in the entire scene in a millisecond and with his adrenaline spiking through the roof from earlier, he was unable to control his rage. A roar escaped his lips and he began firing his pistol. The first two shots hit Denver in the back and head; the second two took out Tinus and Nezh. A couple of the others stirred, one rolling from his bed, trying to grab his gun but – too late – with a bullet shooting straight into his right eye. Walking around the room he double-tapped the rest of them. "You evil, fucking bastards!" he yelled. "I'll fucking show you. We don't leave fucking witnesses."

At that point the door burst open and Edil, one of the other Chechens rushed in. Looking around he yelled, "Engleesh, what fuck you doing?" and dived at him. They both rolled across a bed and onto the floor, his pistol flying with the impact. Edil hit him twice on the jaw but his rage was such he didn't feel a thing and he just threw him off against another bed, drawing his kukri from his belt. Edil rolled to his feet. "You will die for this, crazy Engleesh fucker," and charged again, but ran straight on to the Gurkha knife, stopping him in his tracks. As he fell back, clutching his stomach, the knife was pulled out and sliced across his throat. He was dead before he hit the floor.

Not knowing whom else was in the building, he picked up another pistol from one of the beds and a carbine from under a bed. Checking both had full mags, he set about searching the building. It took less than five minutes; the place was empty and the only place he couldn't check was the bottom basement that he knew was only accessed by fingerprints. With that, he went out to the van and, with a few hacks of his kukri, severed Zane's right hand off at the wrist. Taking it back in to the elevator, he placed each finger against the pad – it was, in fact, the thumb print that started the descent of the lift. The door opened to reveal what looked like a cross between a giant wet room and an operating theatre. It contained benches, an operating table, drains in the floor, various chairs (including one with stirrups normally used to give women internal examinations), saws, drills and blowtorches, all lined up on a table. At the back of the room were two barred cages, both empty.

He returned back up to the second floor and double-checked that everyone was dead. He looked at Sunny lying there and came as close as he ever had in his life to crying. He pulled a sheet off a bed and placed it over her.

He sat on a bed and knew he had to take stock of the situation. He was unaware of how long it would be before anyone else arrived, but guessed he had until 08.00 hours, which gave him a maximum of five hours to plan how he would get out of this mess.

Leaving secretly was something that he had fantasised

about for some time, so he had part of an escape plan already formed. He would have liked more time to work out the finer details, but what had happened in the past hour had changed the whole situation. At least he knew where he needed to get to and as quickly as possible.

Going to the ground floor storeroom where all their large lockers were stored, he opened his and took out his stash of cash that he had been given over the past six months, which amounted to almost three hundred thousand dollars. He then found a crowbar and set about opening all the other lockers, removing all their cash. The cash filled two trunks and his rough estimation of value was over three million US dollars. Adding this to what he had in the Swiss accounts meant that if he ever got out in one piece, he would be a wealthy man, not that being wealthy was ever something that bothered him.

He visited Sunny's office next, which held the computers. There were two laptops and a bank of four hard drives. He unplugged them all, taking them down to the storeroom. From there he went to the retired Major General's office, which Zane had been using recently. Just as he thought, behind a large, framed map on the wall was a safe. He might have been taught lock picking in the Regiment but not safe breaking – however, they did teach him how to use explosives of all sizes. Going back to the armoury, he broke open a store cupboard and took a small quantity of C4 plastic explosives and a short period delay detonator. Placing it around the edge of the safe door, he set the detonator and left the office, shutting the door. Ten seconds later there was a bang. He gave it a couple more seconds before going back in and the safe door was blown off. Inside were all the Unit's passports, along with more cash, some gold bars, a folder containing a large stack of bearer bonds, plus some documents in a folder marked TOP SECRET, which he also took, thinking they may be used as insurance in the future.

He loaded the trunks along with a large amount of

ammunition, a couple of carbines, four pistols and some more explosives, never knowing when he may need them, into the black Hummer, along with a pack of water bottles, some dry rations, some traditional Arab clothes and his own civvies. He checked that it was full of gas but with bad fuel consumption, he loaded some jerry cans with fuel as well.

He took more cans of fuel, emptying them throughout the building, and then, finally, fetching a load more explosives from the armoury, he set about placing them all around the building, including by the bodies of Zane, Fish and Joel he had carried in from the van. He hated doing this to Sunny but had no choice. Setting the detonators for twenty minutes' time, he made his leave, never looking back.

CHAPTER 46

Leaving the compound, he took a couple of left turns onto Tamuz Street before passing the 14th July monument and heading north. Traffic was very light at this time in the morning and he was waved through two checkpoints by guards, recognising that the vehicle was as close to a diplomatic one as possible. He knew it would help him at different times in his getaway but may look too out of place further into the journey. Hopefully, he could keep it until he at least got to his planned destination.

By the time he joined the Mosul Road, he figured the detonators would be firing, hopefully leaving the building wrecked and burnt to the ground with the bodies unrecognisable.

In two hours, he was in the heart of the Sunni Triangle, passing near Tikrit, the home town of Saddam Hussein and the sight of many battles from the First Gulf War, to the more recent recapture from Islamic State.

He pushed on northwards, past old remnants of fighting with wrecked military vehicles and bomb craters everywhere. He was very aware that it was still a largely Sunni province and that meant the Islamic State had considerable support. Iraqi security services claimed they had defeated militants, but murders, kidnappings and roadblocks were still rife.

By five he stopped to refuel from the jerry cans. He was getting close to Azwi City, not far from Kirkuk, which he knew had a bad reputation for terrorists, but he had to take the chance to get as far away from Baghdad as possible. He knew the Hummer would now stand out like a sore thumb but he had his Glock and carbine next to him. Pushing on through the desert, luck must have been on his side because he didn't see another vehicle and, by just after seven, was getting close to Mosul.

His mind kept going back over the events of the past few hours and Sunny. He wished he had got back sooner to save her.

Turning off Highway One and approaching Iraq's second largest city and the epicentre of the fight against ISIS (which has left the city looking like a bombsite), the fatigue was hitting him now. The adrenalin from the night had faded long ago, but no matter how tired he was he would get out of Iraq before stopping. As he crossed the Khabur River, he knew the border wasn't far away, so pulled over to change out of his combat clothes into civvies. He knew this next part of the journey could be the most difficult and hoped that the events at his compound hadn't become national news.

The Ibrahim Khalil border crossing is the only official route from Iraq into Turkey. He knew from planning how to get away from Baghdad if he had to, that security could be tight on both sides of the border but, he knew his work permit from Coeus virtually gave him diplomatic immunity and was sure that five x one hundred dollar bills in the passport would help turn a blind eye to anything he was carrying... The average wage for a solider in this part of the world was about one hundred and fifty dollars, but many earned much more from bribes.

There were lines of tankers, trucks, commercial vehicles and even some private cars, all waiting. The queue stretched for a good eight hundred metres, but he knew there was a diplomatic lane on the far left, so he pulled around to get to it. There was a black Mercedes in front of him at the first checkpoint, which was let through very quickly. When it was his turn the guard came up to the window, looking the Hummer over. He handed *him his passport. The guard, taking the money and smiling, said, "Ah, English, yes. David Beekham, good, yes. You good, you go."*

With that, he gently pulled away thinking, Well, that's the first one out of the way and the next one shouldn't be any more difficult. He was back behind the black Mercedes as he waited to go through the Turkish checkpoint, and to his relief it was as easy – the guard was very pleased with the dollars and waved him on and into Turkey.

The E90 road from Iraq shadows the Syrian border to Cizre where, in 2015, Turkish troops turned the town into a war zone, killing hundreds of civilian Kurds and destroying thousands of homes. Before branching off north on the D380 to Midyat, he stopped and topped up with the last of the jerry cans of fuel. The sun was high and the hilly scenery beautiful. For the first time in over twelve hours he started to feel less stressed. At least he was out of Iraq and the further he got from the border the safer he felt, but his mind was still wandering back to the night before and to Sunny – he should have seen it coming, but there was nothing he could do for her now.

By late afternoon he was nearing his destination of Batman Merkez, a town which, in the 1950s, had a population of about three thousand, but now, thanks to its huge oil fields, has an international population of over half a million.

He hadn't been in Baghdad long before he realised it would be sensible to have a fall-back location where no one would know him and he wouldn't look out of place. After searching the Internet and a few telephone calls with the Swiss Bank, he had rented an old farmhouse with about six acres of land on the outskirts of the town for a year, for less than fifteen thousand dollars. It was the perfect location for him in an area where it was common for foreigners working in the oil industry, to long-term rent and the fact the town was called Batman, which he thought was funny, made it even better.

Using the built-in satnav in the Hummer, he found the address and the keys were, as promised, in a key safe at the side of the house. The first thing he did was to park the Hummer in the barn at the rear of the house and then he took the trunks and weapons in. He ate the last of the dry rations and, having been awake for thirty-six hours, he stretched out on the bed. He rapidly fell asleep, knowing that after what he had seen and been through over the past six months, he could take comfort in the fact that the death of the rest of the Unit was justice. The only way to put that behind him now and to move forward with his life was to get justice for those who couldn't get it for themselves.

CHAPTER 47

Dan was up early and into his office before seven. Brenda was already in and the night shift staff were packing up for the night. He asked her how things were moving with Nightjar and she said they were no further ahead, but at least there had been no more murders.

Both Jane and Bronco arrived shortly after. Dan said, "I've just got Gareth's report on Ernie Gray and he certainly took a beating – four broken ribs and a fractured skull, which caused the heart to just give out. Apart from that he was in great shape for a man only four years away from a telegram from the Queen." Turning to Bronco, he said, "You weren't far wrong, Dave, the Chief would love to help but there just aren't the bodies, excuse the pun. But we have got young PC Edmunds, which is good and two PCSOs, so we will just have to do the best we can. Are there no leads at all from the previous cases, Jane?"

"Well, apart from the fact that they are young, in pairs and on bikes, there was the one time they *did* venture right into the town centre where they robbed a pensioner who was drawing cash from an ATM and we caught it on CCTV. We traced them back to the Millfield but, as always, no one wants to help us. We really don't know much at all."

As Dan was about to comment, his phone rang. "Ah, Julie – great, I was hoping to hear from you." Nodding to the others, he continued, "Really, that's brilliant. OK, yes, yes. Send it over. Thanks, speak soon." He put the phone down.

"Well, that *is* great news. They've done an urgent DNA test on the blood leading out of the subway and from the end of Mr Gray's walking-stick. There are two different ones and one is in the system, a Darren Dawson, aged 20. He has a juvenile record but nothing since, but guess what? He lives on the Millfield. Dave, can you find out if he has any family? I think we need to pay him a visit."

Bronco quickly logged on to his computer and after a couple of minutes called out, "Guv, I've got him! He lives with his dad who has a long record, mainly for petty stuff, breaking and entering, petty larceny; he is currently bound over for receiving stolen goods. There's also a twelve-year-old daughter, Angie."

Dan quickly arranged for some backup – he wouldn't even park his car at the Millfield without it. PC Edmunds was waiting for them downstairs; he travelled with DI Roberts while Dan and Bronco travelled together.

The Millfield Estate was one of the hundreds of council estates built after the Second World War. The Minister for Health and Housing, Aneurin Bevan, promoted his vision of new estates where the working man, the doctor and the clergyman could live in close proximity to each other. It may have worked in the post-war years and even perhaps up to the start of the sixties, but then they slowly declined to where, now, in many parts of the country, they were dangerous no-go areas, where lawlessness and drugs ruled. There were five blocks, all six storeys high, on the Millfield. They were all run down and neglected by one government after another, no matter what party was in power.

As they pulled into the estate, Bronco directed Dan over to block three where a police van was already waiting for them. Jane pulled up behind and Bronco walked over to the two officers by the van.

"Morning, gents. We are paying a visit to number 322,

hoping to find Darren Dawson. His DNA links him with the murder here yesterday. If one of you will cover the stairwell, the far end there with DI Roberts, and one stay here by the vehicles that would be great. PC Edmunds, you can come with the DCI and me. We'll go and see if he's in."

They made their way into the building, passing the elevator door that was covered in graffiti and up three flights of dirty, smelly stairs. Walking along the landing, where some of the flats were boarded up with more graffiti scrawled over them, they got to 322, which was much the same as the rest – grimy and in need of a good wash down and a coat of paint. They could hear the radio blaring out some current pop tune neither of them knew and knocked on the door. The radio went quiet and they heard movement inside. Knocking again, Bronco called out, "It's the police! Open the door."

The door slowly opened slightly and a young girl looked around the edge. "Yea, what do you want?"

Bronco answered, showing his warrant card. "We are police officers. I'm DS Laine and this is DCI Hooper. Are you Angie Dawson?"

She looked him up and down. "What's it to you who I am? I ain't done nuffin' wrong."

"If you ain't done nuffin' wrong, young lady, then you have nothing to worry about, but we aren't here to see you. Is your brother in?"

"Nah, ain't seen him in days."

"In that case, your father?"

"'E's in bed, 'e don't get up 'til late and what you want him for? 'E ain't done nuffin."

"Well, we need to see him now, so you had better wake him."

She went to shut the door but Bronco had his foot there now. "Don't be silly, Angie, we are going to see him."

They heard a hacking cough coming from somewhere inside the flat and a voice called out, "What the fuck's going on? Who is it, Ange?"

"It's coppers, Dad, they want you."

The girl moved out of the way and Dawson stood there, a dirty white vest over a beer belly with stained, dark blue tracksuit trousers and bare feet.

"What the fuck do you want?"

Again, they showed their warrant cards. "We just need a few words, Jack. You haven't done anything as far as I know; it's about your boy, Darren. Is he here?"

Dawson coughed again and pulled the door open. "You'd better come in."

Leaving Edmunds at the front door, they stepped into the hallway. The flat smelt of pot, BO and cheap perfume. Dawson led them into a room with a large, new-looking TV and a very worn, leather three-piece suite. There were takeaway boxes and empty beer cans everywhere and the ashtrays were overflowing with cigarette ends and joint remnants. He slumped onto the sofa while Dan and Bronco preferred to stand.

Dan now took the lead. "Mr Dawson, is your son here?"

He coughed again. "No, he's not. I haven't seen him for days; he treats this place like a fucking hotel, the little shit. What's it about?"

Bronco replied, "We just need a chat with him, Jimmy, that's all. Where would he go if he wasn't here?"

"Don't give me that bollocks – a little chat? You don't get a fucking DCI and a DS for a fucking 'chat'. Don't try to mug me off; I've been around too long for that. This is about yesterday, isn't it?"

"We can't comment on that."

Dawson looked sad. "Listen, I've been a tea leaf all my life, for fuck's sake. My old man was as well; he worked in the docks. If you didn't nick while working there they'd think you were a fucking Jehovah's Witness. I've done jobs and I've served me time. I think they call me old-school these days, but that's what we did, we nicked. If we got caught, we did time. These youngsters, they don't give a fuck about anyone. Daz was dealing drugs when he was twelve. He's a bright lad, never been caught since he was a juvey, but this past year or so he got in with a really bad crowd. There's a couple from Romania or some fucking foreign place, he's got hooked on bad drugs and I can't do fuck all to stop him. If his dear mum had been here, it might have been different, but she passed away four years ago. I don't know where he is – he hardly ever comes here unless he wants something, him and his so-called crew stay in boarded up flats on the estate. Search the place, you'll find him in one of them, I'm sure."

The policemen silently listened while Dawson continued with his tales, finding it useful information. He coughed again, reached for a dog-end from the ashtray, lit it and continued, "You know what? I blame myself, of course I do, but I blame the courts as well. Back in the day, if you were caught, bang to rights, you did time – that's how it was, but nowadays the courts are just too fucking soft; they let too many get off with cautions. It must make your job impossible and if a toerag like me thinks that, I hate to think what you guys think, trying to do your job."

Bronco laughed. "Perhaps you should tell that to the magistrate the next time you're nicked, Jackie-boy. I don't suppose there is any point in asking you to let us know if he comes back, but if you do see him you can tell him we will find him."

After that, they left and PC Edmunds was still waiting outside. "Excuse me, sir, but while you've been in there, I couldn't help but notice the estate is deserted. I know I haven't been around here for long but I've never seen it like this as there are always groups of youngsters either wandering around or by the broken-down playground, but there's no one anywhere – it looks like they have all gone into hiding."

"Obviously word has got around to the gangs and the other folks are more than likely scared and want to keep out the way. I think it's worth a good look around while we're here; so Bronco, if you go with Jane and take one block, I'll keep Jimmy with me to do one, the two PCs can do another and the PCSOs can watch the cars. Who ever finishes first can move on to the next block." They then set about checking any flat that was boarded up.

CHAPTER 48

Angie Dawson listened carefully to what her dad and the coppers were saying. She waited until they had gone and slipped out when her dad had fallen asleep in the chair. She was wearing trainers, denim shorts over black leggings and a stretch crop top under a denim jacket – it was hard to believe she wasn't even a teenager yet.

She quickly made her way down the stairs and turned into an alleyway, which left the estate by climbing through a hole in the wall at the back. Making sure no one had spotted her, she hurried along Deans Lane and turned into a small, run down industrial estate. Halfway down on the left was a derelict building that had once housed a thriving electrical components company. It had most of its windows smashed and was overgrown with weeds. The mesh wire fencing had been cut and pulled back in one part and piles of hardcore and rubbish was fly-tipped there. Looking around constantly to make sure she wasn't seen, she made her way past the fence and the rubbish to the back of the building where there was a door. She pulled this open and made her way up to what had once been an office on the first floor. As she reached the top Darren greeted her. "Ange, what the fuck are you doing here? We are keeping out of the way after yesterday." Leading her into the office there were four others, Darren's best mate, Zoot, and two Romanians, Kronid and Michal, where they all had sleeping-bags on the floor.

"I had t' come, Daz, the coppers have been t' the flat, two

detectives – one of them I'd seen on TV about that murder case – I recognised 'im and they were asking all about you. What have you done, Daz?"

He shook his head. "It couldn't be helped, Ange, the stupid old fucker hit me with his fucking walking-stick, can you fucking believe it? It was me and Kronid, we'd been cruising, looking for someone to turn over and he was perfect, limping along with his fucking bag-for-life. Ha-ha, he didn't fucking need that for long, did he?" The boys all laughed. "The stupid, old fool deserved it. No way would I let him get away with fucking hitting me."

"Are you all mental? You killed him! Are you all fucking blitzed already? It's not even lunchtime. If they catch you, then you will go down for years."

Michal walked over, laughing. "Hey, my little angel, don't worry. Come – let's fuck!" he said, pulling her towards him and rubbing his hands on her breasts.

"Hey, that's my little sister! Back off, Mickey, she's only twelve."

Michal laughed again. "That's why she's so sweet and you know she gives me blow jobs, don't you, angel."

Angie pushed him away. "Just fuck off, Mickey, will you? You might be off your head, but this is fucking serious, can't you see that?"

Darren pulled her away from Michal. "Little sister, don't worry. We have it planned; we're going to stay here for now. Tonight, when it's quiet, Zoot will go for a wander. If it's all clear we'll scoot back to our crib, get our stash and disappear for a few weeks, perhaps go up to Manchester. It's meant to be really cool there and Kronid has family there – they will look after us."

"Just be careful, bruv, there will be coppers looking everywhere for you. Do you think someone's grassed you up?"

"They can't have, there's only the four of us; who knows who did it? It must be something else."

Zoot looked up. "Well, perhaps it's that DNA whatsit stuff. I've seen it on CSI, they can trace you from that."

"Don't be stupid, they need to have you on file to do that. I ain't ever been caught; they don't have any way to check, unless they got it when I was a juvey – I can't remember."

Angie hugged Darren. "Okay, well, just be careful. I'm going back and if I see anything I'll call you. If you go to Manchester I won't even tell Dad, you know how he feels about you now, but call me and let me know where you're at."

CHAPTER 49

It took a couple of hours for Dan and the team to cover the entire estate as, surprisingly, there were about twenty empty boarded up flats, including Linton's, that still had police tape across the door. A few had been crack dens and a couple had been badly damaged by fire. Checking the accessible ones, it was clear that some had been used as squats, but no sign of Dawson or his gang.

They made their way back to the nick with the exception of PC Edmunds to keep an eye on things, with strict instructions to call for backup if anything happened. As they reached the office, they could hear Stan Jones in full flow. "Well, let's be honest, Cornelius is about as welcome as a pork chop in a synagogue or woodworm in a wooden leg. The way he argues and upsets everyone, he could be Piers Morgan's twin separated at birth." There was scattered laughter, which stopped as soon as Dan walked in. "Everything OK, Stan?"

"Yes, thanks, Guv; just saying how nice it is to have a new, easy-going boss to work for after having worked for you." A few in the office were trying very hard not to laugh but failing – even Bronco had to chuckle and Dan's face broke into a huge grin. "Only you could get away with that, Stan. Now, come on, we've murderers to catch."

By half ten Darren Dawson and his pals were wasted, they had been smoking weed all day and were now doing lines of coke. Zoot had been for a look around the estate and came back telling them it was very quiet. They made their way to their empty flat as quietly as they could. Considering the spaced out state they were in, they didn't see a soul. They let themselves in with a key. The previous tenant had done a runner so they had broken in the first time, but found a key inside and so they used that to appear as a lived-in flat. Collecting two rucksacks containing stolen credit cards, cash, jewellery and drugs, they soon returned safely to the industrial unit. Laughing and talking about how well they had done, they made plans to leave in the morning for Manchester and by just after 2 am, all were asleep.

CHAPTER 50

He didn't like last-minute plans but had done enough missions on the fly to not have to worry too much – this was one he wasn't going to miss. Dressed all in black with everything he needed in his trusty backpack, he left just before nine and made his way through the darkened backstreets back to the Millfield. He spent the first hour silently moving from floor to floor looking for any sign of where the gang might be, but knew the police would have done the same. With no joy from the search, he settled down in a gap between rows of large rubbish bins with a view of all the blocks... and waited. A little after ten thirty he sensed movement near block four. He had taken his night-vision goggles out with him earlier and pulled them down over his eyes. The device lit up the area before him with an eerie green light. He could see four people in hoodies walking single file to the entrance of the block. Once they were in, he made his way cautiously after them. Waiting by the entrance he could hear them walking up to the second floor. Hearing the sound of a door being unlocked, he went up after them, keeping in the shadows. He saw the last of them enter the flat. Stepping back into the darkness he waited at the end of the landing, biding his time, waiting until they settled down, but was taken aback when, after just a couple of minutes, they started to come out again. He was back down the stairs and in-between the bins long before they appeared at the entrance. Giving them a few yards' start, he carefully followed them all the way back to Deans Lane and the unit.

He let them go in, checked around the outside of the unit and waited for a half-hour before guardedly making his own way in. He could still hear them talking upstairs so he sat down in a cupboard under the stairs. He didn't think the wait would be long, but knew it would be worth it.

The group had quietened down a little while back and he could hear snoring. Pulling the balaclava over his head and taking a bottle and some cloth from his backpack, he pulled on the NVGs again and glided up the stairs without a sound, into the room they were occupying. The four were lying on the floor – some on their sides, some on their backs. Tipping some of the liquid from the bottle onto the cloth, he placed it firmly onto the first one's mouth, holding it there for a few seconds until he was sure the chloroform had taken its effect. Moving across the room he carried out the same to the second, but the third one began to stir, turning his head just in time to feel a hand cover his mouth and hold him down. The fourth, who was still snoring, didn't flinch as the cloth was put over his face. Using his knife, he cut the clothes off all of them, just leaving them in their trainers.

He secured their hands and feet with cable ties and put strips of gaffer tape over their mouths and eyes. Gathering the rope he had in his pack, he strung them, one by one, up and over a beam until they were all on tiptoes. He found an old bucket filled with urine and threw it over them to slowly bring them round. Reaching in the backpack he took out a Smith & Wesson expandable baton. Flicking it open he hit the first lad hard across his ankles, which shook him awake, letting out a muffled scream. Moving along the line, he did the same to each of them until they were all awake.

"Right, you little bastards, it's time for you to get some payback. Now, I need to know who is responsible for the death of the pensioner in the subway. Now, you may think you are tough but, believe me, you will tell me because I am going to

inflict pain on you like you've never known and if it kills you, then fucking tough shit, you fucking deserve it." With that, he pulled the tape off each pair of eyes. It was very dark and at first, they struggled to see, but slowly their eyes focused. Before them stood what looked like some kind of monster with his night-vision goggles over his balaclava.

"So, let's try to make this easy. To start, who wants to tell me who killed him?" Moving from one to the other, they all kept their heads down, avoiding contact. "OK, no takers. Right, let's start with you then, sonny," and he smashed the baton against his knee. The muffled scream from behind the tape was followed by sobs.

"Now, do you want to tell me?" but no reply, just sobs. He did the same to each of the gang, all with similar results. He did it once more but this time in their ribs, certainly breaking a few as he went, but still no one was prepared to talk.

It was easy to see who was the most likely to crack and who would last the longest. So, going back to the first one who was still sobbing, he slowly took some bolt cutters from his pack, opening and closing them a couple of times, right in front of the boy's tearful face.

He pulled over a chair and climbed onto it to reach the boy's hands, putting the lad's little finger of his right hand inside the cutters. "One more chance; do you want to tell me?" Crying and shaking his head, "Your choice, your finger," and in one swift move his finger was snapped through, falling to the floor as easily as breaking a chocolate finger in half.

He picked it up and waved it in front of the rest of them. "Just a little finger, but next time, how about I cut your balls off?" They all pulled and shook on their restraints, but taking the baton again, one by one, he struck them on their knees and ribs.

"Right, who is going to be the first one to have his balls cut off?" Clicking the cutters in his hand, he walked along

the line, tapping the cutters against their genitals, which made them all lift their knees up and yell. He walked back to the first one who had lost a finger. "Ha-ha! Not much chance of getting your balls, it looks like they've disappeared up your arse; it's going to have to be your cock!" With that, he took hold of the limp, shrivelled appendage and placed it in between the jaws of the cutters, closing them so they just held it in place. The boy started to shake his head and yell a muffled reply. Taking the cutters away for a second, he pulled the gaffer from his mouth.

Crying and frantically sobbing, trying to catch his breath, he spoke, "It weren't me, mate, honest it weren't. Please don't cut me cock off, it were Daz and Kronid, they fucking did it, it's nothing to do with me, we're just mates. Please don't cut it off!"

"So, which two are they then?" Immediately one of the others yelled, but that was what he wanted. "So, I guess it's you two, then. Right – now we can get down to business."

CHAPTER 51

The call came through just before six that morning, with Bronco informing Dan he needed to meet him at the industrial estate, just off Deans Lane. They thought that they had found Darren Dawson and it looked like the vigilante had struck again, but this time it was a bit different. Cornelius was also on his way.

Dan was up and showered in minutes – this was becoming a habit, but after pouring coffee into his travel mug, he was in the Freelander and en route by six fifteen.

As he turned off Deans Lane there were flashing lights everywhere, four police cars, two ambulances just pulling away, a couple of unmarked police cars and a SOCO van. A large section of wire-mesh fencing had been cut back, with police tape already marking off the area. Two PCs were struggling to open a large, rusted roller shutter door to make access easier.

Cornelius was looking very pale, perhaps not used to the early mornings. He stood talking with Bronco and DI Brian Churchill, in a wheezy voice. They were all dressed in their white Tyvek coveralls. He turned when he saw Dan and grunted, "No need for you to be here, Hooper, it's the vigilante alright – you should have stayed in bed."

Dan continued walking towards him. "With respect, Super, if it's Darren Dawson in there then it's as much my case. So, do we want to stand and argue about it or try to find out who is doing this?"

"Well, it's not a pretty sight in there. Laine, why don't you show DCI Hooper the way?"

Dan turned to walk towards the building. "Who called it in, Dave?"

"The night watchman from the factory over the road. It seems someone, and it doesn't take any working out whom, let off a flare just outside the door here. The watchman saw it, came to investigate and, as the flare went out, he looked and saw a finger lying next to it. He called it in and, thankfully, didn't go inside. He said he watches *CSI: Miami* so knows all about crime screens getting contaminated."

Dan laughed as he put his coveralls on and they entered through the side door. Floodlights had already been set up from the door, up the stairs and into the office. Julie was at the top and waved to Dan. "It's OK, you can come up. Just be careful where you walk, it's a nightmare for us here. It's been derelict a long time and, along with it being used as a squat, it means finding anything is like trying to find half a needle in a thousand haystacks."

Turning at the top of the stairs he looked into the office where the floodlights blazed onto two bodies hung by their necks with rope from a beam, both naked and both covered in dried blood from various wounds. Dark purple bruises lurked all over their skin, with the word 'GUILTY' carved into their chests.

Julie continued. "There were two more, also naked, both badly beaten and one with his little finger cut off his right hand. They also have 'GUILTY' carved on their chests. They were hardly conscious and both badly traumatized, they said it was a man like a monster, with a mask and green lenses for eyes."

Dan turned away from the bodies. "Well, it's certainly the same MO, isn't it? And it fits in again with the special forces – the green lenses would have been night-vision goggles."

Bronco asked what the link was with Darren Dawson.

Julie pointed to a broken desk against the other wall. "We found a load of credit cards, purses and wallets in two rucksacks, also a very old, Glycine German wristwatch with the strap cut, which I think ties in with Mr Gray's murder."

Dan smiled. "Well, as much as I hate murder, at least Ernie Gray can rest in peace, God bless him."

Turning around, he saw Gareth walking up the stairs. "Ah, the good doctor. I fear we're seeing far too much of each other."

"We are, indeed, young Daniel, but if these are the culprits of Mr Gray's murder then I feel no pity for them." Looking closely at both bodies, he said, "Well, they both certainly took a severe beating and, judging by the bruises, which I have seen the likes of before, I would think were made with a long, narrow weapon, possibly an extendable baton. I think we can get them down, Julie. As always, I will know more once I get them back on the slab, but it looks very straightforward."

Cornelius came wearily up the stairs and, between deep breaths yelled, "Right, it's not a fucking tea party, can we get things moving around here?"

Gareth turned around. "Ah, Cornelius, what a joy. It must be at least ten years since I last heard your charming voice – obviously that's not long enough, but then to be honest, I doubt eternity would be long enough. But rest assured, I will take whatever time I need, to do my job properly, so don't you dare try to rush me. I would have thought with half a dozen murders to solve, you would have enough to be getting on with. Why, some would say young Daniel here was doing a better job than you, old boy," and with a wink to Julie, who was smiling under her face mask, he turned back to the bodies.

Cornelius was obviously flustered by the comments

from the pathologist and after coughing a couple of times he turned to go back downstairs. "Well, that shut him up," Bronco said.

"Yes, thanks Gareth, but I'm not sure any would say I was doing better, there just aren't enough leads."

Gareth laughed. "It was just good to shut up the loud-mouthed oaf. He was bad enough years ago, but it appears he is far worse now."

Then a PC called up the stairs, "Dr Evans, come quickly, please! It's the Super, I think he's having a heart attack."

They rushed down the stairs and Cornelius was lying face down on the ground. Gareth swiftly turned him onto his back, felt his pulse and immediately started with CPR. "Call for an ambulance, this is serious!" he called, but Bronco was already onto that.

Dan was on his knees next to the doc. "Can I help? What about mouth-to-mouth?"

"It's not used much any more, Daniel, for many reasons, but have any of the police cars got a defibrillator?" Dan called out, asking if anyone had one, but they were only provided to road policing units and armed response vehicles.

After a couple of minutes, Gareth was getting tired so Dan took over, remembering the Vinnie Jones advert with the Bee Gees' *Stayin' Alive*. He only had to do it for a minute or so before the ambulance arrived. The medics wasted no time in baring his chest and setting the defibrillator to work. Dan watched as they tried time and time again, but no joy. Gareth stood, shaking his head. "This is not looking good." The medics stopped with the defibrillator, rolling Cornelius onto the stretcher and lifting it into the ambulance. One medic continued with CPR, as the other got into the driver's seat, setting off for the hospital.

"Well, we didn't expect that today, did we? I hope my dig at him didn't set it off."

DI Churchill answered, "No, sir, this has been on the cards for ages. I don't know how long he has been taking pills for his heart but he still smokes, eats lots of crap food and drinks like a fish. He couldn't drive here this morning because he had been on the sauce all night – it really isn't a surprise."

Gareth replied, "Yes, I could smell the drink, but I didn't think it was my place to mention it. Let's hope he doesn't end up on my slab."

Bronco turned to Dan and said, "Well, for now, at least it looks like you're CIO again."

"Yes it does, I'd best call the Chief and let him know." After five minutes chatting with CS Jackson, he finished and told Bronco that, yes, he was back in charge for now, but not sure for how long.

They made their way back to the nick and called everyone in for another briefing. Everyone in the room appeared sorry but relieved that Cornelius wasn't CIO.

Dan sent DI Churchill to the hospital to interview the other two lads and asked Jane to inform Mr Dawson of what had happened and as soon as Gareth gives the go-ahead to identify the body of his son.

An hour later, the Chief Superintendent came down to Dan's office to inform him that Cornelius had died. Although his attitude upset everyone it was still a sad end to a long career, but one that was all too familiar with officers of that age.

Sitting across from Dan, the CS continued. "The press office has been inundated with calls asking if the so-called vigilante has struck again. Megan is being non-committal, but she can't do that for long; she will issue a statement later, so no need for another press conference. I wish I could tell you what to do, but it's not easy when everything is already being done. All I would say is, with so many press here, be very careful what you do or say anywhere and let's not have any large-scale raids like we had at the Dickens Estate until we are one hundred percent certain."

As the day progressed, Gareth Evans came back with the results from the two boys and it was just as expected – death by strangulation – and both had smashed kneecaps and ankles, broken and cracked ribs, together with fractured jaws and skulls.

Jane had taken Mr Dawson to identify the body, which had also been confirmed by Julie's request for quick DNA test results. Mr Dawson also identified the other body as Kronid; he didn't know his surname but thought he was Romanian. DI Churchill didn't get far with the two in hospital, but did at least get their names – only under threat they would be let out and the vigilante may come back for them. One was Michal Gheata and he confirmed the surname of Kronid as Dalca. The other was Stephen 'Zoot' Gale. Both were placed under arrest for robbery and would be taken to the nick for questioning as soon as they could be released from the hospital.

But by just after six he was no further forward and called it a night, setting the next briefing for nine the next morning.

CHAPTER 52

BATMAN, TURKEY, ONE YEAR AGO

The temperature from the morning sun was rising quickly and it wasn't even ten am yet. By lunchtime it would be in the high twenties, as it was most days. The strong aroma of slow roasted Turkish coffee filled the air, mixed with the sweet smell of the freshly baked Şekerpare, a semolina-based traditional biscuit.

With a Panama hat and Ray-Ban Aviators, he received great respite from the sun. He was also wearing light tan Ralph Lauren chinos, Thom Browne boat shoes and a long sleeved light blue Tom Ford shirt, turned back at the cuffs, showing off a Panerai Submersible Carbotech wristwatch. He looked very much the wealthy oil executive and there were plenty of them in this town. As he sat outside the café watching the world go by on the busy tree-lined Turgut Özal Boulevard, a favourite spot for him, there were some fourteen banks on this road – he had either safe deposit boxes or accounts in eight of them. Once he had finished his coffee, he would be visiting two of them, the first to remove twenty-five thousand US dollars from the safe deposit and the second to pay that into an account in one of his five names he was using here.

Turkey had a reputation for their banks being very lax when dealing with money laundering, which made them unpopular with many countries and, although most international banks in Turkey now have strict rules to stop this, there are still many Turkish banks that almost thrive on it –those are the ones he now uses.

Sat there in the sun, it would have been easy to think 'This is the life'. Batman was a very safe and buzzing city, with great shops and restaurants with a truly cosmopolitan feel. With millions in the banks, both here and in Switzerland, he could live in luxury for the rest of his life. But, that was not on his agenda. Every day his thoughts went back to Baghdad, to Sunny and the rage that still burned in his heart, to bring justice to those who couldn't get it for themselves. It was what he had worked for tirelessly over the past six months and, looking back, it had been some journey.

He had slept better than expected on his first night in the farmhouse; it had been a long and tiring drive from Baghdad. On the first morning he set out to recce the land around the farmhouse, working out escape routes should he ever need them. He knew it would attract too much attention to use the Hummer, so taking enough cash with him he walked the three miles into town to the nearest used car dealer and, after haggling over the price to make it look convincing, he bought a six-year-old Toyota HiAce van, which he knew would fit in perfectly. From there he drove into the commercial centre, getting a prepaid cash card and buying tools, mobile phones, a MacBook Pro and a burglar alarm system with CCTV. Driving back to the house he planned his moves for the coming days.

He wasted no time in setting up the alarm and CCTV and placing various weapons in hidden locations around the house and land, should he ever need them in an emergency. He then arranged for high-speed Internet to be installed the next day. His next task was to set out for a run into the hills, which not only helped him survey the area but it got the blood pumping; it was something he would try to do most days.

Using the MacBook, one of the first things he checked was whether there was any news from Baghdad about the ambush or the compound. There was no mention anywhere about the ambush, but Al Jazeera *had a small piece stating that a fire and explosions in the Green Zone compound had destroyed a building, housing a PMC, and that Iraqi security forces were investigating it. That was good because the ISF has no love for foreign security companies and it was doubtful they would delve too deep into it.*

He knew that the Internet would play a big part in his plans and, although he knew enough to do basic searches, he realised he needed to teach himself a lot more.

For the next couple of days, he spent over eighteen hours a day on-line, hardly sleeping or stopping to eat – he badly needed the knowledge so he could move forward. It surprised him how quickly he was able to find his way on to the dark web by using a CyberGhost VPN to hide his IP address and a Tor Browser. By the evening of the third day, there he was, beginning to get the results he needed. He had found details of which banks were the best if you wanted to launder money, where to get false passports and just about anything else you needed, from drugs to weapons.

With so much cash he was reluctant to leave the farm for long and knew it would take time to get all of it into the banking system, but with the help of YouTube and some building supplies he had had delivered, along with a cement mixer, he set about making a hidden underground storage place for the trunks.

When this was completed, his next job was sorting out passports and this would mean travelling to İzmir, the smuggling capital of Turkey, but this would either mean an eighteen-hour drive or a two-hour flight from the nearby Diyarbakir Airport. He had made contact on the dark web and had agreed to meet Mecho Gruev the next day. He booked his ticket on-line with the prepaid card. It would mean an overnight stop, as there was no return flight until the next morning. He knew he couldn't take any weapons on the flight with him, as they would set off the metal detectors, but he cut a plastic kitchen tray into a blade, covering the handle with gaffer tape for a grip and sharpening the blade to a fine point. It wasn't good but would be better than nothing if needed.

Double-checking the alarm system, he drove to the airport and caught the 8.25 am SunExpress 737-800. They served a typical Turkish breakfast of meats, cheeses and fruits along with some very good coffee. The flight was only half full, which meant he was sat on his own and that gave him time to think about what lay ahead for the next couple of days. Being an internal flight and with no luggage other than his backpack, he was quickly out of the airport, grabbing a taxi to take him to Kadifekale, an area as famous for its ancient fortress with beautiful views, as it is for being a dangerous, gypsy neighborhood.

The Balsa Firin Café was a modern-looking café with large picture windows located in Menderes, in a busy side street intersection. Once the taxi dropped him off he took a quick recce around the area before going in. It was a pleasant surprise for him, with glass display cabinets filled with freshly baked cakes and savouries. A few of the tables were taken, all by men and, at the back a skinny, dark-haired man waved him over, smiling.

"I think you looking for me, my friend," he said in broken English.

"If you are Mecho, then I am," he replied.

"Yes, I am, my friend, and you are English or Australian, I guess. I, myself, am from Bulgaria, but there is more work here for me, but not normally, if you will forgive me for saying, with your kind, most of my work is for Syrians making their way to Europe."

The most confusing thing was that Bulgarians shake their head for yes and nod for no, which took a little getting used to. They sat and talked quietly for about fifteen minutes, both asking questions of the other until they agreed to proceed with their transaction and to do that would be to go to the Bulgarian's office across the road.

It was a bright day and the street was busy as they crossed, with Mecho continuing to talk almost non-stop. Knowing this could be a set-up, he cautiously checked out the area to notice if anyone was paying attention to him, but it all looked safe. The office was on the first floor of the building with a sign of an insurance company on the door. He was led through to a back room with a desk, photocopiers and a printing press. Opening a safe, Mecho showed him some samples of passports; in return, he showed him the passports he had taken from the compound. It was agreed that he would get five new passports; two British, one Irish, one Zimbabwean and one Canadian. In return for the passports he was handing over, Mecho would charge him a reduced fee of twenty-five thousand for the lot. He paid a down payment of ten thousand, agreeing he would come back to the office first thing in the morning when they would be waiting for him. He would then pay the balance. He posed against a white background for photos and was aware that, without a passport, many hotels wouldn't let him stay. Mecho, however, gave him a few recommendations that would take cash with no questions. They shook hands and he left.

Using the satnav on his phone, he looked to see where the hotels were and chose the one furthest away. He was lucky to see a taxi and asked to be taken to the Ramada Plaza opposite the Luna Park. Once he was dropped off, he walked into the entrance of the five-star hotel, stopping to look at the restaurant menu, before making sure the taxi had driven away. He took a short walk to the Guzel Izmir Hotel in a tiny backstreet filled with other hotels and bars. The young clerk on the check-in desk spoke good English and when he asked for his passport he was told he had left it at the hotel he was staying at in Istanbul, but he slid a hundred dollar bill across the desk, which disappeared *into the clerk's pocket in the blink of an eye. Filling the check-in form as John Smith from Manchester, he paid for two nights just in case, which cost the princely sum of fifty dollars. The room was bright, but the sheets didn't look very clean, which was no problem – he would sleep on top of the bed. It was only two pm but it was a good time to catch up on some sleep and, drawing the curtains, he lay on the bed and slept for four hours. Waking after six o'clock he showered in lukewarm water, dried himself on a threadbare towel and went out into the street to find somewhere to eat, taking his backpack with him. There were many places to choose from. He picked the busiest one and enjoyed a meal of saç kavurma, a tasty Turkish dish made with sautéed lamb, peppers and spices.*

CHAPTER 53

On the return to the hotel through the busy narrow streets, he noticed two men were following him. As he crossed to the other side of the street, one crossed after him and the other continued on the same side. He had no doubt that a western tourist on his own, carrying a backpack, would appear to be an easy target. He didn't want to get into a fight with so many other people around so he continued back past his hotel and the Ramada, checking he was still being followed. He then crossed the wide road on to Luna Park, with its tree-lined walkways and large amusement park. The entrance was brightly lit; he followed the palm tree-lined walkway to a large fountain, which he casually walked around, pretending to take an interest in, but all the while watching the two men. They had continued walking towards him, chatting, and their eyes kept going back to him. They were both mid-thirties and just under six-feet tall. One had a dark ponytail, both looking more eastern European than Turkish, but he wondered if they were Bulgarian and had been sent by Mecho.

One man walked one side of the fountain, one the other and, as they got close, in broken English, one asked, "Hey you; you got a light?" As he quickly turned to look the other one came behind him to grab his backpack, but the man was too slow. He kicked him in the side of his knee, sending him to the ground. The other pulled out a knife and ran towards him. He swung the backpack at him, stopping him, and turned and ran through the line of palm trees and onto the grassed area, which was very dark. The man with the knife chased him while the other slowly got up and limped after him. Letting the first one get closer, he dropped the backpack, turned and grabbed the wrist of the hand holding the knife in his left hand, opening the guy up for a straight right jab to the chin, which poleaxed him. He kept hold of his wrist and turned it against the joint, snapping the bone, the knife dropping onto the grass. The second one was almost back but, seeing what had just happened, he turned to limp away but was too slow. Grabbing him by his ponytail, he pulled him backwards onto the ground and punched him a few times in the face, then dragged him by his hair across to the other one. He laughed, saying, "That's what's the same between a ponytail on a man or on a horse – lift it up, there's always an arsehole underneath it!"

The first one began to stir, so he kicked him hard in the head and picked up the knife. Turning to the other he pulled his head back again by his hair, held the knife to his throat and demanded, "Who sent you?" No reply. "I'll only ask once more before I start to cut – who sent you?" Again, no reply; so, placing his hand over the man's eyes and pulling his head back, he started to slowly draw the knife across his windpipe, not deep enough to cut his throat, but enough to draw blood and scare him so much, that at that moment he pissed himself. "The next cut will kill you, so speak now or you'll never speak again. Who sent you?"

He coughed a couple of times and replied, "No one send us, it's what we do; look for easy targets, just steal bags, purses, anything we can get – you look easy target."

"I don't believe you, that's your last chance!" Lifting the knife again, the guy screamed, "It's truth, on life, my mother – it truth!"

Letting him fall back onto the grass, he stood up and kicked him very hard in the side of his head, knocking him out. He then went back to the first guy, taking his left arm this time, *bending it backwards over his knee until it snapped and then he did the same to both the ponytail guy's arms.* Let's see how they steal things with both arms in plaster, *he thought. Picking up his backpack he made his way to the hotel, stopping for a large whisky in the brightly-coloured bar. He downed it in one before going to his room.*

Sleep didn't come easily and he was awake early so he showered and dressed and was out by seven. He wasn't due to get the passports until ten, so first of all he walked back to the Ramada Plaza. Entering the restaurant, he paid in advance for breakfast and ate a full cooked, as close to English breakfast as you could get in Turkey, along with three cups of rich, Turkish coffee. With time to spare, he took almost an hour using his phone's satnav to walk back to the Balsa Firin Café. It was still an hour before their agreed meet time, so he took a table at the back and topped up with even more richly roasted caffeine. At 9.30 he decided to make an early appearance at the office, crossing the road and silently walking up to the first floor office. He could hear noise from inside so he carefully opened the door. The front office was empty, but the back room door was ajar. As he walked towards it, it fully opened and Mecho walked out, almost jumping as he saw someone there. "Oh, my friend, you are early, I do not hear you. I think you move like a ghost, my friend; Casper the Friendly Ghost, perhaps," and laughed. "But, not to worry, I have all you need – come see." They walked into the back room; opening the safe he took out a large envelope and tipped the contents out onto the desk. Handing them over one at a time, he said, "Tell me what you think, my friend. It is my best work for you; I want you to be happy. I think we may work again in the future, perhaps." He carefully looked at each one and was very impressed. "They're very good, I am pleased. Thank you, Mecho."

"Good, good, my friend, they are all in the names we agreed on. They all are genuine names and will accept

background checks, as I tell you. This is my best work. Now for the balance, please." He handed over the remaining fifteen thousand dollars and they shook hands firmly. "I shall call you Mr Whitehouse from now on, not Brownley, Greensted, Grayson or Blackwood, as in the other passports – take this," he added, handing over a handwritten card. "It is my private phone number. If you ever need anything urgently, just call me, I will be there for you, my friend." He thanked him and left, not realising how soon he would be in touch again.

Once in the street he checked carefully around before turning onto the main road. He walked for a few minutes before catching a taxi to the airport.

He had been back in Batman for two days and now that he had passports he started to arrange meetings with banks to open accounts. His first appointment was at the Halkbank at 285 Turgut Özal Boulevard, a street he was going to spend a lot of time on over the next few months, posing as a self-employed consultant in the oil industry, which was the perfect cover story. He was shown into the office of Murat Ata, the branch manager, having explained his story and that he wanted to open an account and had a large amount of cash to deposit. He was assured that his bank was well aware of the delicacies of the oil trade in their country and that they were there to help, so as a new customer, the bank would be happy to receive cash of up to one hundred thousand dollars for the opening deposit and then fifty thousand a week, without having to inform anyone. He also arranged for credit and debit cards. From there he went further down the street to the İşbank at number 272 and went through an almost identical process. Over the next two days he did the same, either opening accounts, or renting safe deposit boxes. Visiting the banks, either paying in or storing cash, would take up a couple of days a week, each week, but it was something he had to do to be able to move on.

And so the months had flown by. When not spreading his

money around the Turkish banking system, he spent hundreds of hours on the Internet and the dark web. He was a quick learner and after a few weeks he had downloaded Brutus, a password cracker to use on Sunny's laptop and the hard drives he had brought with him. It was obvious, as he had thought for some time, that the company was funded by the CIA, as he was amazed by the content, which would allow him into back doorways not only of US National Security, but also British Intelligence, Interpol and much more. It took a couple of months to go through it all, but by then he was able to search files and databases worldwide without any detection. It also allowed him to eliminate his name and details from every possible database; it was as if he didn't exist any more, something that would be a great help as he got closer to putting his plans into action.

His only other trip away from Batman was a big one, and a very important one, to Zurich. He travelled first to the bank where his wages had been paid into and, using his own passport and passcode, withdrew just under three hundred thousand dollars in one hundred dollar bills. They fitted well into the large briefcase he had brought with him. From there he took a taxi to the Julius Baer Bank on Bahnhofstrasse, where trams passed by luxury shops like Prada and Patek Philippe. He had made an appointment to see the new accounts manager, Alexander Briner, and was politely shown to his office on the first floor. Herr Briner was a tall, slim, forty-something gentleman, in what was certainly a grey Savile Row suit, crisp white shirt and silver tie with a Windsor knot. "Mr Greensted, welcome to Zurich, please take a seat. Thank you for coming in person; we do prefer to meet our new clients as we feel it builds a working relationship moving forward. Before we go any further, I must ask if you have brought all the documents we asked for."

Thankfully, a phone call to Mecho had proved invaluable,

as he was able to show tax returns and company registration certificates for First Line Import and Export International with a registered office in The Waterfront Business Park, Cork, Ireland.

Checking through them all and calling his secretary to photocopy them along with his passport, he handed over papers to be signed, which, with a signature he had practiced for the past week, he signed and handed back.

"Thank you, Mr Greensted. I am pleased to accept your application to bank with us. Now, I believe you wish to make a deposit and, while we deal with that, we will be arranging your bank card and passcodes, etc." He placed the briefcase on the desk, opening it and turning it around, confirming how much was in it. This was also passed to the secretary to deal with. He then handed over the bearer bonds he took from the compound. Herr Briner took them, looking through each one carefully and then stood and excused himself for a moment, leaving the office.

Sat there on his own, he wondered if there was a problem? Should he be looking for a way out? Was this where things were going to suddenly go wrong? Standing up, he looked out of the window on to St Peterstrasse, watching people sat outside a café, drinking coffee. Hearing footsteps behind, he turned quickly, only to see Herr Briner coming back in with the bonds still in his hand and a smile on his face. "Mr Greensted, sorry to keep you but I had to verify these bonds. I have had various dealings with similar in the past but wanted to check their worth and, as I am sure you know, these are valued at just over six million dollars." He was shocked, he had no idea they would be worth that much, but he kept a straight face, replying, "Yes, that's correct and that's why I feel the time is right to cash them. I assume you can deal with that?"

"Yes, of course, we would be pleased to; we do take a one percent commission."

They soon finished their business and he left with an empty briefcase, bank cards and passcodes, plus the knowledge that he had no banking link now to America or Iraq.

Flying back from Zurich to Diyarbakir meant a three-hour stopover in Istanbul, so it was late by the time he got back to the farm. He was still up early the next morning and went for a run into the hills before driving into town to extend the rental on the farm for another year. With his finances safely sorted, for whatever lay ahead, he knew that the time was fast approaching to leave Batman for a while and move back to England to put his plans into action. And That's When The Fun Would Really Begin!

CHAPTER 54

The phone rang just as he got out of the shower at six thirty. *Not another one, please,* he thought, but it was a number he didn't recognise. Answering, "DI Hooper," there was a pause and then a shaky voice spoke. "Captain Hooper, it's Jimmy Miller, do you remember me? You gave me your card."

"Yes, Jimmy, I do. What can I do for you?"

"Well, since our meeting I've realised I need to pull myself together and stop feeling sorry for myself. I have even enrolled in a PTSD course, starting next week."

"That's good news, Jimmy. Thanks for letting me know and good luck."

"No, sir, that's not why I've called you. I am also trying to get fit and, although I can't run yet, the leg hasn't healed that much, so I bought an old second-hand bike and have been out riding. Most days I go down Forest Road past the old gravel pits; it's a good ride and the road is quiet, which suits me. Well, twice now I have seen this guy, who I am sure was in the Regiment. We didn't meet but I am sure I saw him at Hereford. I've just passed him, he is down there now in a blue tracksuit. I know you're looking for someone with that background and thought this might help. I wouldn't normally grass up any one of the lads and it might be nothing, but you've got me back on the right path, so I wanted to help."

"That's great, Jimmy, thanks. I will check that out. Take care and keep up the good work." He then called Bronco to let him know, but for some reason he was unavailable, which was strange for Dave.

Hearing the Chief's words about not jumping in too soon, he thought he would just take a drive down there and perhaps even have a run himself. He doubted there would be anything to it, but quickly putting on his tracksuit, he was in the car and on the way in minutes.

It was a dark, cloudy day with light rain in the air. Parking on the loose gravel, he got out and started to run towards the area the BMX riders used, scanning the area as he ran. In the distance he could make out a lone figure running with his back to him, getting towards the end of the humps and bumps and onto the path around the old disused pit. Dan speeded up to get closer and, although the guy was running at a steady pace, he was slowly catching him. He could see now that it was a blue tracksuit, so he increased his pace even more, which soon had him over the humps and onto the path. He was only about fifty metres behind him when the guy stopped to stretch his hamstring. Looking around, he saw Dan heading towards him very quickly. Still stretching his hamstring, at first, he wasn't concerned about the runner, but as he got within twenty-five meters he recognised him. Dan's picture had been all over the papers and TV for the past week and so he just turned and continued to jog on, still feeling the back of his thigh. In a few paces, Dan was next to him. Slowing down, he turned to ask if the guy's hamstring was OK, but the moment Dan looked at him, something clicked. He didn't know what it was, but – like a shock down his spine – he just *knew*.

"No, it's just a twinge. I think I was pushing it too hard, thanks, mate."

"No worries. Hey, this is strange, but I think I know you; what's your name?"

The answer was so sharp and abrupt. "No, I don't think

I know you, mate. What is that, a chat up line? Are you gay or something?"

Dan laughed. "No, mate, not at all. I'm just sure we've met somewhere before. Were you in the forces?"

Looking straight into Dan's eyes, he just replied, "No," and with that, he turned to jog back along the edge of the pit.

Dan stopped for a second, resting his hands on his hips and watched as the guy began running back along the path. He was certainly in a quandary; he didn't know what it was, but something wasn't right and somewhere in the back of his mind there was something telling him that this was the vigilante. He knew then that he had to stop him, no matter what.

He set off after him and, in a minute, had caught up with him. "Hang on for a minute, mate, I want a word with you." No reply, but he kept on running.

The rain was now falling heavily. Grabbing the man's arm, he said, "Will you stop, I am a police officer and I want to talk to you." The man turned, breaking the hold. "Get your hands off me!" he shouted, pushing Dan away.

"I've told you, I'm a police officer, Detective Chief Inspector Hooper, and I have a few questions for you, starting with what's your name?"

He took hold of his arm again, this time much harder, but immediately the man pulled free so Dan made a grab for him and they both started to struggle. They were getting soaked by the rain and slipping on the wet path. Dan tried to grab him in a headlock but was lifted in the air with both of the man's arms wrapped around his waist from the side. This was getting dangerous and Dan realised it was no mistake – this must be the killer – but was he going to be the next victim?

He lashed out as hard as he could with his elbow catching the top of the man's head, which stunned him, making him stagger back. That's when his foot slipped on the muddy path sending both of them backwards over the edge, somersaulting over 40-feet into the freezing water of the pit. They separated in the fall with Dan crashing headfirst and backwards into the murky water. His head hit a wooden submerged structure, knocking him unconscious. With blood trickling from a wound on the back of his head, his world had suddenly turned to black.

CHAPTER 55

He was floating in the air, free falling, floating on thermals; it was like one of the hundreds of High Altitude – Low Opening (HALO)s he had performed over the years, but looking down he could see his Catherine. The sun was shining; she was wearing a light blue dress with her hair pulled back into a ponytail, walking along Brook Street in London's West End, on her way back from her final wedding dress fitting. She was waiting for the lights to change to cross, for a look in Victoria's Secret. But, then he saw the stolen DHL lorry speeding down New Bond Street. Ignoring the red lights, it first ploughed into the people crossing by the Russell & Bromley shoe shop. Catherine was halfway across the road and people were screaming, turning to get out of the way, but it was too late, the lorry continued right through them, scattering broken bodies in its wake. Catherine was left dying in the road amongst other bodies. The truck carried on down New Bond Street, crashing on the pavement with the driver jumping out and running down the narrow alley of Lancashire Court, next to the Boss store, yelling, "Allahu akbar!"

He was still free falling, but now through darkness. The scene changed to him stood next to Catherine's bed in University Hospital as she lay there motionless, the surgeon shaking his head and placing a hand on his shoulder. Bronco stood next to him, turning and hugging him as the sobs wracked his body. Still he fell, now in a panic, struggling, fighting, crying and seeing newspaper headlines: 'Terrorist

Attack London 18 Dead', 'Hunt For Hit & Run Terrorist Goes On' and 'Police Draw Blank in Terrorist Hunt'.

The fall got quicker, falling faster and faster, the ground getting nearer and nearer – there was no stopping and then he woke.

Laying on his back, coughing, shaking, soaking wet, his vision blurred but slowly cleared, not knowing for a second where he was. He saw a corrugated tin roof above him. He tried to sit up but coughed and fell back.

"Take it easy, you very nearly drowned." It then slowly came back to him – the run, the man, the fight and the fall into the water.

"What… you… where are we..? I need to arrest you, you're the vigilante."

"Just rest and hear me out; you're in no fit state to go anywhere. I dragged you out of the water, up about forty steps and into this shed. I even gave you mouth-to- mouth which, to be honest, I really had second thoughts about. I couldn't leave you, Dan. You need to know that you are the reason I am here, the reason for the killings. Just listen to what I have to say and, if at the end of it you still want to arrest me, I give you my word, I will come quietly."

"I don't think I have much choice, do I?"

"No, you don't, so here goes… It might take some time."

CHAPTER 56

"My name is Tom Windsor, not that you will find that name in any database or social media site, as you are about to hear. I think you recognised me when you saw me, which more than surprised me, but we *have* met very briefly before. It was September 2000, Freetown, Sierra Leone. Operation Barras, which, if you remember, was a joint SAS and 1 Para rescue mission to save British military hostages held by a rebel group called the West Side Boys. We flew out from Brize Norton."

Dan shook his head, his thoughts slowly becoming clear. "How could I not remember that? What a mission – fighting those drug-fuelled rebels, many of them just kids, believing they were protected by some spirit god – that was crazy."

Shaking his head again, as if to clear it some more, he said, "Hang on, it's coming back. I *do* remember you – what did they call you? Farmer or Pincher? Something like that."

"You *do* remember me then. Yes, it was Poacher. I joined the Regiment from 2nd Battalion, Royal Anglians; it's their nickname and it stuck."

"OK, so tell me then – how am I the reason you are here?"

Tom Windsor began to tell the story, from going to Baghdad to join Coeus, the murders and brutality he saw there. It was more in the name of greed than war, of bodies being dumped in pits of acid. Of Sunny and how, despite their location and situation, they had grown close. The night when it all happened and how he had dealt with it. His journey to

Turkey and how he had spent his time there and, most of all, the rage he kept in his heart, to fulfill his wish that he would bring justice for those who couldn't get it for themselves.

Dan listened intently, not interrupting or questioning, but enthralled by it all.

Tom continued. "So, six months ago I came back to the UK and began researching, looking for just causes. I have always been proud of those who serve their country and decided that these were the people I would look to get justice for first. With these hard drives there isn't much I can't find out. I was making lists, adding and crossing out cases, when I saw an old newspaper report about Catherine. While reading through it I saw she was due to be married to a former paratrooper, now a detective, so I decided to look into it more. I was amazed to discover the link between Sierra Leone and us. From that point on it was a no-brainer and you went straight to the top of the list.

"I quickly realised though, that if I just dealt with those who killed Catherine then suspicion my well fall on you, so I set about finding other local suitable cases. It was so obvious that justice isn't correctly served in this country for so many good people and to see evil wicked bastards not being charged with their crimes, in some cases, purely for political reasons, or perhaps just because due to cutbacks, the police hadn't got the manpower to do the job.

"So, in just a couple of weeks, I had all the cases I wanted, lined up in this area. The only change of plans was the murder of Ernie Gray and I couldn't let them get away with that. We both know, even if I had just tipped you off to where they were and you nicked them, the most they would have got is perhaps twenty years and be out in ten. Ernie Gray was braver than you and me put together; how many today could go through what Ernie and his comrades went through in 1945? I owed it to him to bring justice.

"I truly believe, and I suspect you do too, that his life was worth more than ten years, living in your own centrally-heated room, three solid meals a day, playing sport, training in a gym, watching television and even taking drugs. Again, it was a no-brainer; I had no choice but to get justice for a real hero."

Dan had heard, slowly getting up to his feet. "I have to stop you; there is no doubt in my mind that you believe in what you're doing, but to me you are suffering with PTSD and, while many of us would sympathise with your wishes to bring justice, the truth is, if everyone did that then the world would quickly descend into anarchy and disorder, where only the vicious or most evil would survive. I appreciate your concern and thoughts for my past, but I need to take you at your word. I've listened as you asked – now it's time to take you in."

Tom smiled and shook his head. "But I haven't finished, so hear me out. I said the reason I came here was you, so don't you see? I not only know who was driving the truck that killed Catherine and all those other people, but I also know who was behind it all."

Dan was shocked. "That can't be; I know that for a fact because I had a meeting with a senior officer at MI5 at Thames House. He assured me that the person responsible had fled the country and was now in Afghanistan and that they would keep the case live in case he ever came back."

"Dan, that's bollocks; he's not only in this country, but he is less than five miles from us as we speak, as is the person who planned the attack. To make it clearer, since her death, they have been behind at least another six murders. I have plans to deal with them both, ready to put into action. Let me go and I will get justice for you and Catherine and, in the process, stop anyone else going through what either you or Catherine went through."

"Tom, I don't think I can do that; it goes against my principles and all I stand for. Just give me the details and let me deal with it."

"You don't get it, do you, Dan? That won't ever happen – MI5 won't let it happen. The only reason I know who they are is that *they* know who they are! You met with Commander Timothy Blair at Thames House; I have seen their records. The reason they won't do anything is political. The person behind it is an Imam with links to Islamic state. He is a double agent and was turned when they caught his son who was the driver of the truck. They threatened to arrest them both and he did a deal whereby he gives them information."

"I don't believe it." Dan paused, thinking. "But then, yes I do. I guess nothing like that should surprise me any more."

"Let me do it, Dan. If it helps I won't even put the 'guilty' sign on them, it can be an accident. No one else need know and I will go, never to be seen or heard of around here again – the vigilante case would just fade away."

By now they were both beginning to shiver as their clothes had dried on them. Dan's head had stopped bleeding but was very sore. "I just don't know, Tom. I am tempted and you make a very good argument, but it's such a lot to take in. I just don't know."

"OK, I understand, I really do and perhaps you need time to think it all over. So, how about this… give it a day; I will be here the same time tomorrow morning. If you want to arrest me then come and get me, I won't fight. But if you want me to go ahead with the plan, don't come and you will never see me again. In two days it will all be over and you can get on with your life, perhaps even with your friend, Sue," he smiled.

Dan thought long and hard for a couple of minutes before holding out his hand to shake Tom's. "Just be clear, if I come here tomorrow and you aren't here, then I will find you, no matter how long it takes and I know enough about you now to track you halfway around the world, if needs be."

Tom took his hand firmly. "It's a deal. I will be here as promised. Now, we need to get out of these wet clothes else we will both have pneumonia tomorrow."

They jogged back to the road together. "Do you want me to drive you back into town, Tom?"

"I think it best not to, just in case anyone sees you. It's best you go and hopefully we will never see each other again."

Tom began to jog back into town while Dan started the Freelander. Putting the heating on full-blast, he drove back to his house. His mind was full of what had happened this morning and it wasn't even half eight yet.

Figuring he didn't need to visit the hospital for a check over, he was home quickly, he showered and just about had time to pour a hot, strong coffee into his travel mug before being on his way to the nick in time for his 9 am briefing. He didn't know what he was going to say to everyone, especially Bronco who he trusted more than anyone in the world.

CHAPTER 57

As he walked into the office, Bronco came up to him and asked, "Are you OK, Guv? I've been trying to call you and, to be honest, you don't look that good. Is everything OK?"

"Yes, Dave, I had called you this morning early, er... just, er, just sort of general thoughts about everything really, but your phone was off. Anyway, I got out of the shower still soaking wet, went to try you again and slipped on the bathroom floor. I banged my head and the phone went straight down the toilet; it's at home in the airing-cupboard in a bag of rice. That's what they recommend, isn't it?"

Bronco looked concerned. "Sorry, I forgot to put my phone on charge last night– no idea why, just thinking too much about the case probably, so the battery went. Did you bang your head hard? Only you don't seem quite right."

"I was out for a few seconds; I don't think it was much more. I'll be fine."

"What did you want to talk about?"

Dan thought for a second; he realised his mind wasn't focused and was filled with thoughts of Tom Windsor. "Oh, just not knowing where to go from here and I must admit, my head is a bit fuzzy. Has anything come in overnight?"

"Yes, that's why I was trying to call you. From all the phone calls we have had, there appears to be a very good one, a sighting in roughly the right area, a bit away from the Dickens Estate towards the Old Town. The caller says that it's a man of the right description who only recently moved in – she thinks it's the vigilante."

Dan's heart pounded almost as much as his head was. He still didn't know what answer he was going to give Windsor, but he almost didn't want him caught before he had made his mind up.

"OK, right, well, let's think… the Chief has made it clear that we mustn't go in guns blazing like we did last time, so it has to be a softly-softly approach. Have we got the address?"

"Yes, Guv, 79 Colvin Street. It's a small terraced house. DI Churchill is checking the details now."

Brian Churchill stood up from his desk and walked over. "Yes, Guv, no real luck, it's another Asian landlord. He reckons the tenant is a Mr Shah, which, let's be honest, in India that's like being called Jones." At which point, Stan Jones did a completely un-PC impression of Peter Sellers singing *Goodness Gracious Me.*

Dan stopped him. "That's enough, thank you, Jones. It's not 1960 any more. Carry on, Brian."

Grinning, he carried on. "Well, he says Mr Shah has lived there for over a year. I don't believe him, he's more than likely subletting and avoiding the tax man."

"OK, thanks, well, as I said, we need to take it carefully, so I think the first thing is to get a surveillance team over there and see if that leads us anywhere. Brian, can I leave that with you? Take Stan Jones for company; that will be an experience for you," and everybody laughed.

Dan just couldn't concentrate – one minute he knew he had to arrest Windsor, the next he wanted to let him deal with the two who had taken Catherine away from him. He just didn't know which way to turn for the best. He had heard that Churchill and Jones were in position, in a car up the road with a good view of number 79, but there was no movement there, which he was relieved about.

By just before twelve, he realised he hadn't eaten since

last night, so he walked up to the canteen. He was pleased, as he walked in, that he had beaten the lunchtime rush and Sue was on her own at the counter. She beamed a huge smile. "Well, hello you! I hear you had a fall this morning."

Dan grinned. "How on earth did you know about that, Sue?"

"Well, *you're* the detective, perhaps *you* should decide. Either I have a hidden camera in your shower room perving on you when I can, or the jungle telegraph in this place is worse than *EastEnders*."

They both laughed and Sue continued, "But you are in luck and not a lot of people know this, but I am a trained lifeguard and am more than happy to guard you every time you shower. I should warn you though, it would be very close contact guarding – I don't mess about."

Dan roared with laughter. "That's really cheered me up on a strange day. Mind you, I'm not sure showering on my own will ever be the same again. Now, I haven't eaten since last night, so I think I will forget the healthy diet and have one of your all day breakfasts, please, and a large, strong Americano, please."

"Coming right up, DCI Hooper." She dished it up and handed him the plate. Keeping hold of his other hand, she whispered, "Seriously, Dan, you know where I am and you know I'm happy to be there as a friend if that's what you need. Don't be scared to call me, oh, and by the way, I'm not really a lifeguard."

Dan just gave her a broad smile, looking straight into her beautiful, brown eyes. "Thanks, Sue. One day, I promise, and it might be sooner than you think."

He sat and ate his breakfast, but not really tasting it. Why did he just say that to Sue? Was he thinking about Windsor's comment from yesterday? He wished he could decide, but then he realised that if the tip-off was correct, the worry might be taken out of his hands.

Back in the office, with no word from Churchill, Bronco suggested they take a trip to Colvin Street, so with nothing better to do, they did. Parking around the corner, they walked around to join the others, both getting into the back seats.

"Thank God you're here, Guv, Stan has recited every bad joke I have ever heard; it's like Chinese water torture."

"No need for that, Detective Inspector, just trying to spread some joy," Stan replied.

They waited with them for half an hour and then decided to leave them to it – and Stan's jokes. They were almost back at the nick when Bronco's phone rang. He replied and listened with a few yesses and, "We'll be right there."

"That's Brian. Just after we left, the guy came out of the house. They separated and followed him, taking it in turns to be the closest. He went into the betting shop on North Street. He has been in there a few minutes and they would like backup before going in, just in case he noticed them."

Dan's heart pounded again. Is this it? Is this the end of the road and, if it were, what would Windsor say about this morning?

They pulled up on double yellows right outside the shop. Stan was reading a paper at a bus stop along the street while Brian was sat inside the Costa across the road. They both made their way to Dan.

Dan weighed up the situation – should he go and warn him if it is Tom? Again, he was in a quandary. He had to decide NOW. "Right, Bronco, it's best if you go in first; my face has been in the news too much and if it's our man it might spook him – plus we don't even know if he is armed or not. Brian, you go in just after and take Stan's newspaper open at the racing page."

Brian gave Bronco a minute and then went in. Dan and

Stan walked back to the bus stop just in case, then Bronco came back out. "I think it's a false alarm, Guv. I doubt it can be him as he works in there. He's behind the counter taking the bets and paying out winnings – what shall we do?"

Dan realised and he breathed a sigh of relief. "OK, I'll come in. I think we need to have a word with him but it's highly unlikely that it is our man."

Dan knew he was playing a game now and he didn't like it, but to keep up appearances he asked all the right questions and confirmed that there was no way this was who they were looking for. Not only had the assistant never been in the forces, he was only there as a relief assistant manager for two weeks, from the branch in Glasgow where he lived. The manager who was visiting family in Poland for two weeks in fact, rented the house.

Stan took his details and would confirm them, but they were all sure it wasn't who they were looking for. None surer than Dan.

When they got back to the nick, Bronco said, "Guv, you obviously aren't right – that bang on the head has affected you. Why don't you go and get it checked out? Then you can get off home, have an early night and come back fresh tomorrow."

"I think you're right, Dave; I'll go now," and with that they agreed to start at nine the next morning.

Again, Dan didn't bother getting his head checked out, he knew that wasn't the reason why he wasn't concentrating on the job; it was Tom Windsor and what to do about him. He thought about it constantly throughout the evening, his thoughts leaning one way then the other. He thought of how Tom had saved his life – if he hadn't pulled him out of the pit he would have drowned. He thought there was no point in trying to sleep, but it had been a long day and eventually he fell asleep.

He was falling again, looking at the truck crashing through lines of shoppers, just going about their day, spinning and falling, before seeing Catherine looking at him with the smile that melted his heart. She held her arms out wide for him. "Come here, you gorgeous policeman. Give me a hug, I love you so much." He reached out, "I love you so–" but before he could finish, before he could hold her safely in his arms, the truck struck her, ripping her away from him forever. But still, he kept falling through darkness and then into the light. He heard the words of the oath he took when he joined the police, "I, do solemnly, sincerely and truly declare and affirm that I will faithfully discharge the duties of the office of constable with fairness, integrity, diligence and impartiality and that I will uphold fundamental human rights and accord equal respect to all people, according to law."

He woke in a cold sweat, shivering. It was 3.30 am and, in that instant, he knew what his decision was. He slowly climbed the stairs, undressing and getting into bed. He was asleep in seconds – no more dreams. His alarm woke him at six and he was up, showered and in the Freelander by 6.45, driving to Forest Road.

CHAPTER 58

Turning into Forest Road he saw Tom Windsor running towards the pits. Pulling alongside, he lowered the nearside window and said, "I think you'd better get in."

Tom stopped, looked up and down the road and got in. "So, is this it? You've made up your mind?"

Dan didn't reply but continued down the road, past the entrance to the pits and turned left into the car park of a sports field that was empty. The early morning sun caused steam to rise from the dew on the grass.

"Well, say something, Dan. I've told you, if you want to arrest me, I'll not stop you."

Dan turned the engine off, undid his seat belt and turned to Tom. "I was about to say you have no idea what I'm going through, but then after hearing your story yesterday I guess you have a fair idea. I have been totally torn in half by this. I think of Catherine every day, of how she died, of the evil bastard that mowed down all those innocent people, yelling 'Allahu akbar!' as he did it and what I would do if I ever got my hands on him. I think of what our wedding would have been like and whether we'd be starting a family now. I have always tried to put on a brave face and got on with life as best I could, but the truth is, no justice has been done.

"But then I stop and think about my police oath that I took, intending always to uphold to the best of my ability. I lost count of how many men you told me you have killed from Baghdad to here. In this country alone, at least six deaths – while to some you may be a hero, a vigilante, to others you're a serial killer – an animal who will no doubt get a life sentence and that means life – and be left to rot in a prison somewhere like Belmarsh or in a glass cell in the dungeon of Wakefield Prison.

"How can I ignore all of that? How can I live with myself if I let a killer go? Am I letting down my friends and colleagues in the job? Am I giving up all that I stand for? Could I continue in the force if I let you go ahead with your plan?"

He stopped talking and took a deep breath, putting both hands over his face for a moment. He slowly turned his head to face Tom. "So, I have made up my mind and, Tom, my decision, right or wrong, if you are certain, if you are in no doubt, then I think the right thing to do is…" He paused and looked around before turning back to look Tom straight in the eyes.

"…Is for you to continue and kill those bastards and get justice for Catherine."

Tom let out a blast of air. "Fuck, Dan, I thought you were going to arrest me. Thank you, Dan, I won't let you or Catherine down and, when it's done I will be gone –you will never see or hear from me again."

Dan, looking Tom steadily in the eye, said, "OK, but just one thing, Tom, you said you would make it look like an accident, not mark them as 'guilty'. Well, to get justice for her I want you to do it and to let the world know just how guilty they both were. I know it will make my job hard searching for you, but if you keep your word and disappear, then in time the case will get dropped."

All Tom said in response was, "In that case, there's nothing else to say but thank you and I hope that once this is over you find the happiness you deserve."

With that Tom climbed out of the car and started to run

back into town. Dan sat there for a while, hoping that he had made the right decision. Before driving back to the nick, he wondered if he would ever know for sure – but it was done now and only time would tell.

Tom pushed hard on the run after a day where he had felt in limbo, not knowing if it was the end of the line for him, or if he could finish the job he had set out to do here. He couldn't wait to get back, get the job done and disappear.

CHAPTER 59

Dan sat in his office; he was even in before Brenda today. Checking his e-mails he saw the postmortem report for Cornelius. It would have been worrying reading for anyone with an unhealthy lifestyle – Gareth Evans' report showed that the Superintendent had been medically obese, had type 1 diabetes, hyperlipoproteinemia, which in layman's terms means ultra-high cholesterol and the onset of emphysema, along with over 200 milligrams of alcohol per 100 millilitres of blood. The drink-drive limit was 80 milligrams; it was a wonder he could even walk. He had just finished reading it when Bronco entered. "How are you feeling, Guv?"

"Much better thanks, Dave," he lied. "I've just read Cornelius' postmortem; it was a death waiting to happen, wasn't it? Just a shame it happened when it did, I think Gareth feels bad about it, although he shouldn't."

Bronco simply ignored this and asked, "What's the plan for today then, Guv?"

"Well, the two in hospital are due to be discharged today, so I think we should bring them straight here for questioning and see what they can remember about the monster with one green eye. It would be good if you and DI Roberts did the first interview – a woman might just intimidate them a bit more. If not, you and Churchill can have a go and if nothing else, we can get them to own up to some of the muggings."

They were brought in and questioned separately, both thinking they were being smart, answering "No comment" to every question. It was only when Bronco reminded Gale that he might need protection from the vigilante that he opened up, telling them everything they wanted to know and more, including who they got their drugs from, which was passed on to the drug squad. They were both charged with the muggings they had admitted to, but not the one where the person had died in hospital. That, they both said, was down to Darren and there was no way he could defend himself. With that, the case of the muggings and the murder of Ernie Gray were closed.

CHAPTER 60

Tom returned swiftly to the house and after a lukewarm shower and a light breakfast he was set up for the day. He really had thought Dan was going to arrest him earlier, but that was behind him now. He would keep his word and as soon as the mission was completed, he would be away from here for good. This was what had taken up most of his planning time and, after having met Dan, he was even keener to bring him justice.

He arranged everything he needed for the night's mission, mostly packed safely in his backpack. Everything else he planned to take back with him was in an old army rucksack. He began packing away everything from the house, cleaning all the surfaces, bagging up the rubbish and disposing of it in some rubbish bins at the back of the shops; he would be leaving no record of who had been there. The van he had used so far would be left locked in the garage, paid for until the end of the year. His transport tonight would be something quite different.

He left just before ten, carrying the kit bag with his backpack on his shoulder. He was walking to the garage, but not the same garage. This one had been rented three months ago, as always, paid for in cash. Inside was an old Parcelforce truck, which he had bought for cash from a dealer in Liverpool, whom he had found on the dark web. It still had the old livery on it, so would not look at all out of place anywhere. The clothes he needed for tonight's mission were already stored in it. He changed into them, dressed all in black with his balaclava rolled up, like a beanie on his head. He double-checked that he had everything, always remembering the Benjamin Franklin quote 'By failing to prepare you are preparing to fail'. The times he had said that to himself before going into a mission, along with the Para's motto 'Utrinque Paratus', 'Ready For Anything', and tonight he certainly was ready for anything. Driving slowly, he was less worried about CCTV this time as he would never use the truck again and there was no way it could be traced back to him.

The Imam's house was next to the mosque on Perth Street. There was a driveway between the two buildings that led to a small car park at the rear, and then behind the house and out on to Elgin Street, which fortunately had a closed down community centre with a car park, and that was his destination. Firstly though, he parked further along Perth Street to watch the house from the front. He had previously checked the place out on Google Maps and Google Street View and then recced it several times over the last couple of months. The bonus was that there was a pathway from the car park directly to the driveway and the back of the house, where there was a gate into the garden – this really couldn't have been better for him. He had a good view of the house; all the lights at the front were out, apart from the hallway to the front door. He sat silently in the truck for about twenty minutes, when he saw a teenager walking down the street towards him. He pushed down in his seat; he certainly didn't want to be seen. However, as the boy got closer, he realised it was Ayaan, the son of the Imam, who turned and went into the house. He breathed a sigh of relief. On the previous nights when he had checked the house the boy had always been home much earlier. It wouldn't have helped his mission if he had gone into the house to get them and only one was present.

He waited another five minutes before parking the truck in the corner of the car park next to the pathway.

Taking his backpack and pulling his balaclava down over his face, he stealthily stepped onto the pathway, forcing the gate's latch with his Fairbairn-Sykes knife, without making a sound. The only light he could see on in the house was the rear downstairs on the right, which meant he couldn't enter via the French windows and so he moved to the kitchen door. He could see through the window that the kitchen was empty. Gently sliding the knife blade in-between the door and the frame, he eased it open. He could hear laughter from deep in the house as he stepped covertly into the darkness. There was no turning back now.

CHAPTER 61

Abdelhay El Boushi was sixty-three years old and had been an Imam at the mosque for fifteen years. He was born in the city of Karima, some four hundred kilometres north of Khartoum on the banks of the Blue Nile, at the time when Sudan was gaining its independence from the Anglo-Egyptian rulers, who had treated Southern and Northern Sudan as separate regions under international sovereignty. The two areas were then merged into a single administrative region as part of the British strategy in the Middle East.

The result was civil war, which drastically affected his childhood. Both his father and uncle were killed fighting the Anyanya rebels near Bahr el Ghazal in South Sudan. It was something that would haunt him throughout his youth and would sow the seeds of extremism.

He would visit the mosque daily and listen to his grandfather reading the Koran. As soon as he could read, he would spend hours every day going over its chapters or surahs. He was sixteen when the first civil war ended, but knew he wanted more than this poor region could offer and, with the flame of anger burning in his heart, left home.

He travelled first to Khartoum, where he attended all of the great mosques until he found Imams with the same radical views as himself, who then helped guide him onwards. First, out of Africa, to Pakistan, then Afghanistan, each step of the way, meeting more like-minded Islamists and finally to London where, in Finsbury Park and Whitechapel, he found a home amongst some of the most radical preachers he had ever met. Soon, he too, was preaching of the need for Sharia law and much more. It was here he took a wife for the first time; she was just thirteen, he was forty. Nine months later she died giving birth to a baby boy. His father named him Ayaan, God's gift.

Soon, with the help of some of the elders, he was given his own mosque, with orders that as Imam, he would need to put on a public face of peace and harmony, but in private, would be able to further the cause with many of his Islamist contacts he had met over the years and throughout the world.

It had been the perfect life; his contacts in Pakistan helped him send many young men and women to madrassas to be trained in terrorism. His son, Ayaan, was reading the Koran in the same way he had as a boy. Every night after prayers he would lecture the boy in the way of the Jihadist.

But it had all changed two years ago. Ayaan was eager to take part in the war that was raging against the infidel in the UK. After much arrangement, they hatched a plan to use a truck stolen for them by friends in Hackney and to drive it through the immoral and decadent heart of London's West End, killing as many as possible.

It had all gone well: eighteen infidels were killed, many more injured and the world's press saw that ISIS could strike at the heart of capitalist London at will.

But two days afterwards when he was at home alone, as Ayaan was staying with friends, he received a late-night visit from MI5, supported by anti-terrorist armed police.

Being held down with a Glock 19 pointing at his temple, he was informed that they had proof his son was the driver of the truck and that he himself was the instigator of the attack. He was to be arrested and would spend the rest of his life in jail. They also informed him that they knew just where his son was that night and had a special services unit ready to go in and get him, with orders to shoot to kill.

But they gave him a choice: if he agreed to continue almost as normal, but to pass useful information on to them, then they would let him go and his son live.

But he only had sixty seconds to decide or else his son, along with his son's friends, would die.

If it wasn't for his undying love for Ayaan, he would never have considered it, but he had no choice.

The MI5 officer took out his phone and, with the video camera pointing at El Boushi, made him confirm that he would be informing for them. This was part one of their insurance in case he changed his mind. If he did so later, this would be secretly released to an ISIS cell, no doubt resulting in his nasty demise. Part two was that, if he did then his son would be killed.

He kept all of this from Ayaan, and only passed on low-level information. Much to his son's annoyance, he only let him take part in protests, saying anything else was too dangerous after the lorry attack.

Unbeknown to him, Ayaan and his friends still carried out six murders, but with all the stabbings happening at the time, they weren't put down as terrorist attacks, which really upset them.

It had been a busy day and he was hoping his son would be home soon. He had worries that his friends were getting more and more radicalized and knew they wanted to travel to Syria to join the caliphates. He was very aware that MI5 would be watching their every move.

He sat at his desk and logged into a secret e-mail account that had never sent or received any e-mails; it was just used to leave messages. El Boushi would leave a draft e-mail there so his contact in Kandahar would read it, delete it, leave his reply and vice versa. It was an old system to stop the likes of

GCHQ in their famous doughnut building in Cheltenham, from intercepting anything. Tonight, there was just an attachment for an MP4 movie file. Opening it, he saw it was from Pakistan. He watched in awe as a 'shahid', a suicide bomber, performed an 'istishhad', a martyrdom operation, setting off his bomb in Pakistan, resulting in thirty-one people being killed and thirty-four injured. He smiled as he watched it, but on hearing the front door open, he paused it to show to Ayaan.

"Come look at this, my son. How great is this shahid? Allahu akbar! Look at the dead bodies; he is now with Allah." They watched it again and again with laughter, not knowing what lay ahead for them that night.

CHAPTER 62

They were watching so intently and getting so excited over the killings that they had no idea anyone had entered the house. Although, had they been stood silently listening for an intruder, it's doubtful they would have heard anything anyway.

He waited for a second in the hallway, listening to their excitement. As they cheered once more, he silently stepped through the open office door, his balaclava covering his face and his Glock 19 now fitted with a silencer, in his hand.

"Enjoy it while you can, it's the last thing either of you will watch," he said in a deadpan, soulless voice.

They both turned round in shock horror – how had someone got into the house? Who was this masked man with a gun pointing at them? The son jumped up and charged at Tom, but it was doomed to be a failure; as he got within three paces, Tom's size ten Oakley Elite assault boot stamped against his oncoming right knee, sending him crashing to the floor, crying out in pain. By then the father was on his feet, turning towards Tom. He yelled, "Are you MI5? We have a deal, what do you want?" and then stepped forward again, but Tom wasn't going to wait to be attacked; they needed to see who was in charge, so he shot the Imam in his sandalled foot. He fell back into the chair screaming, with blood dripping from his foot.

It would be so easy to just kill them both here and now, but that wasn't the plan – that would be far too easy for these two. They would both suffer fear and pain before they died; sadly not as much as those they had killed and those they left behind had suffered, but they would surely suffer.

The boy was laying on his side, holding his knee, tears running down his face. "You fucking infidel bastard, I will kill you and your family for this!" He finished the sentence by spitting at Tom, but missed as he moved to one side and brought the butt of the pistol down onto the side of his head, knocking him out. The Imam roared again, trying to stand on his injured foot but was sent crashing back into his seat by the barrel of the Glock, with the silencer on it cracking across his mouth, splitting his lip. Tom finished with a blow to the temple to render him unconscious as well.

As they slowly came round they were tied back to back, sitting on the floor with gaffer tape over their mouths. As their heads and visions cleared, they looked up to see the man, now without his balaclava covering his face. Tom looked down at them, his steely eyes filled with hatred. "No, Imam Abdelhay El Boushi, as you may have now realised I am not MI5 or 6, or any other department of the British Government and you have no deal with me like you made with them." The son's eyes looked in shock, struggling to try and turn to see his father, willing him to deny it.

"Ayaan, your reaction tells me you didn't know of your father's deal with the intelligence service. Well, it's the truth. Ever since your murderous attack on innocent people he has been passing information on to MI5 in return for your safety – in fact, your life. The funny thing is, it will have been a waste of time because tonight you both die – tonight I will get justice for those who are unable to get it for themselves, but you two evil bastards will suffer first." They both continued to struggle as he carefully removed the Fairbairn-Sykes from his belt, almost teasing them. But as he began to walk closer to them, in an instant it felt as if an explosion had happened in his head and then he knew nothing – just a dark void. A crashing blow had knocked him to the floor and he lay there unmoving, as a figure stepped over him.

CHAPTER 63

Tom's eyes fluttered open, for a second not knowing where he was, until a hand slapped him very hard across his face. He instinctively began to move his hands to protect himself, but they were grabbed and taped up behind his back. The Imam's face was inches away from Tom's, spitting as he screamed at him, "You fucking kafir pig! You think you can just walk in here and kill us? Don't you know who we are? Hit him again, Ashraf." Tom had now spotted the third person in the room. By quickly assessing him, he guessed he was late twenties, just under 6-feet tall, lean but fit, wearing trainers, with a traditional black 'thobe' and a white, cotton kufi skullcap. His weathered face was partly hidden with a beard.

His flat hand struck Tom's face again, sending blood flying from his mouth.

"That's not hard enough!" cried the son. "I thought you were a Jihadist. Ashraf, you hit like a girl, let me do it!" and with that he punched Tom in the face, hitting his right eye and the side of his nose that started to pour with blood. He didn't stop there, though – he hit him again in the same spot, opening a cut above the eye. Ayaan turned to the newcomer and taunted, "*That* is how you should hit him – are you sure you are a Jihadist?"

"Don't question me, boy, I have spent two years in Syria fighting for the cause, killing many – you are not much more than a child and, from what I just heard, your father had to become a traitor to protect you." Bending down to pick up the Glock he brandished it towards him threateningly, saying, "Perhaps I should kill all of you."

The Imam raised his hand. "Stop this now; first, we must deal with this pig, then we will talk and I will explain it all. Thank you, Ashraf, for your divine intervention. How did you know to come to help us?"

"I had left my car in the car park after Asr prayers. I had been to talk with our friend El Shafee and, as I walked back, I saw this kafir park a Parcelforce truck in the car park and get out. I was cautious so I waited to see where he went. I then went to my car for a weapon and all I could find was this piece of wood, but it did the job. I then quietly entered behind him."

Tom was dazed while this was happening, but he had received worse beatings in the past. He tried to block out the pain and work out how he was going to get out of this with his life, because he had no doubt that if he didn't that they would kill him.

As the Imam listened, he picked up Tom's knife from the floor. "It was God's will, Ashraf – thank you," and then, turning to Tom, "So you were going to use this on us, were you, you infidel bitch! You are the one who will die tonight – not us – and we shall enjoy killing you." With that, he drove the knife into Tom's left shoulder joint. Tom tried but failed to mute his scream; his insides were shaking with shock.

"That's good, father. Hurt him, then kill him."

"Yes, my son, but not here, the noise he makes may be heard by our neighbours. We need to take him somewhere where we can take our time to teach him a lesson and then we will kill him. Search him for the keys to his van, we will take that."

Ayaan found the set of keys, while Ashraf looked through the backpack. "Look at this, it's chloroform he must have planned to use on you. Let's use it on him!" Tipping a load of the liquid onto a cloth, he walked around behind Tom, moved his head back and held it over his nose and mouth. Tom knew better than to struggle; he had been trained for just this scenario in the SAS, although he couldn't help but think it would be a release to drift into unconsciousness.

"Son, take the keys and get the truck open. Ashraf will help me bring him out." They pulled his body up to his feet and, with the Imam limping and Ashraf carrying the infidel's backpack, they dragged him out through the garden. It was a very dark night; there was little chance of being seen. The back doors were open and they threw him in headfirst, banging against the inside as he went.

Ashraf slammed the doors and, with Ayaan already sat behind the wheel, he walked around to the side door, helping the Imam to slide into the front seats, who was finding it ever harder to walk. Grimacing through the pain in his foot, the Imam said, "I know just the place – the disused airfield at the end of New North Lane. It will be perfect and there are derelict buildings there where we can torture the pig." Ayaan started the truck, reversing back to the entrance of the car park so he could turn and drive out into Elgin Street.

CHAPTER 64

The moment the back door slammed shut, Tom opened his eyes, or the one good eye that he could actually open. He had only pretended to inhale the chloroform, but didn't breathe any of it in. But he *was* in a mess – possibly the worst mess of his life. With one eye almost shut, his nose certainly broken and a wound in his deltoid where the blood had now congealed, he hurt like hell. He felt the truck start and then reverse, but as it went to pull away the back door opened for a second and then quickly closed. A black shape had rolled in. It was so dark and with only one good eye, he couldn't make out what it was until a voice whispered, "Well, Poacher, what a mess you've got yourself into." Tom was stunned, he could just make out a figure in all- black with a balaclava over his head, but who was it? Then it clicked. "Dan, is that you?"

Lifting the balaclava, he replied, "Well, you didn't think I would let you deal with these bastards on your own, did you?"

Tom was even more confused. "How did you know I'd be here?"

"After what you told me it was very easy to find a mosque with a father and a son, both the right age. I looked into El Boushi, saw what his background was like and knew he was the one. It had to be a night-time mission, so I had planned to be here every night until you came. Fortunately for you, this was my first night. I heard him say that they're going to the old airfield, so we have about fifteen minutes – what do you want to do?"

Tom spat out some more blood from his bleeding mouth. "I want to kill them, that's what I want to do. Could you untie me?" and he rolled painfully onto his side while Dan took his Swiss Army knife from his pocket and cut the tape off.

Looking around, his eyes now accustomed to the dark, Tom quietly chuckled. "Look, the boy couldn't have searched in here properly when he unlocked the door – there's my kit bag – it should have everything we need."

By the light of Dan's phone they emptied the bag. Tom picked up a double-barrelled sawn-off shotgun. "I can only see out of one eye, but I won't miss with this – you take the Taser. There's more chance I'll shoot first before you will, which is fine. I am not here to mess around; they are dying tonight. But just be careful, the tall guy has got my Glock."

In the front the son was getting over excited. "What can we do to him, father? We should crucify him and whip him like they do in Syria and then cut his eyes out. Then when we are done we should behead him and film it! Let me do it, father, let our brothers see me on film showing the Jihadist is winning in the infidel's country."

"We will see, my son, but you need to calm down; there is no rush. We will make him suffer and enjoy his death. We are almost there; pull off to the right here where the fence is broken."

The vehicle went off the road and over a bumpy area of gorse and grass, driving between trees and some fence posts that had been pulled down long ago while scattering some feeding rabbits. A hundred yards to the right was a low rise building that couldn't have been used in twenty-five years. All the windows were smashed and just about anything of any value had been removed for scrap, including all the doors. Ayaan pulled up next to it and couldn't wait to get out of his seat. He was at the back door at the same time as Ashraf. "Let's get the pig!" he cried, reaching for the door handle.

CHAPTER 65

Inside the van, both Dan and Tom were stood ready and waiting for the first movement of the door. They heard the boy grab the handle and, the second the door began to move, they both kicked it as hard as they could, sending it crashing back and knocking the boy backwards to the ground. By now the Imam had made his way to the back and all three were stunned and confused to see two men dressed in all-black, one with a balaclava over his face and the one they had beaten, standing there holding a gun. Ashraf was the first to move. Reaching for the Glock that was tucked in the waistband of his trousers, he yelled, "Ayaan, you fool! Did you not look in the back when you–" They were the last words he ever spoke. He was still pulling the gun out when Tom fired, the shotgun's pellets blasting his stomach and chest at such close range, it could have blown a hole in a barn door – the Jihadist had no chance.

Ayaan was swiftly trying to get back on his feet when the barbs of the Taser hit him square in his chest, sending him back down onto the floor, shaking like a beached fish.

El Boushi stood there with his mouth open in total shock and went to pull the knife from his pocket.

Tom jumped down and hit him with the butt of the shotgun, knocking the knife from his hand and sending him to the ground where he lay in Ashraf's blood, which was still pumping into the dirt.

He shouted at Tom, "You infidel pig! You will pay for

this! My followers will find you and hunt you down like a dog; they will make sure you feel the pain of a thousand deaths before they finally kill you." Tom slammed the butt into his face again, opening the damage he had made earlier in the house.

Dan gave the boy another blast with the Taser before jumping down from the truck. Turning to Tom he said quietly, "Do what you like with the old man but the boy is mine."

Tom stopped and looked across at him. "Are you really sure? What about the oath you took? You don't need to do it; I am happy to."

But from the moment the truck door had opened, Dan had changed. This wasn't a mission with the No 1 Para to Syria, Iraq or Sierra Leone where a cool head was the norm, this was personal and, for the first time in his life, the red mist had descended. His one thought was retribution.

"No, my mind's made up. I thought I couldn't live with myself if I *did* kill him – now I know I would never live with myself if I *didn't* at least take some revenge on this animal." Dan reached down, pulled the boy up from the floor before smashing his fist into his face three, four and five times, finally throwing him on the floor, yelling, "That's for Catherine!" as the tears filled his eyes and he pictured her face.

The Imam shouted something sounding like a threat that neither of them understood, but Tom had now picked up the Glock and shot him in his other foot, shattering his ankle and causing him to let out an animal-like howl. Turning the gun towards Ayaan, he told Dan to move away and he fired a shot into his thigh. The boy screamed and sobbed, "Father, help me, help me."

Through his tears and screams the Imam pleaded, "Take my life, but save the boy. I beg you for mercy, istirḥama, istirḥama. Please don't kill my Ayaan, my gift from God."

Dan looked down at him with pure hatred in his eyes. "You DARE ask us for mercy! You are a disgrace to the millions of good Muslims all around the world, the honest, caring peace-loving ones that end up suffering because of extremists like you. How many lives have been lost from the boys and girls you have sent to Jihad? Do you know how many your son killed in London that day? You delight in killing, torturing – you will get no mercy from me." He proceeded to take the pistol from Tom's hand and shot the son in his other thigh, causing even more screaming, urine spreading from his jeans. It was obvious from the sudden smell that his bowels had emptied in fear. "Look at the pain you have brought upon your only son; how ashamed are you?" The Imam lay back on the rough concrete floor, sobbing like a baby.

Tom turned to Dan and asked, "Have you had enough or do you want some more retribution? I have a special ending lined up for them; what do you think?"

Dan stood surveying the scene, taking in every inch of the three bodies; one with a large hole where his stomach had once been, one unconscious with both legs streaming blood and one crying and talking to himself in Arabic, with bullet holes in both feet. And then Dan turned to look at Tom. What was this man? A murderer or a hero, a vigilante or a serial killer? Standing there with that face, he looked like Tyson Fury had spent a day using it as a punch-bag and, with his left arm hanging by his side, the blood oozed from the shoulder.

He thought of his job, his oath, of Catherine and then of Sue, and he knew what he should do. He picked up the knife, walked back to Ayaan and bent over him, cutting his shirt open to reveal his bare chest. As he brought the knife to the boy's chest, Tom called out, "No, stop! Wait a minute, that's not right." Dan stopped and looked around, unsure what was happening. As Tom climbed into the back of the truck, he was only in there seconds before he jumped back down and handed Dan his kukri. "If you're going to do it, let's do it right," and he beamed through his beaten up face.

Dan took it and slowly carved 'GUILTY' into the chest of his fiancée's murderer, thinking of her with every cut. When he finished he stood up and handed the Gurkha knife back to Tom. "It is your plan – you started it so it's only right you finish it." Without hesitation, Tom walked over and ripped the Imam's shirt, his fat belly shaking. The Imam lifted his arms to try and fight but Dan pulled them out of the way and watched as Tom signed his signature one more time.

"So how does it end?" Dan asked.

Tom took a deep breath; obviously the pain was getting to him. "Well, it's not the location I had planned, but it will serve its purpose, so it will end the only way it could."

With Dan's help, he started to drag the bodies across on to what must have been part of a taxiway to the runway of the wartime airfield. They left the dead Jihadist lying in his own blood, but once they had dragged father and son, they sat them back to back in the centre of the concrete and wrapped gaffer tape around them so it bound them tightly.

Once that was done, they got into the truck with Tom driving one-handed. The pain in his left shoulder was excruciating as he reached to change gear, but he just blocked it out of his mind – the mission was almost complete.

He drove a hundred metres up the runway, did a U-turn and, with headlights on full-blast, he put his foot down to the floor. It took a few seconds, but as they approached the two men sat in their path, the 7.5-ton DAF truck was almost at its top speed of seventy miles an hour. Both father and son were now conscious and screaming, their eyes like animals caught in headlights, knowing they were about to die a horrific death.

The truck hit them with enormous force, bouncing over their bodies as if nothing was there. Tom pulled the truck to a stop and they both walked back.

Both men were crushed; their faces unrecognisable and their bodies a mangled mess, but you could still clearly see the word 'GUILTY' on both of them.

As Dan stood looking down at the mess of broken bones and blood, he thought again of Catherine and how he, hopefully, now had closure.

Tom, standing over the father and son, thought of Sunny and smiled through the pain. He felt as if a huge weight had been lifted from his shoulders and he said to himself, "Finally, I have got justice for those who couldn't get it for themselves." And then, to Dan, while trying to force a smile from his beaten face, "I guess you'll want a lift now." Dan smiled and climbed back in.

They drove in silence towards town, both thinking about the night's events, the past few weeks and what the future would bring.

As they got to the outskirts of town, Dan said, "I think this will do for me, but are you OK? You're in a mess and no doubt you have to get rid of this van."

"No, it's fine, and apart from the beating, it's all part of the plan."

"Thank you, Poacher. I think it's best I just call you that."

"Yes, I think it's best. I gave you my word and I will keep it. After tonight you won't ever see me again."

"Well, that makes sense, but I do owe you one now. You know where I am if you ever need me."

With that they went their separate ways.

CHAPTER 66

TWO WEEKS LATER

It had been a very difficult time for Dan, going back over the events of that night and wondering if he had done the right thing. A missing person's report had been issued for the Imam and his son, but nothing for the other one.

DI Roberts had been looking into it, but there was a rumour they had both left the country, although there were no sightings anywhere.

He waited each day, but there was still no news on the bodies – he knew it couldn't be long before they were found. In fact, the call came in that lunchtime. Bronco took it. "Guv, it looks like he's back! Three bodies have been found on the old Westfield Aerodrome, two with 'GUILTY' carved on them. They were found by a farmer who was out shooting rabbits."

They made their way there in Dan's Freelander. He let Bronco direct him and knew this wasn't going to be easy. It was a familiar scene as they pulled up; Julie Burton was already there and a gazebo erected over two bodies, while photographs were being taken of the third.

As they suited up, Julie walked across to them. "Well, either he's back or it's a copycat. They all appear to be Muslims and they must have been here for a while – foxes, rats and birds have been feeding well on them. The one over there has been shot with a shotgun at fairly close range and the two there have both been shot twice, but there are no shell casings. It also appears they have been run over by a large vehicle. There are vehicle tracks across the grass over there but, apart from that, there's not much to go on."

Dan thanked her and walked over to join Bronco, looking down at the two almost obliterated bodies. "Well, someone did a good job on them, Guv, but there's even less to go on here than the previous ones." They walked to the other body and, as Dan looked at it, he remembered the truck door opening and him and Tom springing into action, the sound of the shotgun firing and the screams that followed.

"I don't get why this one hasn't had 'GUILTY' carved on him, Guv, although the Rasta didn't when Linton was killed. It would seem he certainly knows who he wants for his victims, but the shooting is a first for him."

They continued to walk around the scene, but when they soon realised there was nothing more for them to gain, they said their goodbyes to Julie and, as they drove away, they passed Gareth Evans, with a wave as he arrived.

It was time to get back to the nick for the next briefing in Operation Nightjar.

EPILOGUE

Six months had passed since the last bodies with 'GUILTY' on them had been found. As each month went by and with no leads to follow up on, Operation Nightjar slowly wound down. It would remain an open case for some time, but Dan, Bronco and the rest of the team were assigned to newer cases.

So, a bright December day found Bronco standing next to Dan; neither had said a word for the last couple of minutes, thinking about what lay ahead. In a quiet whisper Bronco asked, "Are you ok, Guv? I don't think I've ever seen you look so frightened."

Still looking straight ahead and almost under his breath, he replied, "Thanks for pointing that out, Dave, but you're right. I'd be less frightened if I was doing a free fall HALO from thirty-five thousand feet into a bunch of armed hostiles."

But there was no more time to talk; it was about to begin.

When the music started to play, he turned, looking over his left shoulder. His heart was pounding and for a second his breath was taken away as he saw Sue Thompson walking down the aisle towards him, with her son Andy holding her arm and Julie Burton walking behind. Bryan Adams' song was playing – *(Everything I Do) I Do It for You*.

She was wearing a stunning, ivory A-line dress of fine lace, with a Bardot neckline and boned bodice. Her long, blonde hair was in ringlets and she had an elbow-length matching veil.

But outshining all of that was her radiant smile. She

beamed as she walked towards Dan, her eyes almost starting to fill – she didn't think she had even been so happy. Turning as she stood next to him, she whispered, "Fancy seeing you here, Detective Inspector. If you're looking for a good time, you've come to the right place."

A smile slowly spread across Dan's face as he looked deeply into her eyes. "Sue, you look so beautiful."

As the music stopped, the vicar began the service. When he asked if anyone knew why the couple should not be joined in holy matrimony, to let him speak now or forever hold his peace, Stan Jones let out a very loud cough, which had the congregation in fits of laughter. But in no time at all, Dan was taking the ring from Bronco and slipping it onto Sue's finger, as they became Mr and Mrs Hooper. After signing the register, with Arthur Jackson and Gareth Hew Evans as witnesses, they proudly walked back down the aisle to the sound of Stevie Wonder's *Signed, Sealed, Delivered I'm Yours*.

Stepping out of the church into the bright autumn sunshine, they were met by a guard of honour with police on one side, including PC Jimmy Edmunds and, on the other, men from the 1st Battalion Parachute Regiment. Walking through them Dan felt the strange feeling come over him, the one that he gets when something is about to happen – he shivered as chills ran down his spine.

The congregation congratulated the couple while coming out of the church and Sue was hugging Jane Roberts who, as always, looked immaculate in a Ted Baker Luluuu dress coat.

Dan stopped and looked around, trying to shake off this feeling, when his eyes latched onto someone stood in the street opposite the church.

Their eyes met and the man gave a slight nod of his head. Dan realised instantly who it was, but was unsure for a second what he should do. He nodded back and waved the person to come over. He took Sue by her hand as the person walked up the pathway. "Sue, my lovely, I'd like you to meet a former comrade of mine from more dangerous times. This is Poacher." Sue smiled as Tom took her hand and kissed her on both cheeks. "Congratulations to you both, I'm so happy for you."

Sue thanked him; thinking how his rugged face with a scar around his left eye and a slightly bent nose, didn't match the perfectly tailored, double-breasted, Prince of Wales Check suit and expensive shoes. Her thoughts were broken by Brenda Shaw waving to her, so she made her excuses and left them to talk alone.

"Well, this is a surprise, but a good one. How are you?"

"I'm good, thanks, Dan. I hope you didn't mind me turning up like this; I've been keeping tabs on you and wanted to wish you both well. How has it been since our 'escapade'?"

Dan sighed. "Yes, well… to be honest, as pleased as I am with how things turned out, I haven't found it easy. I work with good people and I do sometimes feel disloyal to them. But, hey, listen – it's great to see you. Why don't you come back to the hotel for the reception? We can easily make an extra space for you."

"Thanks, but I had best be going. I just wanted you to know that I plan on spending a lot more time in the UK. Take this card; that's my own private number. If there is ever anything you need or anything, I can do to help you any time, just call me."

And with that he turned and walked away, leaving Dan looking at the number on the card not knowing then, that the time would come when calling it, would be the only hope left for Dan.

THE END…

…for now, but the story continues in an explosive way.
Book Two in the Hooper/Windsor series,

PURSUIT OF JUSTICE.

CHAPTER 1

The hand hit him with a loud crack across his face. "Stop crying! The sooner you do as you're told and realise you're never leaving here, the better!" With that he was hit again.

The light was shining too brightly in his face; he couldn't see the man stood next to it, only his silhouette. His mind was trying to block out the man's shouting. He didn't like it. He never liked shouting of any sort – it hurt him, upset him and made him cry. He was crying now, for he didn't want to be here. The man had said he was a friend taking him on an adventure, but it wasn't an adventure, it wasn't nice. He wanted to go back home – he was safe there.

He had lost count of how many days he had been here as time had confused him, but at least he had enough sense to see the man's phone when he left it lying there. He had learnt his mum's phone number by heart, but she hadn't answered by the time the man returned, tearing the phone from his hand and knocking him to the floor. He had been tied to the chair with the light in his face since then.

It was a damp, dark night, as Tom Windsor sped across the Cambridgeshire Fens in his Audi RS Q8, Carbon Black. The destination was a small farm off the beaten track, between Peterborough and King's Lynn.

He had secretly been monitoring Jean Terry's phone ever since he first found out about her son, Sammy, going missing two days ago. In the faintest chance he called her, or there was a ransom demand involved, she had contacted the police and told them he suffered from a development disorder and had the mind of a seven-year-old child. A PC had taken details and said he would pass the information on to the right department. She had heard nothing more from them.

He had been taking note of the growing number of missing persons recently. Over the past eighteen months he had worked tirelessly, building his expertise as a hacker. Using the dark web, he was now able to place a worm into the Police National Computer (PCN) and was receiving updates of any missing persons cases that fitted his criteria. Tracking where the call had been made from was now child's play, thanks to the programmes that were loaded onto the hard drives he had stolen in Baghdad two years ago.

He turned off the main A47, passing many small villages with either Saint or Drove in their names. He wound along B roads with water-filled dikes alongside them and further onto unmade dirt tracks where he turned the lights off and finished the journey in darkness. He stopped about four hundred metres away from the farm dressed in all-black, with his new PIG Full Dexterity Tactical gloves and a balaclava rolled up like a beanie hat. He pulled his night-vision goggles down over his eyes and made his way stealthily towards the farm. Tom had swiftly studied the farm on Google Earth before leaving his base in Northamptonshire and knew, as with all the recent cases he had been dealing with, that there could well be a violent outcome. He had made a pledge, however, to continue to seek justice for those unable to get it for themselves and therefore he was happy to be as violent as necessary to bring Sammy home.

Getting closer he heard dogs barking, but suspected they were either chained up or in a pen. Circling the empty-looking, dark house, he spotted a typical traveller's chrome caravan with a Nissan drop-side flatbed truck linked to it.

Silently passing one of the outbuildings, he paused as he heard shouting and crying inside. There were no windows and only one door. Tom retrieved both his Glock 19 with a silencer fitted and his Taser from his backpack. Sliding the gun in his belt, he removed the night-vision goggles and pulled the balaclava over his face, took a deep breath and opened the door.

The first thing he saw was a man with his back to the door about to hit Sammy. Turning around in shock, he yelled, "Who the fuck are you? What do you want?"

Tom aimed his high-powered Axon Taser at the man and shouted, "Move away from the boy and kneel on the floor now! I won't give you another warning!"

Brendan Boswell was a big man although, only standing at about 5-feet 10-inch in his muddy boots, he must have weighed almost eighteen stone. The sleeves of his checked shirt were rolled up over huge forearms Popeye would have been proud of. He certainly had that look of strength so many farmers and ground workers have. With a couple of days' growth on his face and his unkempt ginger hair, he was the archetype Irish traveller.

He looked at the man stood before him all in black with a balaclava over his face. He knew he wasn't a copper – he would have announced that – so who the hell was he and what did he want with him?

Tom yelled again. "Your last chance – get on the floor!" but Boswell was a fighting man. He started to charge at Tom, but was stopped in his tracks by fifty thousand volts, like running into a brick wall. Every muscle in his body cramped and he fell to the ground, shaking.

Tom quickly made his way to Sammy, untying the ropes around his wrists and said soothingly, "Hello, Sammy. Don't be scared; you're safe now. I'm taking you home."

Sammy was still crying and was just repeating, "Taking

me home, taking me home."

Tom put the gun and the Taser back into his backpack and walked across to Boswell lying on the floor. "You evil bastard, treating the kid like this. You will pay for it!" He then stepped back and aimed his size ten Oakley assault boot into the traveller's stomach, forcing all the air out and making him wheeze. But Tom wasn't finished – he stepped back again, this time kicking him viciously in the head, knocking him unconscious. He deftly tied the man's hands together with cable ties.

Tom turned towards Sammy and said, "Sammy, I'm going to take you into my car and then back to your mum." Leading him out of the building, he put the goggles on again to enable him to see clearly and to return to the car as fast as possible. He unlocked the car and sat Sammy in it. "Now, listen carefully, Sammy. I have to go back to the farm but I won't be long. Stay here in the car and *do not* get out. I will soon be taking you home to your mum; do you understand?"

Sammy nodded and replied, "Yes, understand."

The rain had started to fall as he made his way back to the farm. Before returning to the man he did a recce of the rest of the prefab-style, derelict buildings and wasn't totally surprised to see, looking through the window to five or six men lying on the floor asleep, most of them snoring. *Just as I thought, this really is modern day slavery*, which he knew had been on the increase for years. There was nothing he could do for them now, he had to get Sammy back to his mum, but he would make sure they would get looked after.

Removing his night-vision goggles again, he opened the door, but Boswell, who had come round by now, had somehow got to his feet and charged at him rather comically, still with his hands tied behind his back. It was a fruitless move with Tom managing to easily sidestep away, grabbing him by the back of his head and driving it into the wall.

Boswell grunted and fell to the floor with a large gash now visible on his head. Searching him first and pocketing his mobile phone, Tom took the gaffer tape from his backpack and bound Boswell's feet, legs and arms and, lastly, covered tape over his mouth. There was a doorway in the back wall leading to a storage cupboard, so Tom dragged him into it and then wedged the chair under the door handle to hopefully keep him in there. Finally, using Boswell's mobile and thankful that the gloves were touch screen conductive, he called 999, telling the police, "Come quick! There's been a murder at South Drove Farm. We need help." Afterwards he turned the phone off and stamped onto it, smashing it.

Remembering Sammy, he ran back to the car to find that Sammy had dozed off. He woke him gently, asking, "Sammy, are you OK, mate?"

Yawning, he then smiled. "Yes, thank you, mister. Am I going home?"

"Yes, you are, young man," and they set off. The roads were clear and Tom decided to take the A47, A1 and M11, the longest route in miles, but at the speed he was driving, by far the fastest.

Sammy soon fell asleep again. Tom knew he needed to call Mrs Terry and had a cover story ready that he'd used before. She answered on the third ring. He asked if it was Mrs Terry, who replied in a nervous voice, "Yes, who is it?"

"You don't know me and I am afraid I can't give you my name as I work for a government department that dislikes publicity, but I thought you would like to know that Sammy will be home with you safe and sound in less than an hour. He hadn't been treated very nicely, but I can assure you the person who took him has now been treated far worse. I will tell you more shortly, but have to ask for the utmost discretion – as I say, my department dislikes publicity."

"Thank you! Thank you so much, I don't know what else to say."

"You don't need to say anything. I will see you shortly."

Under sixty minutes later he was pulling up outside the Terrys' house. He woke Sammy and led him to the front door, which opened as he got to it. Sammy was still half-asleep but was quickly hugged by his mum, who had tears of joy streaming down her face.

"How can I ever thank you? I don't even know your name."

"Mrs Terry, there is no need to thank me, but this is an ongoing case, so if you say anything about what has happened, it would jeopardise it, so please, again, just be happy Sammy is safe and leave it at that. If the police ask, I would suggest you say that he was out wandering, got confused and couldn't find his way back home, that he found shelter in a derelict building but fortunately the confusion cleared and he was able to find his way home. It's a bit weak but as he is home safe and sound I'm sure they won't question it."

After a quick goodbye he jogged back to his car, knowing it had been a good night and justice had been accomplished.

CHAPTER 2

Dan woke a second or two before the alarm went off at 6.30 am. It was to be his first day back at work after his honeymoon.

A fortnight at the Sandals resort in Antigua, a beautiful island that boasted a beach for every day of the year, had done them both the power of good. They'd been swimming in the crystal clear, blue sea, walking on the powdery white sand and exploring each other's bodies every night – it was the perfect honeymoon.

It had been a crazy year, with him being first made CIO of the Vigilante Murders, as they became called by the press, which had led to him finding the murderer, only to end up joining *with* him to avenge the murder of his fiancée Catherine and then both of them brutally killing the culprits.

At first, he found the aftermath very hard to deal with; he had killed before when he was a paratrooper in Kosovo and Sierra Leone, but that was for the service of his country. This was different – on the downside he felt he had betrayed his oath as a police officer and he hated lying to his work colleagues and friends. But, on the plus side, he knew that he had taken the lives of evil terrorists who had killed innocent people and would no doubt have killed more. Plus, it had finally given him emotional closure and allowed him to move on with his life and marry Sue.

Dan stirred with the feeling of a fly landing on his cheek. Slowly opening his eyes, he took a second to focus on the blonde hair over his face. He smiled and sighed with pleasure, still feeling this fluttering on his cheek. He quietly whispered, "Sue, what are you doing?"

"Giving you butterfly kisses, my gorgeous, sexy husband. I love you so much, I could eat you and I know just where I'd start. Do you think we have time, lover boy?" she laughed, rubbing her hand over his chest under the duvet.

He roared back with laughter, taking her face in both hands and kissing her gently. "Mrs Hooper, you should be ashamed of yourself, trying it on with a detective chief inspector, especially while your son is downstairs having breakfast and we both need to get to work. Now, let me get up and hold that thought until tonight."

"Tonight? How about a quick one in the canteen kitchen after lunch?" she enquired teasingly, with a huge grin on her beautiful face.

Dan rolled out of bed, saying, "You are incorrigible, you really are, but I love you so much – just wait until tonight."

He made his way to the nick, arriving just before 8 am. He was amazed as he walked past incident room 2 to see all his team already there. As soon as they saw him, they all began to clap and cheer. DC Stan Jones was the first to call out, "Must be nice to be back on your feet again after two weeks in bed," which received a groan from everyone else.

"It was great, thanks everyone, and we did get out of bed once in a while, thanks, Stan. It felt much longer than two weeks away, but it's good to be back and I look forward to being brought up to speed, once I've checked my e-mails and post."

Sitting at his desk, he was going through his mail and picked up a postcard from his DS, 'Bronco' Laine, who was on holiday himself in Belgium. The picture on the front was of the Menin Gate Memorial to the Missing in Ypres, that bears the names of the fifty-four thousand British and

Commonwealth soldiers who gave their lives in the First World War, whose bodies were never found. Turning it over, Bronco had just written, 'What a place, you really need to come here one day, you will never forget it'.

As he finished reading it, his phone rang. It was his boss, Chief Superintendent Arthur Jackson.

"Morning Dan, welcome back. Could you pop up? I have some news for you."

Dan made his way to the Chief's office. "Come in, Dan, how are you? How's Sue? I guess you had a great honeymoon."

"We are both fine, thanks, Chief and, yes, it was paradise and she makes me laugh every day, it's brilliant. How are you?"

"Yes, all good, thanks, and I couldn't be happier for you, but we are having some changes. First of all, DI Roberts has got her promotion to DCI. It was always on the cards and I am pleased for Jane. I think we all know she is headed for the top, but the bad news is she is being transferred to MET Ops Covert Policing *(MO3)* with immediate effect. I think it's part of their long-term plan for her to work as many departments as possible. The other bit of bad news is, she's not being replaced here due to cutbacks, but we are getting another newly promoted DS and I think you will be impressed." Passing a file across the desk, he said, "Here is her file. It will do her the world of good working with you, but I also want Bronco, when he gets back, to take her under his wing. She's due to report to you at 9.00 this morning. Once you've had a chat, bring her up to meet me."

After that news, Dan couldn't wait to open her file as soon as he was back in his office. The Super was right – he was impressed. Letitia Makubuya was 26 years old, born of Ugandan parents in Streatham, South London. She gained a master's degree in criminology from the University of Surrey in Guildford and was fast-tracked into the Met's Operation Trident, a police unit set up to combat gun crime. She was an

All-England School's pole vault champion, holding a Black Belt 2nd Dan in Brazilian jiu-jitsu and, as a hobby, fights in mixed martial arts.

Dan was still reading the file when Letitia was shown to his office. Dan was stunned; she looked more like a supermodel than a detective. She was standing at around 5-feet 10-inches, with her hair impeccably neat in cornrows, wearing black Nike trainers and a smart blue G-Star RAW jumpsuit over a white vest. Walking forward with a huge smile to shake hands, she said, "Good morning, sir, it's lovely to meet you."

Dan returned the greeting, saying, "Good morning, Letitia, and likewise, but first things first, there's no need for sir; I am quite happy with Dan if we are alone or Guv, in company."

She kept smiling. "Thank you, Guv. Well, in that case – second things being second – Tish is fine. I always think Letitia is too much of a mouthful and it really is good to meet you. I've heard lots about you."

They both sat down. "And where have you heard that from, then, Tish?"

"From Julie Burton, Guv. We are old friends and are both in the same club," and with a wink she added, "if you get what I mean, Guv. She said you would understand."

Dan had been friends with his Chief Crime of Scenes Officer, Julie Burton, for some years and, along with Sue, both understood she was part of the *LGBT* community.

Dan smiled again. "Did she, indeed? Well, yes, Julie is a colleague and a very good friend, as I am sure you know. I most certainly do understand and couldn't be happier to welcome you to the team."

"Thank you, sir; I mean, Dan or Guv," she chuckled. "In fact, Julie is one reason why I was happy to be transferred here as we are thinking of moving in together. I'm well pleased you're kosher with it." Her cockney accent was getting stronger as she relaxed.

"That's good. Julie is great friends with my wife, Sue; in fact, she was her maid of honour, so when you're settled you must both come over for dinner."

At that moment his phone rang. Picking it up, his part of the conversation went something like, "Yes, yes… Where? OK, we're on our way." To Tish he said, "Right, time to start. There's been an armed robbery at Bezenstocks Jewellers in town. Let's go."

They took Dan's Freelander, stopping in the High Street behind two patrol cars that still had their blue lights flashing. Two PCSOs were putting a tape barrier up across the High Street to keep a large crowd of nosey bystanders back. Getting out of the car, the first officer Dan spotted was one of the younger PCs, Jimmy Edmunds, who Dan knew from previous cases and had great respect for.

Walking towards the shop, he said, "Good morning, Jimmy. What have you got for us?"

Striding alongside him, Jimmy replied, "Morning, sir. I was the first one to get here. I was down the street and heard the alarm go off. Mr Bezenstock is a nice, old chap. He said that a tall, IC-3, dressed in all-black, black cap and had a mask over this mouth – I think he means a bandanna – entered the shop, grabbed the young, 22-year-old assistant, Chelsea, and held a knife to her throat, demanding cash out of the till. This was a waste of time as the shop had only just opened and almost all their transactions these days are on card, so he made the old gent take four Rolex watches out of the window and, pushing the girl to the floor, he grabbed them and fled."

Inside the jewellery shop, Dan nodded to the two PCs already there, who were talking to the girl. He introduced himself and Tish to Mr Bezenstock who was visibly shaken.

"What is the world coming to, Chief Inspector? I have

been here for almost fifty years and I have been robbed more times in the last five years than the previous forty-five. I'm getting too old for this, it upsets me and especially to see young Chelsea put through all this. I'm starting to think it's time to sell up and retire."

Dan nodded and said, "I totally understand, sir–"

Tish interrupted. "Excuse me, Guv, Mr Bezenstock – could you describe the man again?" and then, turning to Chelsea, she asked, "And could I hear your description, as well?"

The jeweller seemed unsure what to say. "Well, he was… ah, how do you say? Hmm… ah…"

She grinned. "It's OK, you can say black. I have heard it all before."

He seemed relieved. "Yes, he was black," and then went on to give the same description PC Edmunds had just provided. Tish turned towards the young woman. "Chelsea, have you got anyfin' else to add to that?"

She stood up from the chair, placing a half-empty glass of water on the counter. "Well, yes. Although you couldn't see much of his face he had two eyebrow slits above his left eye and a tattoo on the back of his right hand between his thumb and first finger."

Tish nodded. "That's great, Chelsea. Thanks, babe, you're a star." And then to Dan, she added, "Guv, we need to go outside; I think I clocked him when we arrived."

Walking out, her eyes searched the crowd until she saw him standing across to her right. Their eyes met and it was like he knew that she knew. He turned to walk away but quickly started to sprint. He was fast, but she was soon after him. He was knocking people out of the way and she was dodging them. Dan and PC Edmunds were trying to keep up but couldn't. They turned off the High Street into Fore Street, a long, straight, tree-lined road, but he soon realised, no matter how quick he was, this girl was quickly catching him up. Turning into a side alley, he pulled out the knife from his pocket, turned it towards her and said, "Fuck off, bitch, else I plug ya!"

She didn't pause. In a heartbeat her right leg shot out, connecting with a crack on his wrist and sending the knife flying. In one continuous movement she spun in a full circle and the next kick hit him hard in his solar plexus, doubling him over, at the same moment that Dan and the PC arrived. With a single pace forward she took his right arm, turning it against the joint and pushing him flat into the ground. "You couldn't plug in a kettle, you wanker! You're nicked," and with that she handcuffed him and read him his rights.

She looked up to see the DCI and the PC standing there open-mouthed with hands on hips. "Alright, Guv, I think he's the one," and she pulled out the Rolex watches from his pockets. Pulling him up to his feet and pushing him towards PC Edmunds, she said, "He's all yours, Jimmy, don't lose him. Not a bad start, eh, Guv? Another case solved. I guess the coffees are on you." Still grinning, she pointed across the road to the Starbucks.

"I guess they must be, Tish, then it's back to the nick. You haven't met the Chief Super yet; isn't *he* in for a treat?"

"OK, Guv, in that case, can I have a cupcake, as well?"

Tish finished the cupcake in seconds as they drove back to the nick. When they walked past the main office, Stan Jones stood up in a jokey kung fu pose and started singing, "Everybody was kung fu fighting…"

They all chuckled in amusement as Dan said, "Another word from you, DC Jones, and I will set our new secret weapon on you." Dan then introduced Tish to the rest of the team including Brenda Shaw, the office manager, before taking her up to meet the Chief Superintendent, with a huge smile on his face, thinking, *Working with this girl is going to be some adventure!*

ACKNOWLEDGEMENTS

There are so many people to thank for helping me on my journey to get this, my first book published.

Firstly, I must thank you the reader, without whom, the entire process would be pointless. I realise that it takes a lot to try a first time author, and I really hope you weren't disappointed. I know my writing is a work in progress, something that I will be working hard to improve, with each book in the series, and I really hope you will join me on this journey.

If I could ask you one favour, it would be, could you please leave a review. Reviews are like gold dust for authors, especially for new ones, and it really would be a great help if you could find time to do so, and even better if it's a positive one.

If you would like to know more about future books, character backgrounds and other interesting projects, please check out my website www.neilsandsbooks.com, you will also find me on Facebook, Twitter and Instagram at @NeilSandsBooks.

On a more personal note immense thanks to, Jill, my wife of fifty years, who has been there with help, advice and inspiration, day after day. Stefan, James, Gabriel, Caroline, and all the great team at Spiffing, for their advice and professionalism, in guiding an excited novice through this unique process. Martin Parsonson, who is not only the perfect next door neighbour, but a very experienced police officer, who let me constantly bombard him with questions. Terry Ellis a friend of forty years, a retired police officer and diver. I have used his real name in this book and the incident with the eel really happened to him. Brother-in-law, Pete Wheeler, an avid reader of action adventure books, who after reading the first few chapters gave me the reassurance to keep writing. Nicki Gower another long term friend, who was the first to read all of the first draft, and despite her being a brilliant English teacher, could not have been more complimentary.

Last but certainly not least, is my wonderful family. The New Zealand wing, of Jemma, Grant, Myla, Riley, and the Surrey wing of Jamie, Laura, Autumn and Rex. Who bring constant joy and happiness and make me believe that grandchildren are Gods greatest gift.

Thank you all.

Made in the USA
Middletown, DE
13 August 2022

71309868R00172